# SIDELINED

# SIDELINED

## Kara Bietz

POPPY
LITTLE, BROWN AND COMPANY
New York Boston

Poppy
Hachette Book Group
1290 Avenue of the Americas, New York, NY 10104
Visit us at LBYR.com

First Edition: September 2021

Poppy is an imprint of Little, Brown and Company. The Poppy name and logo are trademarks of Hachette Book Group, Inc.

The publisher is not responsible for websites (or their content) that are not owned by the publisher.

Library of Congress Cataloging-in-Publication Data
Names: Bietz, Kara, author.
Title: Sidelined / Kara Bietz.
Description: First edition. | New York : Poppy/Little, Brown and Company, 2021. | Audience: Ages 12 & up. | Summary: "High school seniors Julian Jackson and Elijah Vance reconnect on the football field after three years apart, learning to both trust and love each other again."—Provided by publisher.
Identifiers: LCCN 2020051551 | ISBN 9780759557512 (hardcover) | ISBN 9780759557499 (ebook) | ISBN 9780759557505 (ebook other)
Subjects: CYAC: Friendship—Fiction. | Dating (Social customs)—Fiction. | Gays—Fiction. | High schools—Fiction. | Schools—Fiction. | Meridien (Tex.)—Fiction.
Classification: LCC PZ7.1.B533 Si 2021 | DDC [Fic]—dc23
LC record available at https://lccn.loc.gov/2020051551

ISBNs: 978-0-7595-5751-2 (hardcover), 978-0-7595-5749-9 (ebook)

Printed in the United States of America

LSC-C

Printing 1, 2021

*For SLB and the broken guitar string*

# · one ·

# *JULIAN*

When Coach Marcus postpones after-school football practice until sunset because of the heat, I take the long way home. I don't hurry down Main Street with the rest of the kids from my neighborhood, but instead cut through the soccer fields and head into the scrub pines behind Crenshaw County High School.

My grandma, whom I've always called Birdie, used to tell me when I was little, "Idle hands are the devil's playground, Julian." In fact, she said it so often and with such an accusatory tone, I was convinced that the devil himself was just waiting for me to become bored so he could use my hands to commit some heinous crime. I used to sit in church with my palms under my thighs, silently repeating *not today, not today,* scared out of my wits that the devil knew I was bored and was ready to come up from the depths of hell and lead me into a life of debauchery...right there in front of the entire congregation of the Crossroads Church of Meridien. And then they'd all know how really bored I was. I pictured Ms. Brownie, whose real name had been lost to years of the entire town calling her Ms. Brownie, shaking her head and saying in her thick Texas twang, "I always knew that boy had idle hands."

As I got older, Birdie didn't repeat it as much. Maybe it was because I learned how to behave myself and she felt I didn't need the warning. Now that I'm grown, I know that idle hands aren't necessarily the devil's playground. You know what is, though? Meridien, Texas, in the thick of the early September heat.

The dried pine straw cracks under my feet as I reach the clearing in the woods near the end of Kirkland Road. I can see our old backyard from here, the sunlight dancing on the tire swing and dappling the mixture of dead grass and sand underneath. The lone tall oak casts a shadow onto the roof and right across my old bedroom window. It's not much to look at, this old house with its yellowing paint and red shutters. A shotgun house, Daddy called it, long and narrow. Every so often when I walk home this way, memories flash of me and my father in the backyard, tossing a football back and forth.

"Fingers between the laces," he taught me, even though I could barely get my six-year-old hand around the narrowest part of the ball. "Get that pointer finger on the seam, Julian." One fluid motion. Release the ball at the highest point and step through. Every time I throw a pass, I remember his instructions.

"My boy is going to be a star," he said once, carrying me

around the yard on his shoulders. "Hear that crowd cheering for you? Everyone's going to know Julian Jackson: the best quarterback in Texas."

I don't remember anything about my mother, who left us just weeks after I was born. And I really don't have a ton of memories of my father, either, but that one is really bright.

I touch the chain-link fence that separates the yards on Kirkland Road. I wish I could see him as vividly as I sometimes remember his voice.

I notice that the woman who lives in the house now is sitting on the front porch, a tattered paperback in her hands.

"Afternoon, Julian," she says without looking up, her glasses perched near the end of her nose.

"Afternoon, Miss Jean."

"Some tea for you?" She points to an ice-filled pitcher next to her without lowering her paperback.

"No time this afternoon, Miss. But thank you," I answer.

We have the same exchange every time I take the long way home and she's there. I never say yes, and she always asks. I wonder what would happen if I did say yes one day. I haven't been in the house since the morning my father died.

I reach the end of Kirkland Road and throw a look over my shoulder at the house at the end of the street before I turn onto Main and head for home. The sharp contrast between the quiet of Kirkland and the bustle of Main Street is jarring. I'm walking at a snail's pace now. Without the woods for shade, the sun beats relentlessly on my back, and I can feel the sweat running down toward the waistband of my shorts.

I wind my way past the town line, the rusty WELCOME TO MERIDIEN sign blown off-kilter after years of fighting a losing battle with the Southeast Texas wind. If I were walking in the other direction, I'd be passing huge ranches lined with white vinyl fences framing freshly mown grass and dotted with tall trees. On this side of the county, the road leads to rows of tract housing, overgrown chickweed, and bobbing pumpjacks. Officer Calvert sits in the Crossroads Church parking lot at the edge of town, just waiting for someone to come barreling down Main Street on their way to the beach, too busy looking at their phone to notice the sharp drop in the speed limit. The road is patched together with a dizzying pattern of thick tar that still stinks in the late summer steam. Empty storefronts, their windows covered with brown paper and sometimes duct tape, dot the main drag between the businesses that survived the big oil downturn a couple years back. Jake's Convenience, Ron Redd's Rapid Repair, the Meridien Motel and Diner (parking in rear), Mabel's Beauty Box. Burger Barn rises up like some turquoise beast at the corner of Main and Rudy Street. I ignore the stream of kids hanging out there on the pink picnic tables and turn right on Rudy Street to head home.

The TV is blaring when I come in the front door. Ray Remondo, Corpus Christi Action 8 Weather, is standing in front of a map, gesturing to a storm churning down near Barbados.

"Birdie," I call. "I'm home."

"There's my boy," she says, her voice coming from the kitchen. "Come on in here and help your grandmama."

I drop my backpack on the brown plaid couch, worn thin

in spots from years of Birdie's hospitality. As far back as I can remember, there has always been a visitor or two a few meals a week in this house.

Birdie is standing on a chair trying to reach a heavy bowl above the refrigerator when I appear in the kitchen. Her heavy frame teeters on the edge of the seat, and I notice it starting to flex and bend underneath her.

"Birdie! Here." I guide her down gently. "What are you reaching for?"

"I need the good glass bowl," she says. "We've got special company tonight!"

I step up on the chair and grab the big bowl in one motion. I set it gently in the sink and start washing it out with soap and warm water. "Who is it?"

Birdie calls everyone special company, even if it's just Ms. Brownie coming over for gossip and a muffin in the morning. Though she's not a regular dinner visitor, and I doubt we'd be getting out the good bowl for her. Maybe it's Pastor Ernie and his husband, Thomas Figg. Figg, whom no one except my grandmother refers to as Mr., only Figg, has been teaching calculus at Crenshaw since the dawn of time. Maybe earlier.

Or maybe it's my least favorite visitor, my football coach. When Coach Marcus and Birdie get started on offensive plays and passing-game strategies, sometimes I have to leave the room. I don't know that anyone has ever met a booster club president more vocal than Birdie. No one in Meridien loves Crenshaw County High School football more than she does. Including Coach Marcus.

"No football practice today? I thought for sure you'd be out there getting ready for the Taylor game," she says, sucking her teeth and shaking her head.

"Coach Marcus says it's too hot for practice this afternoon, so we're playing under the lights tonight at seven," I say, yawning. I pull my soggy shirt away from my back and try to fan a little fresh air under there. It doesn't help. "Plus, we've got four weeks before the Taylor game, Birdie. Stephens City is our first game, this weekend."

"Oh, I know that," she says. "But you know Taylor is the game we all have our eye on."

Don't I know it. Everyone who's lived in Meridien for longer than five minutes knows it. Our rivalry with Taylor High School is something that seems to have started around the time Moses parted the Red Sea, if you listen to any of the folks around here.

"Never too soon to start preparing for those Taylor Titans," Birdie mumbles. "You know they have morning *and* afternoon practice some days up there at Taylor?" She shakes her head. "They're getting ready for us. We ought to be getting ready for them. Give that Coach Marcus a piece of my mind next time I see him. You're going to have to have your wits about you this year," she admonishes.

"I always do," I tell her, trying to smile. Birdie sometimes rides me harder about football than Coach Marcus does, and that's saying something.

"Ooh, sounding more and more like your daddy every day."

She rolls her eyes. "You've got to get that homework done, then. Time's a-wasting," she says, swatting me on the backside with a dish towel.

"You going to tell me who the special company is?"

"Never mind that," she says, tucking the towel into the waist-band of her full flowery skirt. "You keep your head in the game. You'll see 'em soon enough, when you get home after practice. Now get." She pulls me close to her for a kiss on the forehead and then gently shoves me in the direction of my room.

I grab my backpack on the way. What kind of company will still be around after practice ends late on a Monday? Maybe someone is spending the night? Someone from Birdie's book club or a church friend? Why would that be a surprise, though?

I put my backpack on the floor by my desk and straighten out the green blanket on my bed. I lay out the homework I have in order of difficulty, starting with calculus because it's the easiest for me and ending with English because it's my least favorite. I sit down at the desk with a sharpened pencil and my notebooks. The work is mindless, and I'm still distracted by Birdie's secrecy about tonight's guest. Does Birdie have a boyfriend? Is that why she wanted the good glass bowl and she's wearing her favorite church skirt?

I quickly put the idea out of my head. Surely I would have noticed if some guy had started coming around.

Well, there *is* that one man at church who's always hanging around her. Mr. Cooper. Only problem with that is Mr. Cooper is about eight hundred years old, and we just had a big birthday blowout a couple of years back for Birdie's sixtieth. Maybe it's someone from the other side of the county. Some lonely rancher who's looking for a wife who can talk football.

I let myself settle into that fantasy, living the good life on some big ranch on the other side of town. I picture myself riding a horse and living in one of those houses behind the white vinyl fences while I finish up calculus and physics and at least look at my English lit assignment.

Birdie is sitting in front of the TV when I come out of my room. Ray Remondo is drawing colored lines from the massive blob near Barbados all the way up to the Texas coast. Birdie chews a fingernail. Ray Remondo graduated from Crenshaw County High School around the time my dad was there, and a few years later he was one of those dudes they stick out on a pier during a hurricane on the Weather Channel to show you how bad the wind is. He came back home to Texas recently and started working for Action 8 in Corpus Christi. He's Meridien's little claim to fame. Plus, he's been known to wax poetic about Crenshaw football now and again, which makes him one of Birdie's favorite people. I think he even writes a sports opinion column in the weekly Meridien newspaper that only the old people read.

"What's old Ray Ray gesticulating about today?" I pat myself on the back for using an SAT word.

"Storm out there brewing in the Caribbean. Maybe it'll give us some relief from this ridiculous heat wave," she says, throwing her hand up toward the TV.

She points the remote at the screen and clicks the power

button in a huff. She pulls a towel from the laundry basket at her feet and starts folding.

"You think it's something we need to pay attention to?" I ask.

"Not just yet. That thing may take ten days to get on up here. And you remember what happened with *that Ashley*," she says, rolling her eyes.

Everyone on the Texas Gulf coast knows about *that Ashley*: the Hurricane That Wasn't. Statewide panic and a bread-and-milk shortage all for a couple of clouds and a barely there thunderstorm that took a turn toward Louisiana at the last minute. Folks in Meridien talk about *that Ashley* the way they talk about *that one uncle* who ruined Thanksgiving or the Dallas Cowboys: with complete and utter disgust.

"Did you finish up all your homework?" she asks, wiping the sweat from her brow and pulling another towel from the laundry basket.

"Yes, ma'am." It's just a little white lie. I can finish my English assignment tonight after practice. It'll help put me to sleep.

"You work hard out there," she tells me, straightening my T-shirt and inspecting my shoelaces.

"I always do."

"And you tell Coach Marcus he's got a weak spot on defense on his left. He needs to fix that mess before Taylor." She winks and squeezes my shoulders while guiding me toward the front door.

"What time is company coming?"

"Should be here within the hour, I suspect," she says, her

voice a little uneven. She looks out the window and wrings her hands. "Now get on out there and do what needs to be done."

"Still not going to tell me who it is?" I raise my eyebrows at her like I used to when I was small and I wanted a piece of candy or an extra cookie after dinner.

"Get!" She laughs, opening the front door and pointing down the driveway.

I sling my football bag over my shoulder and, with a quick smile back at Birdie, hustle down Rudy Street.

# · two ·

# *ELIJAH*

I walk myself to the bus station. It's not as dramatic as it sounds, as we live only a few blocks away. Three blocks in the afternoon Houston steam with a black duffel bag slung over your shoulder, however, can feel like forty days in the jungle if you let your imagination get away from you.

The 2:45 bus to Corpus Christi isn't completely full. I set my bag down on the seat beside me and put in my earbuds before we even leave the station. I watch people step onto the bus and make up stories about them in my head. It keeps me distracted enough to not think about my sister, Frankie, and my niece, Coley, for at least ten whole minutes.

Frankie wanted to walk with me. She wanted to bring Coley and wave from the station as the bus pulled away. I told her I think she's watched too many Hallmark movies.

"Come on, Elijah," Frankie begged. "Coley loves anything with wheels. She'll love seeing the big buses."

"I can do this on my own," I told her. I left out the real reason I didn't want her there with my niece: that I thought it would rip my heart out to see Coley waving at me from the platform as the bus pulls away. Maybe it'll be only a few weeks until I see her again, but it will definitely be the longest I've been away from her since the day she was born.

It was bad enough that I had to say goodbye to her after lunch and before her nap. She was cranky and upset with me, her dark curls sticking up in seventeen different directions while she made a mess out of a bowl of macaroni and cheese. I tried to help her, tried to guide the spoon to her mouth, but she wasn't having any of that.

"No, Uncalijah," she whined, stretching out her name for me into a million syllables. "I do it myself." The tears started about halfway through the bowl. We had spent the morning playing in the little splash park near our apartment, and I knew all that running around in the sun and heat was going to leave her happy but zonked. Even waiting ninety seconds for Frankie to nuke a bucket of Easy Mac and warm up a few green beans left her curled in a ball in the kitchen with crocodile tears rolling down her cheeks.

I put her down for a nap after her lunch devolved into a long string of tired cries and whines that the macaroni was "too slippy." Sticky golden cheese was still clumped on her chin and in her curls. It wasn't the most charming way to remember her, but it still makes me smile as the bus pulls onto the highway, pointed south.

"Uncalijah will see you soon," I told her, kissing her fore-head, the only part of her face that wasn't caked with powdered cheese.

"Nooooo," she said, her eyes already closing.

"Text me pictures," I said to Frankie when I left. "I'm sorry I'm leaving her with you like this."

"A nap will fix her right up," Frankie said, hugging me tightly. "We'll be there soon."

"Bye, Ma." I waved toward the back patio, where she was surrounded by moving boxes and rolls of packing tape.

"Be safe, Elijah. Call us when you get there," she said without getting up. "And you tell that Ms. Jackson thank you, you hear me? Her taking you in for a few weeks is the nicest thing someone from Meridien has done for us in years."

"Yes, ma'am."

Maybe it was going to be weird living with Ms. Jackson and Julian. Even if it was only for a few weeks. Who was I kidding? It was *definitely* going to be weird. But when Ma made the decision that we needed to get back to Meridien, there was no way I was going to start school again in Houston and then switch after three weeks. Ma got on the phone with Pastor Ernie, Figg, and Coach Marcus the same day she decided.

I was sitting in the living room the day Figg called her back.

"Really? Well . . . isn't that something," she said, a slight smile brightening her face.

A short pause.

"Well, you be sure and tell her thank you," Ma said quietly.

A longer pause.

"I appreciate you both, Thomas. I'm sure Elijah will be thrilled. You're right; they were friends for a long while."

Friends? Did I ever have real friends in Meridien? I started to think about the things that happened there before we left the first time and—

"Please tell Pastor thank you, too."

A twinge of sadness pulled at my chest, but I swallowed it down. I looked at my mother as she hung up the phone, some of the stress visibly falling from her shoulders.

"What am I going to be thrilled about?" I asked, setting down my book.

"Ms. Jackson has offered to take you in for a few weeks," Ma said.

"Ms. Jackson? Julian's grandmother?"

"Yes," Ma said. "Isn't that wonderful news?"

Wonderful isn't what I would have called it that afternoon. Or even the next day or the next. I wouldn't even really call it wonderful right this very second, but here I am on a one-way bus trip to Meridien with plans to be at Ms. Jackson's house this evening.

School was sorted out with a few phone calls. Football, too. Coach Marcus agreed to let me come to practice and work out with the team as a sort of tryout, but he hinted that it was mostly a formality. I haven't touched a football in three years, and I suspect I'm going to get a ton of mileage riding the bench, but it doesn't matter. Being part of the team might be the thing I'm looking forward to the most about going back to Meridien. Or maybe the only thing; I don't know. Some days it felt like a fantastic idea. And some days it felt like this was quite possibly the worst idea Ma has ever had, and that's saying something.

"You okay with all of this?" Frankie asked me one night while I helped her give Coley a bath.

"Yes? No. Definitely maybe," I told her.

"It will probably only be for a few weeks," she said. "Ma can't quit her job here until the first of the month," she reminded me.

"I know. It's just...*Julian*."

Frankie lowered her head. "I get it. Maybe...maybe you could just walk in there and be your usual Elijah self and act like none of that ever happened? A clean slate is what you need," she said.

I don't necessarily agree that forgetting any and all bits of the past is the best plan for a new start, but I haven't come up with anything better in the few days I've had to pack everything important into my biggest duffel bag.

I thought about Julian all the time. From that early morning three years ago when Frankie and Ma and I disappeared from Meridien until this moment right now as I sit on this bus, I've thought about him.

"Listen, don't say anything about me and Coley while you're in Meridien, okay?" Frankie told me right before I left.

"How come?"

She pursed her lips, and her eyebrows squinched up in the middle of her forehead. "I just don't want people gossiping about me before I'm even there. It'll be my story to tell when I get there, okay? Promise?"

"Yeah, okay. I promise," I told her, even though I didn't

completely agree. Being a teenage mom shouldn't make someone a pariah. "But God help anyone who's got something to say about you," I said, my hands balling into fists at my side.

"Hey, fresh start. Remember?" she said, grabbing my wrist and shaking my hand out of its fist.

I lean my head against the bus window and watch the broken white line stretch for miles. What was Julian doing right now? What was he thinking? Did he spend as much time remembering me as I spent remembering him?

Three weeks without Coley.

Three weeks with Julian.

I don't know which I'm dreading more.

## · three ·

# JULIAN

"We've got a major weak spot on the left side," Coach Marcus yells while we scrimmage. "Tighten up, boys!"

The center hikes the ball to me, and I back up a few steps, looking for an open pass. I spot an open receiver downfield about twenty yards, heading toward the end zone. I pivot right and let the ball go, watching it fall gently into his hands. Just as I exhale, I'm hit, hard, from the left. I fall to the ground in an ungraceful heap, my ribs buzzing.

"Late hit! What the hell was that!" I yell, pushing the defender off me. It's one of our new guys, a freshman. He looks at me, eyes wide.

"I'm so sorry, Julian. I'm so sorry," he says, his voice shaking. He extends his hand to me, but I smack it away.

"Good way to get yourself kicked out of a game, newbie," I

say, pulling myself up off the ground, my ribs burning. This kid is huge.

"It won't happen again, Captain Jackson. I swear," he says, talking around his mouth guard.

Captain Jackson. I snicker to myself as he lumbers away. "Captain Jackson" sounds like I'm the commander of the starship *Enterprise*. Coach Marcus introduced me as such to the freshmen on the first day of practice, but I'm still getting used to it.

"Last play! Make it count. Let's stay on our feet out there, QB!" Coach yells from the sidelines, as if I fell down because I was clumsy. I twist a bit, try to get a little blood flowing to the pulsating pain on my left side. It's stiff, but it'll be okay. "Rub some dirt on it and get back in there," my dad would've said.

I call for an easy play and set up, knowing I'm kind of copping out here, but I really don't want to get hit again. I don't exactly have a ton of confidence in my offensive line yet. The center hikes the ball perfectly, and I make an easy handoff to my running back. The play goes as planned, and I back away from the defense as soon as I hand the ball over. The RB makes a valiant effort to get through, but the defense is just too strong for the wimpy play I called. He's driven back a few yards for a gain of zero. Coach Marcus blows the whistle.

"That was no good. You had Connors wide open downfield, Julian," he says as everyone trudges off the field, sweaty and out of breath.

"Yes, sir," I answer, twisting a little.

"Don't you do that to us on game day," he grumbles. "Use your head out there."

"Yes, sir," I say again.

I stand by the big fan and grab a water bottle while the defensive coach, Andrews, trots over to Coach Marcus, shaking his head. With the loud fan blowing in my ear, I catch only snippets of their conversation.

"...gotta do something about that left side." Coach Andrews removes his cap and wipes the sweat from his bald head.

From the few words I manage to hear over the fan, it almost sounds like we're about to get a new player. Maybe they're bringing someone up from the junior varsity to help out on that left-side defense. I keep my ear trained to their hushed conversation as I step away from the fan and collect the water bottles my teammates have tossed by the bench.

"We'll see how it goes tomorrow." Coach Marcus checks his watch.

Coach Andrews's eyebrows pinch in the middle of his forehead. "I hope you're doing the right thing," he says, shaking his head again and putting his cap back on. The two of them walk toward the locker room.

"Want to throw a few for me?" One of my wide receivers, Nate Connors, taps me on the shoulder. "I want to run a few of the formations I'm having trouble remembering." He spins a football in his palm.

"I can do that. Maybe we can also have some of the cheerleaders hold up the routes on giant posters during the games." I grab the ball from his hand and jog away from him, knowing I'll at least get a punch in the shoulder for that smart-ass remark.

"Jackass," Nate says. He laughs and catches up to me, indeed giving me a solid punch in the shoulder.

My side burns a little bit while we're working, but I'm putting it out of my head for a few minutes to help Nate. Especially if I don't have to worry about getting nailed by a yeti-sized lineman while I throw him a few.

I call a couple of plays and help Nate remember the running routes, tossing some long bombs out to him as he runs toward the end zone. We connect on more than half by the time Nate decides he's tired.

"Okay, I'll call the cheerleaders and tell them to stop making posters. I think you've got a good handle on the routes," I tell him as we collect the balls together. The lights overhead buzz in the late-night heat.

"You're a real peach," he deadpans with a smirk, throwing the full ball bag over his shoulder. "You think we're ready for Stephens City?"

"Absolutely," I tell him. "I don't remember Crenshaw ever losing a game to them."

"Taylor's the real threat anyway. Everything leading up to that feels like a peewee scrimmage," he says, laughing.

"Got that right," I agree.

"So, what are we doing this year, Cap?"

"What do you mean, what are we doing? We're playing football, we're graduating, we're—"

"Oh, come on, don't mess with me." Nate laughs again. "It's

our senior year! Don't tell me you haven't decided what pranks we're pulling before homecoming. They've gotta be good and we've gotta strike first."

"I haven't given it a lot of thought, to tell you the truth." It's not my thing. The senior class always tries to pull off a string of outrageous pranks before the Taylor game. I always thought it was a stupid tradition. But in an even dumber tradition, those pranks have to be decided upon and led by the team captain.

As a senior who would like to eventually go to college without some prank-gone-wrong on his permanent record, I'd like to give the wiseass who came up with this a piece of my mind.

"My dad said that in his senior year, they filled the Taylor quarterback's truck cab with popcorn. That's not exactly the most epic prank, but he still remembers it." Nate shrugs. "I guess I just hope it's something *we* remember when we're forty years old, you know?"

I get it. I do. I just don't see why it's up to me to figure out what's going to be memorable enough. There's this spirit of one-upmanship at Crenshaw, and I don't know that I'm the right guy for that job. Last year's seniors somehow figured out how to swap the cards the Taylor marching band was supposed to hold up that spelled out GO TITANS so that, instead, they spelled out CRENSHAW during their homecoming halftime show. How you top that, I have no idea.

Taylor usually gives as much as they get, too. They decorated the trees in front of Crenshaw in their school colors three years ago, and last year they somehow managed to kill off the grass in front of our gym in a pattern that spelled out TAYLOR TITANS.

And way back when, when my dad was still in school, they spray-painted their mascot onto all of our bleachers in red and black.

"Hey, if you think of something, how about you let me know?" I tell Nate on our way into the locker room.

"No way, man. That's the captain's job. I'm all in on whatever you decide, though," he says, shuffling toward his own locker. "It's on you, Cap." Nate salutes me and then turns on his heel and marches across the room.

My ribs are really burning by the time I get in the shower. I try to talk myself out of it. If I can ice them and rest tonight while I'm finishing my English homework, I'll be as good as new in the morning. But I'm still one of the last ones out of the locker room, and the drill team is getting out of their practice at the same time.

My best friend, Camille, catches me on my way out. Birdie says Camille can talk the hind legs off a donkey. Since I don't usually have a lot to say, we're a good match.

"How was your practice?" she asks, stretching her long frame and shaking her curls out of the tight ponytail they were in. She ties her Crenshaw County Guardettes satin jacket around her waist. I always wonder why they didn't just call them the Guardswomen instead of the Guardettes. Seems like a lame name for a drill team.

"Probably about as good as yours," I say, noticing how tired she looks.

"You're walking funny; you okay?"

"Newbie made a late tackle, caught me off guard. I'm all right," I say.

She raises her eyebrows.

"I'm fine, I swear. Tell me about your practice. You look like you've been hit by a truck," I say, changing the subject.

"You're not kidding," she says, and starts in on a story about how Jannah Sykes took a tumble during the opening number and laughed and how they had to spend the rest of practice doing that one combination because the drill coach is a sadist and when *you're* the one who has to do three back handsprings in the opening combination and you *have* to do it a million times until you're so dizzy you can't tell what's the ceiling and what's the floor, it can get annoying. *Especially* if Jannah laughs every time she falls, and Coach gets more and more mad.

I don't think Camille breathes once while she tells me this story.

"Connors reminded me that I need to start thinking about the senior pranks," I tell Camille when I can finally get a word in. To be honest, I half hope she has some brilliant idea that I can just steal and use.

"Ooh, what are you going to do?" Camille claps her hands in front of her like she's a kid at the circus. "Coach still talks about the pranks the year she graduated, even though she said she's supposed to discourage us from participating."

"Oh, yeah? What happened in her year?"

"Well…" Camille starts, throwing her arms out wide in a dramatic gesture. "Hey, wait a minute." She stops midstride.

"You're just fishing for ideas." She wags a finger at me and starts walking again. "I know how you operate, kid. None of that. They all have to be your idea. Otherwise it makes it less special."

"Less special? Oh, come on, Camille," I say. "You know this isn't my thing. You gotta help me out!"

"Loosen up," she says, shaking my shoulder while we walk. "It's supposed to be *fun*. You remember fun, don't you? It's that thing you used to have in elementary school? Before *this* happened?" She gestures around me with her hands like a mosquito is buzzing nearby.

"What? Before what happened?"

"*This*," she says, gesturing again. "This Mr. Study Until We Die stuff. This Mr. No Fun Until the Work Is Done stuff. Before that."

"Oh, you mean before I realized there's a great big world outside of Meridien?" I ask sarcastically. "Before I decided I wanted to be a part of it? Before I knew that the only way to make that happen is to work my ass off and maybe get a scholarship? Before all that?"

Camille rolls her eyes. "Oh, calm down, Juls. I'm just saying—this prank thing isn't supposed to be some anxiety-inducing mess. It's just a laugh. Stop worrying about it! Something will come to you." Her grin turns mischievous. "But it better come to you quick."

I set my jaw, and we walk all the way to the corner of Rudy Street without talking. Camille is always on my case about loosening up. But I didn't get to be the captain of the football team by loosening up. Or into four AP classes.

Most of the kids from my side of the county end up in one of three places:

1. Stuck in some dead-end job in Meridien working for crap money.
2. Locked up or on probation for doing something they thought was going to be fun but was actually just stupid.
3. Out of here with a scholarship and a gold-lined path to bigger and better things.

As much as I love Meridien, I'm going for option three. And I'm too close to my gold-lined path to throw it all away for some stupid town tradition.

"Birdie had someone over for dinner tonight," I say after we walk a few yards in silence. I know neither Camille nor I will let the tension from earlier turn into anything major. We've been friends too long and are both pretty good about letting stuff like that go.

"Oh yeah? Pastor Ernie and Figg again?"

"No, I don't think so. She kind of acted like it was supposed to be a surprise?"

"Ooh, maybe it was Mr. Cooper." She giggles. "I've seen him giving Birdie the eye in church on Sundays."

"Knock it off." I laugh, giving her a little shove on the shoulder at the top of her driveway.

"Text me!" she shouts, hiking her bags up and jogging to her front door. "I want to hear all about this mysterious guest!"

I turn and head down Rudy Street toward home. From a few houses away, I can tell there are no extra cars in our driveway, but I do notice that there are an awful lot of lights on inside the house. It's all lit up, like for a party.

"Birdie, I'm home," I say, stepping into the front room and closing the door behind me. My ribs ache when I turn, and I grimace.

"Julian? We're in the kitchen!"

I drop my bags on the couch.

In the kitchen, both stools are taken. Sitting on one is Birdie with a cup of tea. On the other is a tall boy with shoulder-length wavy hair, wearing basketball shorts and a tank top. The boy turns toward me, and my heart jumps into my throat. I swear I can feel it pounding against my tonsils.

"Elijah Vance?" I say, my voice sounding small over the sound of my heartbeat banging in my ears.

"Hey, Julian." His voice shakes, and a crooked smile touches his full lips.

My skin prickles from my shoulders all the way down my back when I look at his smile. It's still familiar to me, even after all these years, but it also looks strange on this older face sitting in my kitchen.

"Elijah."

## · four ·

# *ELIJAH*

I can't read the expression on his face when he first sees me. His eyes sweep from the top of my head to my shoes, and I can feel the heat creeping up my neck as he stares at me. The room fills with tension that I can feel in my bones.

"Hey, Julian," I say, my voice more timid than I want it to be.

His face is soft for a minute, and I try to smile, even though I know it's crooked. My stomach lurches.

"Elijah."

"It's so good to see you, Julian," I say, the words tumbling from my chest and out of my mouth faster than I can stop them.

I stand up and take a step toward Julian. To what? Hug him? Shake his hand? I'm moving toward him without really knowing why when I notice his face has turned from soft to stormy in the blink of an eye. I stop short in the kitchen doorway.

"Why are you here?" His brow furrows and his jaw tenses.

It's like a punch in the gut.

"Julian!" Ms. Jackson admonishes, putting her hand on my shoulder. "Elijah's going to be staying with us for a while. And there's no call for that rude tone."

My stomach flip-flops. I try to catch Julian's eye, but he's not looking at me. Instead, he's looking at Ms. Jackson, a storm brewing just below the surface.

"He's starting back at Crenshaw, and he needs a place to settle until the rest of his family gets here in a few weeks," Ms. Jackson says. I watch the looks pass between them, and I know Ms. Jackson is saying a lot more with her eyes than she's saying with her mouth. Her eyes are saying things like *Don't you dare say anything ugly, Julian, or you won't be able to sit down for a week.* I've seen my own mother's eyes say the same thing a million times. Even Frankie is learning to perfect those eyes that talk.

"Ma and Frankie and...everyone will be here in a couple of weeks. When my mother's job starts," I say, my voice a little stronger than it was a few minutes ago. "They're packing up the apartment and stuff." Julian takes his eyes off of Ms. Jackson long enough to look me in the eye.

There is dark stubble along his jawline, but his close-cropped dark hair is cut exactly the same as it always was. Same piercing blue eyes that look like they're looking right through you, too. I wipe the sweat forming on my brow and brush a strand of my hair behind my ear.

"Why are you here before they are?" Julian asks, jutting his chin out at me.

It's a simple question, but the acid behind it makes my chest ache.

"I wanted to start school as soon as possible. I didn't want to have to transfer a few weeks into the semester. So, Ms. Jackson said..." I trail off when I notice the look on Julian's face.

"I said we would be happy to have him stay with us for a few weeks," Ms. Jackson says. "And you call me Birdie like you did when you were little, Elijah. It's okay," she finishes, putting her hand on my shoulder again and squeezing lightly.

"Thank you, Ms....Birdie," I say, remembering the way it felt to call her that when I was younger. Like something warm settling around my shoulders.

Julian cuts his eyes toward his grandmother, his face full of fury. "Why didn't you tell me sooner?"

"Ms. Vance and I only just worked out the details a few days ago. I thought it best to keep it quiet until all our ducks were in a row."

"I won't get in your way," I say quietly.

"Oh, now don't you go fretting about that," Ms. Birdie says, giving me a playful swat on the back with her dish towel. "Come on now, I've got dinner waiting for all of us."

Ms. Birdie sets out a feast of pork chops, mashed potatoes, and peas. Julian digs in without even looking at me. I try to relax, but everything feels wrong. I don't know why I thought Julian would be okay with any of this. I feel too big for this room. Like I'm taking up too much space and too much oxygen. I pull the smallest pork chop from the plate Ms. Birdie passes me and only one scoop of potatoes, even though I know I could probably eat the whole bowl by myself.

From the dining table, I can see the brown house across the street. My stomach churns, and I have to work to swallow a mouthful of peas. The brown shingles are the same, though they look like they've seen a few touch-up paint jobs. The white trim on the front porch isn't flaking, and there are two bright white rockers and a bunch of hanging ferns near the front door. I wonder what kind of family now lives inside. Wonder who is sleeping in my old room and whether they look out the window into Julian's front yard and think about him the way I used to.

I catch sight of him across the table, head down. The curve of his ear, the movement in his jaw while he eats, it's all so familiar and so foreign at the same time.

"Things must look a little different than they did when you were here last, Elijah," Ms. Birdie says in a voice too loud for the room.

"Yes, ma'am."

"First Federal Bank has closed, where your mother used to work," she says.

I just nod.

Ms. Birdie keeps up a steady stream of chatter, noting what's still the same about Meridien and what may have changed since I lived across the street.

Julian gets up from the table in the middle of Ms. Birdie's tour of Meridien, puts his plate in the sink, and heads down the hallway. There's a heavy rock in my chest I can't swallow past.

"He'll come around," Ms. Birdie whispers.

"Does he know about Coley?" I ask, throat still tight.

"Not my story to tell," Ms. Birdie says. "You can tell him when you're ready." She smiles at me and then reaches across the table to give me an awkward hug. I melt into her. "I'm so happy to have you here. Don't you worry about Julian. Now you show me some pictures of that sweet baby girl while I get these dishes."

I follow Ms. Birdie into the kitchen and pull out my phone. I scroll through the most recent pictures of Coley and Frankie while she fills the sink with warm soapy water. Her second birthday back in March. Coley wearing Ma's heels and carrying Frankie's gigantic purse. Coley and Frankie on the beach in Galveston this summer. Coley posing in my glasses. Ms. Birdie makes the appropriate "aww" noises and mumbles "so precious" at least twenty times while she washes the dishes. Coley's bright green eyes shine at me through the phone screen, and I feel a tug in my chest.

"I think I'd like to get settled in and go to bed," I say. "Thank you for the delicious meal, Ms. Birdie."

"Don't you mention it, sweet Elijah," she says, pursing her lips. Her eyes look like they want to say more, but instead she calls for Julian.

"Yes, ma'am?" He appears in the kitchen doorway shirtless with a towel around his neck.

"Can you show Elijah into the guest room, please?"

He doesn't answer right away, and I see a look pass between him and Ms. Birdie.

"It's this way," he says without looking at me.

I grab my black duffel from the couch and follow Julian down a short hallway. The muscles in his back flex while he walks, and my fingers remember what it was like to touch his warm skin. Does he remember?

"It's here," he says, flicking on the light and pointing to the next door in the hallway. "That's my room."

"I remember," I say, a pit in my stomach.

His eyes are angry and hurt and sad and confused all at once. I search my brain for something to say, anything, that will brighten his face. Make things between us okay.

"I'm...I won't get in your way," I say again, knowing that's not the right thing but desperate to say something.

"Whatever," he says, shaking his head and disappearing behind his bedroom door.

I drop my bag just inside the guest room doorway and glance inside. The bedspread is white with pink rosebuds and yellow daisies. The window overlooks the patchy backyard, the rickety shed, and a clothesline stretching from the corner above my window to the massive oak ten feet away. A bag of clothespins dances on the line in the evening breeze, lit up by the light spilling from the kitchen window. I pull the heavy, matching curtains tight, drowning out most of the light, and switch on the rosebud lamp on the night table.

I sit down on the bed and think about Julian just next door. I stare toward the door and wonder if he can feel me thinking about him through the wall. I desperately want to knock on his door and make a joke or say something sarcastic. Just to see him smile at me once.

I pull my phone from my pocket and call Frankie. I texted both her and Ma when the bus pulled into Corpus Christi, but I really just want to hear her voice.

"Hey," I say when she answers. "Just got done with dinner."

"Jeez, I miss you already. This is going to be a long few weeks." She laughs a sad laugh.

"How's my girl?"

"She keeps wandering around the apartment looking for you. I think the boxes are confusing her. I told her you weren't here, but I don't think she believes me." She sighs.

"I'm sorry," I say, my throat tight.

"Hey! None of that! We'll be there in a few weeks, and Coley won't even remember this. Don't you think like that. You go to school and play football and do your thing, and don't even think twice about us. We'll be there soon," she says.

I don't answer. Not thinking about Coley or Frankie or even my mother for a few weeks isn't really even an option.

"How are things..." she says.

"What things?"

"Don't make me say it. You know what I mean." She sucks her teeth.

"With Julian? Not...um...not great," I say, a slight hiccup in my voice. My throat feels thick, and I blink a few extra times.

"Oh, 'lijah." Frankie sounds genuinely sad.

"Maybe this was a mistake," I whisper.

"You know things are always darkest before the dawn. We knew this wasn't going to be easy when Ma said she wanted to move back to Meridien," she says, her voice quiet but steady.

"I know," I say, my gut swirling while I fiddle with the switch on the lamp.

I remember Ma sitting with her laptop at our tiny kitchen table with the month's bills spread out around her and a job website open on the screen.

"What are you up to?" I asked her, filling a glass with ice.

"Do you know I could make almost double what I'm making right now if I took this administrative job at Dirk Murphy's insurance agency?"

"Murphy? Darien Murphy's dad? In Meridien? Why would you want to move back there?" I asked her. My stomach dropped to my knees at the thought of seeing anyone from that town again, but especially Julian.

"This is not the place we should be raising Coley." She shook her head and looked around our cluttered apartment. "We can do better than this."

Next thing I knew, she was talking to Dirk Murphy on the phone and telling Frankie to start collecting boxes and milk crates from her part-time grocery store job.

"Stiff upper lip," Frankie says on the phone, drawing me out of my thoughts. "School. Football. Keep your head on straight, and me and Coley and Ma will be there before you know it. It's going to get easier, 'lijah."

"Maybe he'll come around," I say. I don't actually believe that, no matter how many times Ms. Birdie says it.

"Do you think it's because of what happened before we left? Or is it something else?"

"I honestly don't know. He's barely said two words to me that Ms. Birdie hasn't forced him to say."

"You can do this, you know. Everything will work itself out. I know it," Frankie says, her voice strong and confident.

I wish I felt the same.

## · five ·

## *JULIAN*

I can hear his voice through the wall. I can't hear any words, but his distinct low mumble floats through the cheap insulation and drywall and dances through the air right to my eardrums. I lie on my bed with my English homework, but I can't concentrate on anything with that deep hum lingering around in my head. It sounds like before.

His eyes are the same.

And that crooked smile.

But his hair is longer, falling in golden waves across his forehead and curling behind his ears. When I first saw him sitting on the stool in my kitchen, my first instinct was to touch him. Hug him. Put my hands on his skin in some way. But when he stood up and his frame filled the kitchen doorway, all I could remember was that he left without telling me where he was going, or even saying goodbye.

Things had been complicated before he left, but had I not meant anything to him at all? All those years we were friends, and maybe something a little more than that, and he just disappeared from my life overnight.

He had never exactly been a model citizen or a great student. It wasn't that he actually went out and got in trouble every day or anything, but he always seemed to be around when bad things happened, you know? The teacher's candy stash disappearing in third grade. Fights in the middle school hallway. Elijah always seemed to be in detention for something. Or sitting in the hallway outside of class because he was mouthing off or otherwise annoying someone. Never serious trouble, but enough that he had a reputation of sorts. He was a joker. A class clown.

But we were still friends.

We had been friends since we were seven years old and played peewee ball together. We kind of grew apart for a few years after fifth grade. We were still in each other's orbit, just not connected at the hip as we had been when we were really little. It had started to bother me that Elijah didn't take things as seriously as I did. Later on, I realized that maybe that was one of the things I liked best about him, too.

We started hanging out again that summer after middle school. Elijah showed up on my front porch one morning, and that was it. From then on we were always together, tossing the football back and forth or riding our bikes down to Jake's

Convenience for Cokes and bags of hot Cheetos. We compared the hairs on our chins and made bets on who would be able to grow a beard first. We dared each other to eat the ghost pepper wings at Sir Clucks-A-Lot. Elijah taught me how to jump from the Main Street bridge to the banks of the creek below without breaking an ankle. I taught him Morse code. That summer, we were as close as we had been when we were seven. Never saw one of us without the other.

Maybe that's why it hurt so much that I was the one who found him there that day a few weeks into our freshman year, the window already broken, shards of glass scattered across his raggedy tennis shoes. He had seemed to turn a corner the summer before we started ninth grade. I'm pretty sure the change in his attitude had something to do with football. He knew, as we all did, that the high school coaches didn't put up with any crap and they'd replace you in a heartbeat if you screwed up in school. Even if you were Elijah Vance, Meridien Middle School's Defensive Player of the Year.

But that night, there stood Elijah outside the school, wearing Crenshaw football shorts and a bright red tank top, the rock already thrown into the football coach's office window.

I was the one who turned him in.

I don't know if he knows that or not.

I left an anonymous message on the school's tip line. I still remember what I said. "Elijah Vance broke the window into the football coach's office. He was trying to steal the car wash money."

Even now, three years later, I'm not sure that I did the right thing.

I remember Birdie jumping up from her La-Z-Boy later that night when the spinning yellow light from the school resource officer's car streaked across our living room.

"What in tarnation..." she whispered. "Julian, what in heaven's name is going on over there?"

I didn't answer her, but I did follow her onto the porch.

It seemed like all the neighbors were out on their porches on Rudy Street that night, wondering what the officer was doing in the Vances' driveway. It wasn't like the Vances were strangers to officers showing up at their doorstep, but most of their troubles disappeared when Mr. Vance was put away for good up in Huntsville.

I felt a tiny pinch of guilt, watching Ms. Vance open her front door to Officer Kapinski. The shame on her face was visible even as the sun dipped below the horizon and started to turn the world purple.

Camille whispered to me the next day in fourth period, "Elijah got *suspended*. For a *month*."

I tried to look shocked. I tried to look sorry.

All I felt was numb and confused.

And now he's in my house, and I still can't decide what I'm supposed to feel. There were things we shared three years ago, before he broke the window. Things that can't be erased by a monthlong suspension and a three-year move to Houston. But he still left me. Without an explanation and without saying goodbye.

I throw my English homework on the floor. There's no way I'm going to be able to concentrate on anything else tonight. My head is filled with Elijah.

I find Birdie in the living room, a stretch of quilting across her lap and her glasses perched on the end of her nose. The TV is on, but the volume is turned way down, as some late-night talk show host in a fancy suit delivers his monologue.

I sit down next to Birdie on the couch and let my head fall back. The burning in my ribs has mostly dulled to a slight buzz now. Maybe there will be a bruise there tomorrow.

"How was practice?" she asks, her voice quiet as she works the needle in and out of her squares at a dizzying pace.

"Fine."

"Now, Julian, let's not be like that," she says. "The good book says to love thy neighbor."

I try not to roll my eyes, because even though she's not looking right at me, I'm convinced Birdie can hear things like that.

"The good book says thou shalt not do a lot of things that Elijah Vance has done," I mumble.

"Listen, I know you're upset," she says.

"Upset? I'm not upset," I say.

"Now, Julian..." That's twice she's "Now, Julian-ed" me.

"Why didn't you tell me?"

Birdie lets out a long, low sigh. "Pastor Ernie told me about the Vances' situation last weekend. I told him I would get in touch with Ms. Vance and see if we couldn't work something out. Robin wanted Elijah to start school at Crenshaw right away instead of waiting until they were ready to move back. She was in a bind, Julian. We've got the room. I wasn't going to turn my back on a family in need."

"But three years ago—"

"That boy has more than done his penance for that now. And that's the last I want to hear about it. Yes?" Birdie's tone goes firm.

"Yes, ma'am." I know when I'm about to get "Now, Julian-ed" again.

We sit in silence for a few minutes, the muffled canned laughter from the TV the only noise in the room. "Where has he been for the past three years?" I ask.

Birdie shakes her head next to me. "Elijah will tell you in his own good time."

I wonder what Birdie would think if she knew I was the one who got Elijah in trouble in the first place. Even though we were friends. Even though at some point we were probably on our way to being much more than friends, right before he broke that window.

"He left without even saying goodbye to me," I say, trying to keep the edge out of my voice. I don't want to admit that even three years without him can't dull the hurt I feel now when I see him. As painful as it was the day I realized he was gone.

"He'll only be living with us for a short time. Maybe it'll do Elijah some good to spend time with you again," she says, her face softening into a smile. She squeezes my shoulder. "You're a good boy, Julian."

I grab a bottle of water from the fridge, shake a couple of ibuprofen into my mouth, and head back to my room. I take a long look at the guest room door. No light shines from underneath, so I'm guessing Elijah has gone to sleep.

I crawl into bed and pull the blanket up to my ears.

## · six ·

# *ELIJAH*

I've got bats in my stomach when I wake up on Tuesday morning. Maybe worse than bats. Maybe barn owls or vultures.

Ms. Birdie puts a plate of pancakes in front of me with fresh fruit on the side. "Going to need a little energy for your first day back," she says. "This isn't an everyday breakfast, but I thought you could use a little comfort food this morning." She winks.

"Thanks," I mumble, trying to swallow a bite or two.

"You've got nothing to be nervous about, you know," she says, sitting down across from me. "That old Coach Marcus is going to let you on the team. Don't let him fill your head with that 'unofficial tryout' business. You're tougher than a pine knot, Elijah."

"I haven't played in three years," I admit to her, dragging a piece of pancake through the warm syrup. "Coley and Frankie needed me at home."

"I firmly believe football is like riding a bike. Once you lace those pads up, you're going to be fine. Muscle memory. Don't you get yourself all worked up before you even get your cleats in the grass. You'll be okay," she says, rubbing her palm across my back.

"What about Julian?" I ask. "Does he know?"

"Not yet," she says.

I'm about to protest when she suddenly stands up from her kitchen stool, cutting me off. "And speak of the devil! Good morning, sunshine." She laughs.

Julian grunts from where he stands by the doorway and grabs a protein shake from the refrigerator before heading back down the hallway toward the bathroom.

"He's about as friendly as a porcupine in the mornings." Ms. Birdie smiles at me when he disappears. "But don't you worry about him. I'm sure he'll be thrilled to have you back on the team. You can tell him on your walk to school."

Twenty minutes later, Camille Robles is waiting for us at the end of the driveway, and I still haven't told Julian.

"Elijah Vance," she says, running up to me and wrapping her arms around my neck. "Oh my GOD. We all thought you were dead! Or in prison!"

I try really hard not to roll my eyes. I heard the whispers from some of the people in Meridien right after I was suspended. Loudmouths who made comments about me eventually sharing a cell with my father and making bets on how long it would take before I did something bad enough to be shipped up to Huntsville just like him. It was the cruelest of the cruel remarks we endured in the few weeks between my suspension and when we left Meridien. For some reason, I don't think Camille realizes just how much it stings, and I almost forgive her for it. Is that me getting numb to it? Or just forgetting how nasty things got right before we left?

"Uh...not dead. Or, uh...or the other thing," I say, feeling my cheeks flush. I haven't seen Camille in years, but she doesn't seem to have changed much. Same giant curly hair. Same long, skinny frame.

"Let me look at you!" she says, holding my arm up like she's checking under the hood of a car. "That hair! I'm loving it!" She touches the top of my head and ruffles it a little bit.

"Camille, knock it off," Julian says.

I try to throw him a *thank you* glance, but he's not looking at me. The apples of his cheeks are pink.

"So, where have you been all these years?" Camille says, adjusting her backpack and falling in step between Julian and me.

"Uh...well," I mumble.

"Out with it," she says, knocking me with her elbow.

"We were in Houston," I say, biting the inside of my lip and hoping she doesn't ask any more questions.

"Oh, I have people in Houston," she says, launching into a long description of aunts, uncles, and cousins twice removed.

I'm glad Camille is so good at filling the silence, because Julian hasn't said two words to me since last night when he showed me the guest room. He did wait for me this morning before heading out to walk to school, but when I said good morning, he just kind of smirked.

As we get closer to the school, the football field is the first thing I see. A tiny nugget of happiness breaks open in my chest when I see the yards and yards of green grass and the bright yellow goalposts at each end of the field. I can't wait to get back out there.

"And my cousin Annie's family moved to Sugar Land when I was just a baby. Right after that hurricane." Camille is still talking about people she knows in Houston. "My mom says she tried to convince her to come here, but Annie says there's no way she's going to live near the ocean anymore. And who can blame her, really? All that water nearly swallowed up her house, and my mom wants her to live right on the shore again? Shit," Camille says, sucking her teeth. "For a college professor who is supposed to be smart, sometimes my mom makes zero sense." Camille's mother has been teaching women's and gender studies at Coastal Texas Community College our whole lives. Her dad is the middle school Spanish teacher. It's only because of him that I know how to properly say *"No hablo español muy bien."* I can also ask directions to a library if I ever find myself lost in Puerto Rico. *¿Dónde está la biblioteca?* It's only because of Camille that our entire third-grade class knew all the good Spanish swears. Camille would charge us twenty-five cents per swear lesson. Honestly, half of my third-grade class could have taught us those swears, but Camille was the first to suggest it and then monetize it. By the time she got caught at the end of the school year, the whole third grade at Meridien Elementary School already had a full repertoire. When she finally did get caught, our teacher, Mrs. Bowles, told Camille she had a real keen eye for business. Third grade with Mrs. Bowles was probably the last time I liked school. Or felt like maybe I was kind of good at it sometimes. It wasn't that I didn't *try*. It was more like trouble found me a lot of the time. Around the end of eighth grade, though, it was pretty obvious that I was going to have to try a little harder. Smiling my way out of things wasn't going to work in high school, and I knew football would be the first thing I'd lose if I screwed up.

I wouldn't exactly say I'm about to be sick as we approach the front steps of the school, but I can't rule out the possibility that I will lose that stack of Ms. Birdie's pancakes, either. I leave Camille and Julian standing on the front steps as I enter the building, barely able to mumble a goodbye as I turn and pull open the door. Camille waves and practically shouts that she'll see me later, but Julian simply stares after me.

I stand just inside the front entrance, throngs of kids passing by. A few of them bump into me like I'm not even there, but I can't move yet. I concentrate on breathing and try to remember how to get to the guidance counselor's office from here. Pointing my feet in the right direction, I join the fray and keep my head down.

"You new?" a boy with scruffy facial hair says to me right outside the guidance office.

"Not exactly," I say, searching my head for the right words to explain exactly what I am.

"Oh, jeez. Vance?" The kid sticks out his hand for me to shake. "Connors!" He points to his chest.

"Nate? Hey, man...it's good to see you," I smile. Nate

Connors and Julian and I started playing football together when we were seven years old.

"I didn't know you were coming back. What are you doing here?"

I shrug. "Shit, I don't know."

Connors laughs. "You find me if you need anything, all right? Hey, you coming back to the team?"

"I've got an unofficial tryout with Coach Marcus this afternoon," I tell him as the bell overhead rings, and he backs away from the office toward his first-period class.

"Excellent!" He pumps his fist above his head and takes off jogging the rest of the way down the long hall.

*Excellent.* Let's hope I get the same reception from Julian when he finds out I'll be at football practice this afternoon.

I get a pretty good schedule from my guidance counselor, Ms. Woods, plus a ton of unsolicited advice about keeping my head on straight and staying out of trouble. She throws in a few jabs about the football team, too. I remember she was always in the front row of the bleachers for every single game, face paint on her cheeks and her bright blue pom-poms in her lap.

"See if you can help them out on that left-side defense." Ms. Woods scowls at me as I leave her office.

"Yes, ma'am," I answer, holding my paper schedule in my hand and trying to remember which way to turn to get to the English classrooms.

Most of my first day back at Crenshaw goes exactly the same as the morning. I shuffle my way through the hallways, looking down, trying to remember how to navigate the labyrinth of classrooms. A handful of kids recognize me and smile. Another handful of kids recognize me and scowl. Mostly I'm ignored, which is perfectly fine with me. The less attention I draw to myself, the better.

A lot of my classrooms overlook the big expanse of green grass behind the school, and I find myself just staring at it and then my watch, counting down the hours and then minutes before I'm back on the field. It has been an embarrassingly long time since I've held a football or dug my cleats into the grass.

"Why don't you try out for the team here?" Frankie asked me one summer afternoon before tenth grade. She was rocking back and forth, holding a three-month-old Coley up on her shoulder in our cramped apartment.

"I don't really miss it," I lied, watching the way my niece's curls already framed her tiny little face as she fussed against the crook of her mother's neck. I knew that playing football again was going to take up every second of my free time. And there was no way I was going to leave Frankie to care for Coley all by herself. Ma was always so exhausted when she got home from work that Frankie tried not to ask her to help out with Coley too much. Frankie was alone with the baby all day long while she finished high school online. Helping out with Coley, feeding her, and playing with her when I got home from school was the least I could do. There was no way I could tell Frankie that. She would have felt guilty and tried to force me to try out for the team anyway.

The truth was that I missed football every day. Just like I missed Julian every day. When Coach Marcus decided a monthlong suspension was what I needed after I broke the window to his office, Ma started packing up the house. Frankie was the only person who ever knew why I was trying to break into the coach's office. I sometimes wonder if Coach Marcus would've suspended me if he'd known I was trying to steal the car wash money for Frankie and the baby.

I know it was Julian who tip-lined me. He was standing right behind me after I broke the window. I have no idea if *he* knows that I know it was him. He asked me flat out as we stood there if I was breaking in to steal the car wash money we had just locked up in Coach Marcus's desk. As much as I wanted to deny it, I was like a deer in headlights. I couldn't lie to him; instead, I just pathetically nodded my head when he asked. Frankie had already started hiding her growing belly from her bad-news boyfriend, Ty, and the rest of Meridien, under long T-shirts and leggings.

"We need a fresh start. Your uncle Jacob has gotten me a job in Houston," Ma told us as she put together the moving boxes.

I started to protest.

"I don't want to hear another word about it, Elijah. Frankie needs to raise her baby away from that boyfriend and Meridien. This town doesn't seem to be doing you any favors, either." She handed me a suitcase and told me to start packing.

One day, we just left. Five AM disappearance. Like we were never here to begin with. That morning, I watched Julian's front door, willing him to wake up and see us leaving. Watch us pack everything we owned into a small U-Haul and my mother's minivan and drive away.

"Just go knock on his window," Frankie said, loading another box into the back of Ma's minivan.

I didn't, though. I couldn't.

I thought about Julian all the way to Houston. I thought about him when we unpacked our things in the shitty efficiency apartment Uncle Jacob found for us after we lived with him for two weeks. I thought about Julian when we moved into a slightly bigger apartment a few months later, Frankie's expanding belly knocking things off the shelves. I thought about him when Frankie got too big to tie her own shoes, and I definitely thought about him when Coley was born, a mess of dark curls and a cry that could peel paint from the walls. I honestly just couldn't *stop* thinking about him while we were away.

On the bus to Meridien just yesterday, I thought about Julian again. What it would feel like to put cleats on and play with him again. In Houston, football would have meant getting onto the field without him. But now that I finally have the chance to suit up with him again? All I feel is sick to my stomach.

# · seven ·

# JULIAN

I spend the day on the lookout for Elijah. I'm so focused on knowing where he is at all times, I'm barely paying attention in class. He hasn't shown up to any of my classes by lunchtime, and all that's left are US history and football.

At lunch, all anyone can talk about is Elijah.

"I heard he was in prison, just like his dad," a girl whispers, scooping a heap of syrupy fruit cocktail onto her lunch tray. I roll my eyes. That "Elijah ended up in prison" theory made the rounds when he never returned from his suspension, and it's just as stupid now as it was then. Maybe even more so.

"He's in my physics class. He sat in the back and never even took out a pencil," another guy says when I pass his table.

"I can't believe Ms. Jackson is letting him stay at her house."

"I can't believe they're letting him back on the football team."

"Wait, what?" I stop short at a table full of marching band kids. Camille's drum major ex-boyfriend, Evan, is holding court in the middle of the percussion section. I've always thought Evan was a giant ass, and I'm very glad Camille finally came to the same conclusion last year.

"Yeah, I heard Coach Marcus in the hallway this morning. Something about everyone deserving a second chance, blah blah blah," Evan tells me. "Everyone better hide their wallets," he says to his friends. They all reward his smart-ass comment with hearty laughter.

"Are you sure you heard that?" I ask him.

"You mean you didn't know? Aren't you the *captain* of the team?" he asks, raising his eyebrows.

I walk away from the table without a word. The conversation I overheard at last night's football practice between Coaches Marcus and Andrews must have been about Elijah. Does Birdie know? As booster club president, sometimes she knows things about the team even before the coaches do.

If even Evan knew before I did...I try to shake it off. Elijah was good at football. He worked hard. Maybe he'll be good for the team. The defense *could* use a little help.

I mumble that to myself all the way through lunch and history. *It'll be good for the team. It'll be good for the team.* It doesn't help. I'm fuming mad by the time I get to practice during seventh period. Birdie *had* to have known.

She could have told me last night. I'm the captain of this

team. Shouldn't that afford me some kind of privilege? Someone could have told me that Elijah was not only coming back to Meridien but was going to start playing on my team again. *My* team. The team I've been a part of for four years. I feel like I've been building this family since ninth grade. *After* Elijah left without saying a word. And he's just going to waltz onto the field and start playing again?

I swing the heavy locker room door open harder than I intend to, and it slams against the wall.

"Take it easy there, Cap," Bucky Redd says to me, tightening his shoulder pads. I'm not sure why we all still call him Bucky instead of Brian, even though orthodontia worked its magic in middle school, but I guess when you're saddled with a nickname in second grade, sometimes it just sticks.

I flop down on the bench between him and Nate Connors and throw my bag on the floor.

"What's eating you?" Nate asks, straightening his socks and pulling on his grass-stained cleats.

"Did you know Elijah Vance was going to be on the team again?" I turn to both of them.

Nate nods, looking everywhere but at me. "I just found out this morning. I ran into Elijah outside the guidance office before first period, and he told me Coach Marcus was giving him an unofficial tryout this afternoon."

"And you didn't think to tell me this?"

"Sorry, Cap. I thought you knew," Nate says.

"What about you?" I ask Bucky, not even trying to keep the accusatory tone out of my voice anymore.

"I found out from Connors at lunch." Bucky swallows hard.

"You told *him* and not *me?*" I stick my thumb out at Bucky and stare at Nate.

Nate busies himself with his other shoe and doesn't look up.

"Didn't either of you think that this might be information I might be interested in?" Now neither one of them will look at me. I roll my school shorts and sneakers into a ball and throw them into my locker. The heap makes a satisfying *ping* against the metal. "There's a new player on the team, and no one thinks to tell me about it?" I slam the door and spin the lock before walking out of the locker room and onto the field.

Behind me, I hear Bucky. "Yikes. Someone better calm his ass down or we'll be doing bear-crawl warm-ups all afternoon."

Bear crawls. Now, that's not a terrible idea.

I've always worked my ass off at football. It makes sense to me. There are rules and formations and a playbook to follow. Dad started teaching me the basics practically as soon as I could walk, and Birdie regaled me with stories about his football career at Crenshaw, and later Coastal Texas. I knew I could be just like my dad if I worked hard enough. Birdie thought I could be even better.

"I've never seen anyone work so hard," she'd tell me after peewee and middle school practices. Football and grades. They were what mattered. Those two things, I hoped, might be my ticket to bigger and better things. It had been drilled into my brain since I was knee-high to a grasshopper that football could take me places if I put in the effort. All that work has always been for one reason: I want to be the kind of man my father would have been proud of.

And now, here comes Elijah and my head is all over the place.

I take a few minutes to look through the playbook on the bench before the rest of the team trickles out of the locker room. I've had most of the formations and running patterns memorized for days, but I always take a look at them when I have an extra minute. There are a few that I'm having trouble remembering, and there's no such thing as too much studying.

Bucky and Nate join me at the bench.

"Hey, I'm sorry I didn't tell you about Elijah when I found out," Nate says. "I really thought you already knew. Especially since you guys were...you know. I thought if anyone already knew about it, you would have."

"Sorry I blew up at you," I tell him. And I do feel guilty. "I just don't like feeling surprised."

"Honestly, I was a little ticked that *you* hadn't told *me*," he says with a little punch on my shoulder. "Anyway, sorry."

I shake my head at him. "Nothing a few hundred bear crawls won't solve."

Bucky throws his arms up in the air. "Man! Not this week!"

I laugh and squirt my water bottle in his face.

I notice Elijah has come out of the locker room by himself and is milling around near the ice buckets, staring nervously around at the other players.

I know I should find a way to make him feel welcome. A good captain would do that. I've never been the new kid. Or the returning kid. Or whatever he is. I don't know what that feels like, but from the look on Elijah's face, I don't think it feels too good.

He bounces on the balls of his feet and chews on his lip, pulling his hair back into a tiny ponytail at the back of his head. He tightens the pads on his chest and throws on a mesh jersey, his eyes darting around the group as we all stand around goofing off.

Coach Marcus gives two quick blasts on his whistle, and we all spread out across the grass. I take my place in front of the team and start leading them in stretches, trying to pay attention to my ribs. This morning, a small bruise popped up on my side. I put some tape on it before I got dressed for school, and every time I move, I can feel the curling edges of the tape scraping against my jersey. It's driving me nuts. Finally, I just rip it off and tuck the sticky ball into the waistband of my football pants.

My eyes fall on Elijah while he stretches.

He was a football star from the time we were seven years old. A few weeks after my dad died, Birdie dressed me in a bright blue jersey and brand-new white football pants and shoved me out onto a field at the park with a bunch of other little boys whose helmets were too big for their heads. Elijah was the biggest kid in the grass that day, in a pair of Batman sneakers and grass-stained football pants from the charity bin at church. He was the first person to talk to me.

His size caught the coach's eye right away. "You're definitely on defense, Vance. We're going to put those shoulders to good use," the coach said after sizing him up. That same coach looked at me and screwed up his lips into a smirk. "Offense, I guess? Maybe try quarterback? Can you even throw the ball?"

I remember standing right off Elijah's shoulder anytime the

coach gave him a high five, hoping to lap up some of that praise, too. He never had to work for it the way I did. He was just naturally good at football. I studied the hell out of the plays, read books from the library about throwing the perfect spiral, and watched countless YouTube videos about what makes a good quarterback. I was the third-string quarterback through almost all our peewee years. But Elijah could just read the field on defense, even in elementary school. He knew exactly how to watch the tics, feel the tension from the opposite side, and put himself right into the middle of a major play. As he got older, he just got better.

I watch him stretch and wonder if he still has those same instincts.

"Bear crawls! Go!" I yell and watch the rest of the team groan while I retreat to the bench and grab my water bottle. One of the perks of being captain is that I can sit out of a warm-up exercise every so often and no one really says too much. Today my ribs are thankful for that.

I keep my eye on Elijah. He's at the back of the pack, sweat trickling down the side of his cheek in the late-afternoon sun. Even though he's clearly not in the same shape he was three years ago, the look on his face is a mixture of pure joy and gritty determination.

## · eight ·

# *ELIJAH*

I feel fifty pairs of eyes on me when I walk out of the locker room and onto the field. I stay off to the side, near the ice buckets, while I try to settle my stomach, but I can feel all of it. The judgment. The way some of the guys cut their eyes at me.

Nate Connors, who seemed genuinely excited this morning when I told him I was coming back, spends the entire warm-up just two inches from Julian. Neither of them even wave or smile in my direction. I stay in the back, try to blend in, while I drag my out-of-shape ass through the warm-up and endless bear crawls. I shouldn't be surprised that Julian is the captain. Since we were seven years old, he's always been the kid that works harder than anyone else.

Coach Marcus calls for a water break after the eighteen thousandth bear crawl, and I try to creep into the background again. I just feel like I'm in the way.

I watch as Coach grabs Julian by the front of his helmet and talks to him with his other hand on his waist. Even though I can't hear any of the words, I can tell by Coach's body language that he's giving Julian hell for something.

Eventually, Coach lets go of his helmet and Julian slides up next to me.

"When were you going to tell me that you were coming back to football?" he asks, his voice just oozing with anger.

"I thought maybe you knew," I say. Only a little white lie. "I thought maybe Ms. Birdie had told you."

"Still. You could've said something." Julian's tone is accusatory. "Like *See you at practice* or something. I had to find out from some jackass in marching band?"

I want to say something, but all I can manage is a mumble. Something that resembles, "I'm not on the team yet."

And then my stomach is all wonky again. I want to be pissed at Julian for pinning this on me. Ask him when, exactly, was I supposed to tell him about football? When he shut the door in my face last night, or when he ignored me all the way to school this morning?

Instead, I bite the inside of my lip and fiddle with my belt.

He sets his jaw, grabs his helmet, and heads off to the opposite side of the bench. I can hear the exasperated sigh escape as he leaves me standing by the ice buckets.

Coach Marcus blows the whistle again, and we all take a knee. "Some of you may recognize a familiar face here today. We're using this practice as an unofficial tryout for Elijah Vance. Let's welcome him back and clap it up."

The team turns and looks at me, clapping in unison. Nate lets out a deep, "Yeah, Vance!" and my cheeks burn. Okay. Not *everyone* hates me. I try to hold on to that while I watch Julian. He's not clapping.

"Stephens City on Saturday afternoon," Coach says. "It's not going to be our toughest game of the season, but it'll give you a little taste of what's to come. Now let's get out there and fight hard. Defense on the fifty-yard line, offense with Coach Williams. Fight on me, fight on three," he says, lifting his hand up over his head. "One, two, three."

"Fight," the team grunts together.

"Elijah, come on over here," he says as the rest of the team disperses.

"Yes, sir," I say, my gut sloshing around like a washing machine on the spin cycle. I try to push any thoughts of Julian aside because I know I'm going to have to pay attention and work hard if I'm going to get back onto this team. These guys have been working together for years by this point, while I've been changing diapers and singing "Baby Beluga" seventeen times a day up in Houston. Not exactly the best football prep.

"Did I have you at free safety as a freshman? Correct me if I'm wrong," he asks, surveying the defensive drill happening on the fifty-yard line.

"Yes, sir," I tell him.

"Let's try you at cornerback for the time being. I might change my mind a few times before Saturday, but go on and join the defense out there. Tell Coach Andrews I want you on the left side," he says.

"Before Saturday? Does that mean I'm not going to be sitting on the bench? I can play this weekend?"

"You and I both know you were one of the most talented players we had on the field three years ago. Shame I didn't get to coach you much before you moved away. Anyway, of course you're going to be a Guardsman. Let's just keep it between us for the rest of the practice, all right?" He winks.

"Yes, sir," I say, trying to bite back a smile.

"This doesn't mean you're going to be out there right after the coin toss on Saturday." His tone becomes more serious. "You're still going to have to earn your playing time." He nods, wagging a finger at me.

"I understand, yes, sir," I say, turning to join the defense on the field.

"And I'm going to need that sixty-dollar uniform fee by Monday, okay?"

"Yes, sir," I say, pulling on my helmet. Coach Marcus called Ma last week and reminded her about the uniform fee, but she wasn't able to give it to me before I left Houston. Between my bus ticket and moving expenses, there wasn't a whole lot left for extras. I brought a little bit of cash with me, but I've got to make it last and I don't want to touch it unless it's an emergency. I'm hoping I can put Coach Marcus off for as long as possible until I figure out how to get myself a job.

"Hey, Elijah," Coach Marcus calls to me as I jog away. "Have fun," he mouths, winking again.

I nod and swing my helmet up to my head. As soon as I pull it over my ears, things just click into place. My gut finally settles, and any thoughts of Julian or the rest of the team staring at me earlier disappear when the cheek pads touch my face. I pull the chin strap a little tighter and run out to the fifty-yard line.

The defense is going head-to-head in a tackling drill, and I take my spot in line behind what must be a middle linebacker. The dude is massive. I'm glad he's on my side of the line and not the opposing side. I was always the biggest one on the field during my peewee days, but it looks like some of these guys have had a growth spurt and a half since I left. No way I can bring down a guy that size. At least not without a ton more practice.

"All right, new cornerback. Let's see how you do." Coach Andrews blows the whistle, and I hustle to the fifty-yard line and attempt to take down the guy on the other side. I haven't done drills in three years, and it shows. I'm slow to react, and the defensive end takes me out in no time flat.

"Hey, welcome back," he says, offering me a hand up.

I grab it and let the big guy help me up. "Thanks, man. Feels good to be back."

My hip stings where it hit the ground, and I'm going to be pulling turf out of my helmet for days, but I've never felt so good. It takes a few trips through the line, but I finally take down another cornerback in the tackle drill. It doesn't matter that the kid is probably a freshman and I'm twice his size. I fight the urge to jump up and down, and I can feel the blood pumping through my veins. Suddenly all I want to do is scrim-mage. I just want to get back into the groove of anticipating plays and burying the offense into the grass.

I want to forget the look on Julian's face when he confronted me on the bench a few minutes ago. Forget what happened three years ago. I just want this feeling again. Like I'm a part of something. Like the team needs me. Like I'm important. And tackling that cornerback gives me that feeling.

Coach Andrews sends us for another water break, and I pull my helmet off. My hair is drenched in sweat, and I try to wipe some of it off as I run to the sidelines. I hadn't noticed how long it was, but now that it's plastered to my face, I realize I'm going to have to cut it soon.

"You look a little lost out there," Julian says when I run past him. I'm riding such a high from my one tackle that I almost didn't notice him.

His words still sting, though.

"It's been a while," I say, trying to smile back at him. Did I really look that bad? Maybe the first time I went through the tackle line, sure. But did he see me actually make that last tackle? It felt good. Did it not look that way?

"It feels good to be back out there," I finally say, trying to look more confident than I feel.

"Oh. Well, I guess *that's* important, too," he says, shrugging with one shoulder and jogging back out to the field.

I try to brush it off. So, he's ticked because I didn't tell him I was going to show up to football practice today. It's not my problem.

But as we set up to scrimmage, his words dig into my skin and get me right in the chest. Maybe this *was* a bad idea.

Coach Marcus throws me a yellow practice jersey and tells me to set up. I don't know the plays yet, but I know what a cornerback is supposed to do.

I watch Julian call the play and catch the snap, and I take off after the wide receiver. The kid is seriously fast, and he zooms right past me and cuts to his left. There's no way I can keep up. The receiver catches the perfect pass from Julian and practically skips into the end zone while I chase behind him as fast as I can. Julian lets out a loud whoop and salutes me from behind his helmet.

"Don't let it get to you, Vance," the giant middle linebacker says to me after the touchdown. "That guy's got wings on his feet. None of us can ever catch him. Just keep digging in."

I try to shake it off, but I know it's affecting me every play. By the end of practice, I'm convinced Coach Marcus is going to realize what a huge mistake he's made and tell me there's no way I'm going to be playing on Saturday. No senior football player should look this bad on the field.

Coach Marcus blows the whistle three times. "Bring it in, boys!"

We hustle to the sidelines, grab water bottles from the student trainers, and take a knee.

"It's going to be a busy couple of weeks, boys. Academics are always your first priority, of course, but there are a ton of booster activities coming up. Remember, all of these extras might seem like they have nothing to do with football, but they're about raising money for the program and improving our connection to the community. I expect to have your support and to see your faces at as many of these activities as you can. Talk to me privately if you have conflicts, and we'll see what we can work out," he says.

He mentions that tonight is Bingo Night at Crossroads Church and Thursday night is Football Family Dinner, plus a few after-school football clinics with the peewee league are on the calendar for next week. "And don't forget that you are all expected to attend the Guardettes' '80s-themed dance on Friday night. Not only will you all attend, but you will behave like gentlemen," he says, while a few of the players elbow one another and laugh. "No funny stuff. And you know I will hear about it if there is. Coach Andrews will be there in his finest acid-wash denim and Bon Jovi T-shirt, so you all better be on your best behavior." He laughs, elbowing Coach Andrews in the gut.

He dismisses us to the locker room, and I watch Julian trot off the field with most of the offensive line. There's a pull in my chest as I watch him walk away without me. Three years ago, we would've walked off the field together. I gather my things, wondering if part of the reason I loved football was because of Julian. So much of today didn't feel right, and I can't tell how much of it is related to him.

"Elijah, let's talk." Coach Marcus claps me on the shoulder.

"Yes, sir?" Here it comes. I know it. I'm a huge disappointment and he made a mistake.

"How'd you feel out there?" he asks as we start walking toward the locker room, as slow as molasses in January.

"A little rusty, sir. I'll try harder," I say, hoping he gives me another shot before cutting me out completely. Maybe I should make a stronger plea.

"Elijah, you have so much talent," he says. I sense a *but* coming and try to steel myself for the inevitable heartbreak. "I know you haven't been on the field for three years, but that's what workouts are for. Sure, you're a little out of shape, but that's easily fixed. I can see the way you're tackling out there, and I know you can do this. You've got to get out of your head, though, son. You're thinking too much," he says.

"No one has ever accused me of that, sir," I say. "I felt like I had two left feet out there."

Coach Marcus laughs. "Let it go. Have fun. Let your natural instinct for the game kick in. Tomorrow it will be a little bit easier, and the next day and the next. You'll see."

Tomorrow? The anxiety falls away from my shoulders, and a smile pulls at my lips. "Yes, sir. Tomorrow will be better." I nod.

"It will. Mark my words," he says, swinging the locker room door open for me. "You've got this."

I walk toward my locker with my chin held up. I feel his words sitting right in my chest.

# · nine ·

# JULIAN

**He's rusty. Really rusty.**

I have to admit, it felt so good to let that long bomb go to my wide receiver, Darien, when I knew that there was no way Elijah was going to catch him. When that kid is on, *no one* can catch him. He runs like a damn gazelle when he gets his hands on the ball. If only we could make that happen reliably, we'd be the freaking state champions.

The buzzing in my ribs after I let that pass fly and it landed right in Darien's sweet spot was totally worth it. I watched him cradle it all the way into the end zone and fought the urge to do my victory dance right in Elijah's grass-stained face.

I know I'm going to have to ice my side tonight, but I've certainly played with worse injuries than this. I'm not even going to mention it to Coach Marcus. First, he'd yell at me for somehow being tackled incorrectly, and then want me to rest or go to the trainer and probably bench me for a week. For what? Sore ribs? How would it look if the second-string quarterback got the start in the first game of the year instead of me, and for something as dumb as sore ribs? Ray Remondo would rip me apart in the Meridien paper, and I know not one single Crenshaw graduate or booster would let me live it down.

I take my time in the shower and getting dressed, taking a good long look at my side. The bruise isn't huge, but it's turning a nasty shade of purplish red. Got to remember that ice tonight.

The cloudless sky is thick with humidity, and Elijah is waiting for me outside the locker room door after practice.

"Hey," he says when I open the door. "I waited."

My gut goes soft, seeing his smile.

"Listen, I don't want things to be weird like this between us," he says. "I want you to know I don't blame you for, you know...ratting me out that day."

I swallow hard. I didn't even know that he knew it was me. "Don't blame me?"

"Yeah. Things are a little—uh—tense between us, and I just thought..." His voice trails off. "I know it was you that tip-lined me. And I don't—um—I don't blame you," he stammers.

We walk along Main Street for a couple of silent blocks, the sun shining on our backs. We pass a couple of storefronts, and the empty one next to Ron Redd's Rapid Repair is coming up quick. The one with the windows partially covered in brown paper and the peeling blue paint inside. Where I usually cross the street and walk on the other side. I know Elijah will notice if I suddenly cross Main for no apparent reason, and I don't feel like explaining all that right now. Not to him.

The air is too heavy between us, and I don't know how to respond to Elijah's admission that he knew it was me. There's a pinpoint of light inside my brain that says *Now is when you should ask why he left you the way he did*, but everything else inside me is screaming to just ignore it. Nothing good can come from that conversation.

"Remember when we ate nothing but hot Cheetos for an entire summer?" I nod toward Jake's Convenience in the distance, past the empty storefront with the peeling paint inside.

Elijah lets out a too-loud belly laugh, and the inside of my chest melts. "It's a wonder we didn't ruin our taste buds for good. I think my fingers stayed orange until Halloween."

I glance sideways at him and then run ahead, my eyes trained on the sticker-covered glass door of Jake's Convenience. I hear Elijah's footfalls behind me, but I know he won't catch me before I get into the air-conditioned comfort of the stuffed little shop.

The bell over my head tinkles my arrival just as Elijah catches up, breath heavy. I find a bag of hot Cheetos and grab two bottles of Coke from the fridge while Elijah follows.

"What are you doing?" he asks. I can hear the smile on his face even without turning around.

"Nostalgia," I tell him as I pay for the items.

I settle myself on the curb outside the shop and open the Cheetos. My fingers are immediately atomic orange. I offer the bag to Elijah, who sits down next to me. I take a long sip of Coke and let the burning powdered cheese flavor drift down my throat.

"Why didn't you tell me you were coming back to the football team?" I ask him.

"I'm not...." He takes a deep breath. "Last night didn't really feel like the right time. Or this morning. You just...you seemed pretty angry. With me. Or something," he says. I can feel him tense up beside me, like he wants to say something else. Instead, he clears his throat and shifts uncomfortably on the warm concrete.

"Do you know *why* I seem angry?" I refuse to look his way. I don't know what I'm going to say next.

Elijah is quiet for a long time. I can hear him fiddling with the cap on his Coke bottle. "Is that a trick question?" he finally asks.

Does he even remember? Did it mean nothing to him at all?

It was after a particularly grueling football practice our freshman year, the day before he broke the window. I stood in the locker room under the lukewarm shower longer than usual that night, letting the water wash away every inadequate feeling that had built up over the course of the last few hours. Coach Marcus had been yelling at me at practice for weeks, and it had finally culminated in a night when nothing I did seemed to be good enough. I was ready to throw it all away. Throw my hard-earned Crenshaw Guardsmen jersey with the bright blue number eight on the back right into the trash can and join the chess club. Or the show choir. The freaking fishing team. Anything to get me away from football.

I finally turned off the shower and loped toward my locker, dejected. When I heard a locker slam shut a few rows over, I went to investigate, stepping carefully on the wet floor in my slides.

"Elijah?" I asked, coming around the corner. He was sitting on the bench in front of his locker, his head in his hands.

He jerked his head up quickly, surprised to see me there. "I thought I was the only one still here," he said, wiping his face with the back of his hand. His eyes were bright and rimmed with red.

"You okay?" I asked, sitting down next to him on the bench.

He shook his head no but offered up a little smile. "*You* okay?" he asked back.

I shook my head no and smiled, too.

We sat there talking in the empty locker room for almost an hour.

"Remember that game at Liberty Middle last year?" he asked me.

I laughed at the thought. "When the mascot accidentally wandered onto the field midplay and you mowed him down?"

Elijah threw his head back and laughed, clapping his hand on my knee.

I stopped laughing right away and turned toward him. Elijah had been out since seventh grade without apology and without any fucks to give. And maybe he realized in that moment what I had known for at least a few months about myself but hadn't been able to admit out loud yet. Or maybe he knew before that moment. Maybe it didn't even matter. What did matter is that right in that second, as two scared and tired fourteen-year-olds laughing about football in the school locker room, we both felt seen. Understood.

I don't remember if he leaned forward first or if I did. I don't remember if he kept his hand on my knee or if his fingers drifted somewhere else. I don't remember what I did with my hands. I don't remember what I was thinking in that exact minute, or if I was thinking at all.

I do remember his slow, warm exhale as our lips touched. I do remember the feeling of letting go. The way my shoulders relaxed, and I wasn't scared, and everything made sense, even though nothing made sense all at the same time.

He pulled back first. "Maybe I shouldn't have done that?"

"No, I... it was okay," I said.

It never happened again.

Not because I didn't want it to happen again, but because things changed after that. He ignored me completely the next morning. Didn't even walk to school with me like we had been doing for weeks. I thought he hated me. I thought he regretted that kiss so badly that he couldn't even stand to look at me anymore.

It was that same afternoon that I found him with broken glass on his shoes, getting ready to climb into the coach's office and steal the car wash money.

I think about it a lot, why I called the tip line that afternoon.

I spent three years convincing myself that it was because Elijah was breaking a rule and it was my duty to make sure there were consequences for that. But really it was because Elijah's complete rejection had cut me to the quick.

"It's not a trick question," I say, taking a long sip and avoiding Elijah's eyes.

"Uh... I think maybe I do know, probably," he says, his voice shaky.

I take a chance and glance toward him. His eyebrows are pinched in the middle of his forehead, and his lips are set in an uneven line. He stares out at the cars whizzing down Main Street, and never glances in my direction.

"We probably ought to head home," I say, folding up the Cheetos bag. "Birdie's probably waiting on us."

Elijah swallows the last of his Coke and throws the bottle in the trash can. He wipes the Cheetos crumbs from his hands across his black shorts. "Aw, man," he says, trying to brush off the neon orange dust but only making it worse.

He doesn't remember.

I've spent three years thinking about him and wondering what I could have possibly done differently, and he hasn't given me a second thought at all.

A huge wave of sadness washes over me as we round the bend from Main Street onto Rudy Street.

"Oh, good. You're both here!" Birdie greets us at the front door. She's wearing her GUARDSMAN GRANDMA T-shirt with my name and football number in silver glitter on the back. "It's Tuesday! You didn't forget, did you Julian?"

Booster Bingo. I totally forgot.

Birdie calls bingo every Tuesday night at Crossroads Church. Not only is it the highlight of her week, but it's the highlight of *everyone's* week in Meridien. I would reckon the multipurpose room at the church is more packed on Tuesdays than the pews are on Sundays. The second Tuesday of every month is Football Booster Bingo, and almost all the proceeds go to the Crenshaw football team. Birdie and Coach Marcus expect the team to volunteer selling hot dogs and popcorn and passing out extra cards.

"I didn't forget," I lie. "I just need to change my clothes, and I'll help you pack up the car."

I leave her and Elijah on the porch, Birdie reminding him how important Tuesdays are to the whole community. I've heard the spiel before, and I can only imagine Elijah's reaction to the news that he'll be selling bingo cards with me all night.

I comb my hair and put on a clean Crenshaw polo shirt.

"Aren't you a sight!" Birdie says, waiting in the living room. Down the hallway, Elijah's door closes, and I assume he's changing his clothes. "Tell me about practice. How did Elijah do?"

"He's pretty rusty," I tell her, setting my jaw. I'm still annoyed she kept this secret from me.

"Now, don't be mad at me for not telling you sooner," Birdie says in a hushed voice, throwing a look down the hallway toward the guest room. "I honestly didn't know if the boy was going to go through with it. He was so nervous this morning about upsetting you and making a mistake. Practically had to talk him off the ledge at breakfast before you got up," she says.

"Well, he certainly looks like he hasn't played in a while," I say, letting my anger for Birdie subside a little bit.

"Oh, I'm just glad he put on a helmet and got out there! He'll get his legs under him, sure enough," she asserts. "Is he at cornerback? Left side, I hope."

I laugh. "Yes, Birdie. He's playing the left side."

"Now if they could only fix your protection. You might actually have a fighting chance against Taylor this year!"

"Hey, now! That hurts!" I laugh again.

"A quarterback's only as good as his protection," Birdie quotes, carrying the bright pink wheel of tickets out to the car.

Elijah comes out of the guest room in a clean shirt, his hair pulled back into a tight ponytail again. "Is this okay? Do I look nice enough for bingo?" he asks me.

His shoulders strain against the frayed sleeves of his V-neck T-shirt, and I notice a few tiny stains on his khaki pants. My gut hums in protest as my eyes follow the worried lines on his forehead down his freshly shaven cheek. "You look fine."

"It's the nicest thing I have with me," he says, a concerned look settling across his full lips.

"I promise, it'll be fine. You'll be sitting down at a table for most of the night, anyway. Help me with this cooler," I tell him, heaving up one end of the heavy ice chest Birdie has left in the kitchen.

I sit in the back seat in the car while Birdie and Elijah talk about practice all the way to the church. Well, Birdie talks. Elijah nods along in agreement and offers a word or two when he can get them in.

I help Birdie set up the bingo cage on the stage near the lectern while a few of the other football players trickle in. Nate and Bucky help me pull a few tables in a line near the door to sell cards, and Elijah and Camille soon get to work putting chairs out.

I avoid talking to Elijah, even though he's barely left my side all night. He's there while I set up the popcorn machine, breathing loudly and not talking. I'm not sure what to say to him. The realization that he really doesn't remember what happened in the locker room three years ago, or at least that he doesn't care to talk about it, circles around in my head, and I can't get past the bright, stinging buzz of it.

Camille's dad sets up the audio for Birdie, and her mom busies herself with the cash box and the bingo cards and daubers.

I help Professor Robles-Garcia stretch a long white tablecloth over the front table and set it up with the cash box. "You remind me more and more of your father the older you get," she tells me. My cheeks burn and I look at the floor. I never know how to respond when someone tells me how much I am like him. It makes me feel like I have something to live up to, which makes me feel both proud and anxious. "We should have you and your granny over for dinner soon," she says.

"That sounds nice," I tell her. "I'll have Birdie give you a call."

"You can even bring the Vance boy, I suppose. Camille tells me you've got Elijah living with you for a bit?"

I start to answer, but the professor doesn't wait for me to form the words.

"Elijah Vance. Hm. I hope he's not up to his old tricks," she says, her face pinched.

Her words don't sit right with me, but she walks away before she can see the look on my face. Elijah might be a lot of things, but he's not the bad seed some of the people in this town think he is.

People start arriving in droves soon after we get the room set up. Camille, Elijah, and I are sitting at the front table, handing out bingo cards and daubers as Mr. Robles collects money. Almost every person who comes through the door has a handy football tip for me, or a warning about the Taylor game, which is still almost a month away at this point.

"That Taylor quarterback is going to spell trouble for you," Ms. Brownie says, pointing a wrinkly finger in my face. "He's just a sophomore and already being courted by Alabama."

The whole town turns into armchair coaches and experts as soon as football season comes around. I never hear Ms. Brownie warning baseball pitchers or the basketball team about their games.

"Since when are you in charge of the scouting report?" Ms. Brownie's sister says, poking her in the ribs with an elbow.

"I've been reading the newspaper. That Ray Remondo fella knows what he's talking about," Ms. Brownie says, nodding her head.

"Oh, sure he does." Mr. Cooper comes through the line behind the sisters. "Last year he predicted Taylor would beat us by no less than twenty-seven points! They still beat us, but only by two!" He laughs so hard that he starts coughing.

"Both of you hush, now. You'll see in a few weeks when those Taylor Titans come to town. I'd put money on us losing that game if I had any!" Ms. Brownie is the grumpiest woman in the county, and the only self-proclaimed "fan" of Crenshaw football that would openly bet against us.

Ms. Brownie's proclamation brings on another bout of laugh-coughing from both her sister and Mr. Cooper.

"Our boys have got this in the bag." Pastor Ernie joins the conversation as he follows Mr. Cooper in the line. "Isn't that right, Elijah?"

"I'm going to do my best, sir," he answers, handing the pastor two bingo cards.

Figg slides into line behind the pastor and puts his hand gently on his back. "Never say they've got it in the bag. Remember what happened twenty years ago?"

A chorus of groans erupts from every old-timer in the line. The paper predicted the Guardsmen would win by like a million points, but a massive brawl broke out on the field before the homecoming game even started, and Crenshaw had to forfeit. I've asked Birdie what started it, but she refuses to tell me. All of Meridien is very hush-hush about the whole thing. Like it's an embarrassing town secret or something. The only thing the whole town agrees on and is very vocal about is that the Shame of the Century was brought on by someone predicting that Crenshaw "had it in the bag."

Add that to the running list of things Meridien is stupidly superstitious about.

The group of adults moves toward the tables, and we hand out a ton more cards to the throngs of people coming in, each one of them with a handy comment or tip as to how I can guarantee a win against Taylor. I smile politely and thank each and every one of them for their support of Crenshaw County football, but by the time the line wanes, I'm ready to punch someone in the teeth. Does anyone even remember that we've got three games coming up before we even have to start thinking about Taylor?

I grab a handful of cards when the line slows to a trickle and wander through the crowded tables, leaving Camille and Elijah to handle the entrance for a little while. I'm glad Elijah's not within spitting distance, because I don't think he'd like to hear what people are saying about him.

"I heard he was back in town," Ms. Brownie says. "That family is nothing but trouble. Can't really expect much with Eric Vance's DNA running through your veins," she says under her breath, so Pastor Ernie doesn't hear.

"I can't believe that Coach Marcus let him back on that football team. Is winning that important? More important than morals now?" someone else says.

"He's just a boy and boys make mistakes. Let's not go crucifying the child," Mr. Cooper says.

"Just you wait until it's *your* money that goes missing," Ms. Brownie says.

Most of the people sitting near her nod their heads and mumble quiet "mmmhmmm"s of agreement.

"Now, you cut that out. No money disappeared; the boy only broke a window." Mr. Cooper puts his hand down on the table.

The talk stops after that.

Bucky Redd and a few of the freshman are running the concession stand. "Hey, Julian! Come here," Bucky stage-whispers to me. He holds out a hot dog covered with relish. "Can you bring this over to Camille? Tell her I made it just for her exactly how she likes it."

I roll my eyes. Bucky has been in love with Camille since kindergarten. They're probably the most mismatched pair on the planet, but Bucky will never give up. He's very careful not to be pushy about it, though, and Camille will sometimes flirt back here and there. I doubt anything will ever come of it after all these years.

"You made it just the way she likes it?" I ask, raising my eyebrows.

"A little well done on the grill with extra relish." He smiles. "Come on, how many other guys would know her exact preferred hot dog order?"

"You are definitely one of a kind, Buckster." I laugh.

He adjusts his plastic gloves while I carefully carry the perfect Camille hot dog over to where Camille and Elijah are closing up shop.

"Special delivery from Bucky Redd," I tell Camille, setting down the fancy hot dog in front of her. "He says he made it exactly how you like it."

"Extra time on the grill and more relish than necessary? Oh my god, that's just the sweetest!" Camille takes a big bite and flashes a thumbs-up to Bucky, who is watching her from the concession window.

He tips his hat and takes a bow.

"He will never give up on you," I tell her.

Camille shrugs with just one shoulder and pops the last bite of hot dog in her mouth. "He's sweet."

"Are you saying there's a chance you might finally let him take you out somewhere?"

"Anything's possible, my friend," she says, rolling up the hot dog napkin and tucking it in my front pocket.

Camille mouths "Thank you" to Bucky, and then turns to Elijah and me. "You wanna play?" she asks, shoving fifteen dollars into the cash box and pulling three books of game cards from my stack. "Come on, let's get a chair."

"I've never played before," Elijah says shyly. "I mean, not since kindergarten or whatever."

"Sit by me; I'll teach you everything you need to know. And maybe I'll be a good luck charm, too," Camille tells him, patting the chair next to her.

I sit down across from the two of them, my blue dauber ready to do some damage. I never win at bingo, but it doesn't stop me from hoping every time I sit down and listen to Birdie call out the numbers. Even though I'm a minor and can't collect the prize if I do win, I know standing up and yelling out "Bingo!" is something I'm missing out on.

"I 24. I 24. I . . . 24," Birdie calls out into the microphone, and there's a chorus of whoops and groans.

"Everyone's really nervous about the Taylor game, huh?" Elijah asks after marking through I 24 with his orange dauber.

Camille rolls her eyes. "That's all anyone cares about around here. Oh, sure, they'll show up for Stephens City this weekend and all the other games, but Taylor is the one they're all waiting for."

Elijah's knee starts shaking under the table a little bit.

"It's overhyped," I say, hoping he'll stop shaking. "Meridien loves their football, and Taylor's the thing that keeps them all talking."

"I'd hate to be the guy who screws it up. I mean, they're still mad about a game we lost twenty years ago! I wouldn't want to be the reason people are complaining at bingo twenty years from today," he says, biting his lip.

"O 71. O 71. O...71," Birdie calls.

"Hey, you've almost got bingo." Camille points to Elijah's card. "You're just missing G 47."

Elijah looks down, and his smile lights up his whole face, and my chest aches in spite of itself. I find myself missing that thing. No, not the final bingo number. That thing when you trust someone and there's an unspoken bond between you. That thing when just a shared look can mean more than an entire conversation.

"G 47. G 47. G...47," Birdie calls.

"Oh my god! Camille! Look!" Elijah, his cheeks bright pink, shoves his card toward Camille.

"Yeah! You won! Call out bingo before someone else claims it!" She gently pushes his winning card back toward him.

Elijah jumps up excitedly, his chair tipping and clattering to the floor. "Bingo?" he squeaks out, the pink in his cheeks turning to bright red in an instant.

"Well, are you sure?" Birdie says into the microphone. "Loud and proud if you're sure, Mr. Vance!"

Elijah laughs, and his face returns to its normal hue. "Bingo. BINGO!" he yells.

## · ten ·

# *ELIJAH*

"Hey, let's walk home," Camille says to us as we're wiping the tables down after bingo. "I could use a milkshake."

"Burger Barn?" Julian asks her, loading the last of Birdie's things into the trunk of her car.

"Absolutely. Elijah, you up for it?" Camille asks.

"Oh. Um. I don't have to come with you," I say, glancing toward Julian. His face isn't exactly friendly or vicious. Just sort of…blank.

"Don't be ridiculous." Camille sucks her teeth. "*Of course* you have to come. Winners get milkshakes. It's a rule I just made up."

I look at Julian and he shrugs. "I don't care."

Not exactly the ringing endorsement I was hoping for, but I'll take it. My stomach sank to my knees earlier this afternoon when he asked me outside of Jake's Convenience if I knew why he was angry. I put him off as best I could, but he seemed to disappear after that. When he led me into Jake's and bought snacks for both of us, it was like I had the old Julian back. As I watched him pay for all of it, I had it in my head that I was going to apologize to him. Put all that stuff in the past behind us. I couldn't tell him about Coley just yet, because of the promise I had made to Frankie, but maybe I could explain a little bit. At the very least, I was going to say that I was sorry.

*Because of course* I knew why he was angry.

I left. Poof. Without an explanation. Without saying goodbye.

Disappearing without warning was probably a decent reason for someone to be angry with you. Especially after what we shared in the locker room. Things got massively complicated after that, and I was fourteen and overwhelmed. It's not a great excuse, but it's what happened.

I tell Camille I'm in for Burger Barn, and we drag a few more bags and boxes and the big ice chest out to Ms. Birdie's car. She shoves a five-dollar bill in my pocket when no one is looking. "You have fun, now. And don't you worry about Julian. He's just a big grump. Everything will come out in the wash." She winks at me.

It's a short walk down Main Street to the outdoor tables at Burger Barn. A handful of kids are hanging out, but we settle ourselves away from the crowd at a small round picnic table with a bright blue umbrella after we order our ice cream at the window.

"Homecoming is only a few weeks away," Camille says, taking a long sip of her banana milkshake. "Do y'all have any plans?"

Homecoming. I missed it by a couple of weeks when we lived in Meridien before, and I didn't participate in any of it at my school in Houston, either. Frankie and her friends always loved everything about it, though. The mums the girls wore around their necks and the garters the boys wore around their biceps at school the Friday of the football game. The dance the next night, when everyone wore sparkly dresses and dry-cleaned suits and took a million selfies outside the decorated gym. The alumni barbecues on Sunday afternoon.

"Don't remind me." Julian shakes his head and dips his plastic spoon into the sundae he's devouring.

"What's wrong with homecoming?" I ask, licking at my swirled cone.

"Don't listen to grouchy pants over here." Camille laughs. "He's just sour because he's got to plan the football pranks."

"I just think it's a stupid tradition is all. I mean...filling a quarterback's car with popcorn? TPing the trees in front of Taylor? How is any of that going to help us win a football game?"

Camille rolls her eyes. "Well, it's not, honestly. But it's not just about that! It's a tradition, Juls. Something Crenshaw and Taylor have been doing for a million years. Don't you want to put your mark on it somewhere?"

"I think the tradition is dumb," Julian says, throwing his spoon into the bottom of his empty sundae cup.

Camille sighs hard. "Aren't you tired of being Oscar the

Grouch *all* the time?" She rolls her eyes. "It's just for *fun*. It's supposed to be silly. Lighthearted. Entertaining. Merrymaking. Let's see, how many SAT prep words can I think of for fun? Elijah, you want to help me out here?"

"Delightful? Pleasing?" I say, and Camille laughs. My gut warms.

Julian's face is a storm cloud, though.

In all honesty, I can see his point. The traditions that he's expected to uphold don't really serve any purpose other than good fun, and I don't know that Julian has *ever* been the type to do something just because it's fun. On the other hand, why *not* do something just because it's silly? Does everything have to make sense?

I think about Coley. She laughs every single day. About bubbles in the sink. About the funny voices Frankie uses when she reads her favorite book. Sometimes she laughs at nothing. One of the best sounds in the world is the sound of her laughing at something I've done.

Julian has been serious since the day I met him. Sure, he laughs and has fun at football, but there's always been this undercurrent of work in everything he does. I start to wonder if he's ever had a moment of just pure joy.

"What about the camping trips the football team takes to Port Aransas? Or homecoming mums? Do you think those are dumb? Those are traditions, too." Camille juts her chin out, daring Julian to take a swing at homecoming mums.

Julian rolls his eyes again. "Those ridiculous dinner-plate-sized flower arrangements girls wear around their necks before the homecoming game? Those don't exactly have a point, either," he says.

"I didn't hear you complaining about them two years ago when you had that gorgeous garter arrangement from Reece around your bicep." Camille raises her eyebrows.

I stop midlick. My stomach flip-flops, and I see the tips of Julian's ears turn bright pink. Reece? Who is Reece? And why does the mention of his name make Julian's ears turn pink?

"W-who's Reece?" I clear my throat.

"Julian's old boyfriend," Camille singsongs. "He was just the sweetest thing, and he made the most gorgeous homecoming garter for Julian sophomore year. I was so jealous."

"Camille, stop," Julian says, his eyes fixed on his empty Styrofoam sundae cup.

I've suddenly lost my appetite for my swirl cone, and I leave it dripping on a napkin. Julian had a boyfriend. Not long after I left, either. The thought of someone else touching him, putting a garter around his bicep, looking at him...it's enough to make the tips of my ears turn pink, too. I don't know what I expected. That a guy like Julian would sit around and pine for me after I left? After one kiss?

It wasn't something I had time to think about when I was in Houston. But now, seeing him in front of me and seeing how just the name *Reece* affects Julian, it makes me wonder. Did he react that way to my name before he saw me again? Did the thought of me turn his ears pink?

*That's ridiculous, Elijah. It was one kiss. You're the one that walked away without saying goodbye. Julian moved on. Obviously. With a boy named Reece who would probably never leave without saying goodbye.*

Maybe I wasn't exactly nice after that one kiss.

Maybe there was more going on at home than my fourteen-year-old self could handle, and maybe I wasn't exactly the picture of maturity.

Maybe I hadn't known what to do with that newfound thing with Julian.

I had known I was gay since I was a little tiny kid. Can't really put words to that, honestly, but sometimes it's just something you know in your bones. It was for me, at least. I'd been out since seventh grade. Everyone really kind of knew, anyway. Coming out wasn't a huge deal. Frankie cried, but they were happy tears. The next day she bought me a pride flag and hung it on my bedroom wall with thumbtacks. Dad was gone by then, and Ma just kind of said, "Oh. Okay," and smiled at me. Maybe I was hoping for a little more than that from her, but my mother wasn't exactly known for her warmth. Ma was always busy or harried or just not available. Especially after my father went away. Frankie and I tried to stay out of her way for the most part. It's not that she didn't love us or care about us; she just had a very different way of showing it. Putting food on the table and making sure we had a safe roof over our heads was her way. I don't fault her for that.

Kissing Julian was a whole new level of me saying to the world, *Hey, I'm gay.* A level that I wasn't quite sure about. I had never even thought about kissing him until right that very second, sitting next to him on the bench in the locker room. I touched his knee, quite accidentally, and a jolt of electricity shot right up my arm and through my gut. And in that moment that our lips touched, and I could feel his warm breath mingling with mine, all I wanted to do was lose myself in it.

The day before that kiss was the day the world came crashing down around me. I found Frankie crying in my room when I got home from practice, a positive pregnancy test in her lap. I didn't know how to help her, but I knew I had to think of something. I promised her I would figure something out. And that was when I remembered the car wash money that we had locked in Coach Marcus's desk the day before.

"Did your high school in Houston have a bunch of weird homecoming traditions?" Camille asks me, slurping up the last dregs of her milkshake and interrupting my thoughts.

"There were mums," I tell her. "But I don't really know about any of the other stuff. I kind of just went to school and kept my head down."

"You never went to the homecoming dance or the football game or anything? Did you ever wear a mum?" Camille looks shocked.

"No," I say without further explanation. I'm afraid if I say too much, Camille will start asking questions about Frankie. "Hey, it's getting kind of late, and I've still got some homework to finish up," I say, looking at my watch.

Camille looks at her wrist, too. "Jeez, it *is* late! As much as

I'd love to sit here and talk about mums all night with you losers, I've got a Powder Puff meeting in the early morning before the game tomorrow. Eek! I'm so excited."

"Powder Puff? Like girls playing football?" I ask.

"Yep. Girls playing football." Camille laughs. "More specifically, it's cheerleaders and drill team girls playing football."

"It's another fundraiser, really," Julian says. "The cheerleaders form their own team and the drill team girls form *their* own team, and tomorrow afternoon they play against each other to get everyone excited about *our* first game of the season. Just flag football, of course. No tackling involved. I'm supposed to be coaching the drill team."

"Sometimes I wish it *were* tackle football," Camille says. "There are some cheerleader bitches I'd like to mow down. And if Jannah Sykes happened to get in my way, I might plow through her, too."

Julian throws his head back and laughs. "If you do, you'll get kicked out of the game. But that might just be something I'd pay to see."

"That sounds like a lot of fun," I say.

Julian shrugs again. "It is fun. It's good hype for our first game, and the girls get really into it."

"Hey, why don't you come and help Julian out with the coaching?" Camille bumps me with her elbow. "I think the girls would be happy to have both of you."

I notice Julian's jaw flex as he throws a look at Camille.

"I'd like that," I say. Camille's been really friendly, and it does sound like something that would be fun. And maybe spending a little extra time with Julian won't be such a bad thing.

"See? Powder Puff is a tradition you don't hate!" Camille chides Julian.

"Powder Puff isn't something that's going to put a black mark on my permanent record if I screw it up," Julian says as we step onto the sidewalk and start toward Rudy Street.

"Ooh, the dreaded permanent record." Camille waves her hands in front of her, and I can't help but laugh. "Hey, speaking of cheerleaders..."

"Were we talking about cheerleaders?" Julian says.

"Keep up, Julian." Camille deadpans. "I should totally *not* be gossiping, but guess which cheerleader is about to have a few extra pounds to carry around?" Camille raises her eyebrows and makes a sad face. "Dani Patrick." She pats her stomach.

"No way. She's pregnant?" Julian's eyebrows rise all the way up to his hairline. "Man. So irresponsible."

My stomach sinks to my knees.

"Hey there, Mr. Judgmental. Take it easy," Camille says, giving him a dirty look.

"What? You're the one gossiping about her," Julian says.

"I'm just relaying information," Camille says with a slightly guilty look. "But I feel bad for her....She's probably going to have to quit cheer for the year, and that was kind of her whole life, you know? I'm sad for her."

"She's probably going to have to quit more than that. She's basically ending her life before it even starts." Julian snuffles and shakes his head, too.

Camille rolls her eyes. "She's not ending her *life*. For Pete's sake, Juls. Maybe it's not the ideal way to start a family or whatever, but jeez, it's not like she's dying. Back me up here, Elijah."

I search my head for something to say. Is that how Julian really thinks? Is that what he would think of Frankie? Even my own parents had Frankie when they were still in high school. Does he think that way about my mother?

"I don't think she's ruining her life," I finally say quietly.

"Well, whatever," Julian says, waving my comment away. "Maybe *ruining* is too strong a word. But now she's got to put everything on hold while she takes care of a baby? She was really smart, too. She always talked about going to Baylor and being a doctor and stuff. Man, that's disappointing."

"She can *still* do all that stuff." Camille sighs. "Maybe she'll give the baby up for adoption or not even go through with the whole pregnancy. But even if she didn't do either of *those* things, who says she can't be a mom *and* go to Baylor and be a doctor? Jeez, Juls."

Julian just shakes his head. "Maybe. I don't know. It just seems like she could have made a better choice."

My stomach is in knots. On the one hand, I'm really glad I decided to keep my mouth shut and not say anything about Frankie and Coley to Julian. On the other hand, I can almost see where Julian is coming from. I may have even had the same beliefs as him before Coley came along, even though my own parents were still in high school when they had Frankie. But I can't imagine what my life would look like right now if Coley wasn't in it. And I can't imagine Frankie not being a mother. It just fits her, you know? And she still managed to finish high school, and she's going to start college classes once she gets back here to Meridien.

And maybe my father wasn't exactly the best example of teen parenthood, but my mother does just fine for herself. She finished high school and college and managed to do a decent job raising Frankie and me. Julian's got it all wrong. I hate that he's so vocal about all his opinions, though. It makes him sound like an insensitive ass, and I don't really think that's the case. I think maybe he just talks without thinking sometimes.

We walk down Main in silence for a few minutes. Outside of Ron Redd's Rapid Repair, there's a giant poster with COUNTDOWN TO THE TAYLOR TITANS written in bright red marker. Underneath is a great big 32, counting down the days to homecoming.

"This is the kind of thing that makes me nuts." Julian points to the sign in the dusty window. "Does anyone even remember that we have three other games before the Taylor game?" Julian sighs.

"Are you still thinking about your permanent record there, cranky pants?" Camille elbows Julian.

"Maybe you think it's a joke, but football and grades are my ticket out of here," he answers without a smile. "I'm not willing to sacrifice my chances of going to college or whatever over some dumb tradition everyone thinks I should be in charge of. All it would take is one screwup, and I can kiss a scholarship goodbye."

"I think you've been taking Officer Kapinski's first day of school speeches *way* too seriously," Camille says.

We walk Camille all the way home before doubling back and going toward Ms. Birdie's. Julian's. My temporary home. Whatever I should call it.

Once we drop Camille off, Julian and I don't have much to say to each other. He seems lost in his own thoughts, but I can't find anything to say, either.

Not only am I reeling from what he said about the cheerleader, but I haven't been able to find a way to put Reece out of my head since Camille spilled that little gem at Burger Barn. The thought of someone else touching Julian and knowing him the way I wish I did makes my gut ache.

*I* should have been the one to make Julian his first homecoming garter. I thought about our kiss so often while I was away, and it hurts to think that Julian has someone else's kisses, and who knows what else, to daydream about.

## · eleven ·

# *JULIAN*

I pull my polo shirt over my head this morning with just a quick glance at my ribs. The bruise is yellowing, and even though it's still a little sore to the touch, it's barely noticeable. I decide not to tape it up today and just pop a couple of ibuprofen before heading to the kitchen.

"Hi," Elijah says, eating a granola bar at the counter with Birdie.

"Hey," I say without looking at him. I bend down and kiss Birdie on the cheek.

"We've got the Powder Puff game today after school, Birdie," I remind her. "Elijah's going to help out, too."

"Oh, that's wonderful. I'm so glad you're getting involved." She reaches across the counter and squeezes Elijah's hand. "I'll be at the church this morning getting ready for the senior citizens' potluck and the consignment sale, and then at a meeting with Pastor Ernie over on Main Street this evening. You boys are on your own for dinner tonight, okay? There are plenty of leftovers," she tells me.

"You're meeting with Pastor Ernie on Main Street? How come?" I ask her, peering into the fridge looking for something I can eat on the way to school.

"Oh, Pastor's looking into doing something with that empty storefront next to Ron Redd's." She waves her hand dismissively.

"The empty storefront where Daddy was going to—"

"So, you're sure you can make your own dinner tonight, then?" she interrupts, way louder than necessary. Her eyes are talking again. Right now, they're saying, *Don't ask any questions; I'm not going to answer them yet anyway.*

I look at her a second longer than is comfortable. I think about trying to ask again. Birdie stares back. We're having an entire disagreement just with our eyes, neither one of us willing to give in and look away.

I finally cave. "We'll manage dinner," I tell her, downing the last swig of orange juice and grabbing a cold breakfast burrito.

"You okay?" Elijah asks me.

"Never better. We need to get moving," I say, squeezing Birdie's shoulder. "Have a good day, Birdie. Love you."

"Aren't you going to heat that up?" Birdie follows us toward the front door in her bathrobe.

"No time!" I tell her, heaving my bag over my shoulder. It whacks me in the ribs, and I wince.

"Love you both!" she calls as we shuffle down the driveway.

Elijah waits until we turn onto Main Street before he asks, "What's the empty storefront next to Ron Redd's?"

I chew on the inside of my lip. Years ago, when I was little, Birdie and my father bought the space on Main Street next to Ron Redd's Rapid Repair. It had been a pawn shop that went out of business before they bought it. The plan was to turn it into a youth center or an after-school program for middle and high school kids. Sports, homework help, music, and maybe dance classes; my dad had all kinds of plans. We spent a couple of weekends there painting the walls and doing some cleanup. It's one of those clear-as-day memories I have of my father: him handing me a spongy paintbrush while he climbed up the ladder, his favorite music blaring through a portable stereo. I probably got more paint on the floor and on my clothes than on the wall, but I remember that I felt very important. What we were doing felt important.

I wish I could remember his words to me while we painted and cleaned. After he passed away, Birdie struggled with what to do with the space. Just this past spring, she mentioned selling it, but I may have had a reaction to that news that Birdie wasn't expecting.

Maybe.

"You can't!" I remember yelling at her. The first time I had ever yelled at her.

"Julian, we can't just keep it empty," she said, holding her arms open and trying to give me a hug.

I stepped away from her. "That was Daddy's place. You

told me he wanted to turn this town around, give back to the community."

"Of course he did, but things have changed, and I don't have the means to run a place like your father dreamed about all by myself."

"If you sell it, someone's just going to turn it into another junk shop or a nail salon or something. It was Daddy's," I said, all the fight draining out of me.

"I won't make any rash decisions, Julian. I can promise you that," Birdie said, finally gathering me in a hug.

Late spring eventually became late summer, and I assumed Birdie had abandoned her plans to maybe sell the place. Her admission otherwise makes my stomach sick again.

"It belonged to my father and Birdie," I tell Elijah. "He was going to turn it into an after-school spot, like a community center for kids, but when he died that plan kind of died, too."

"Oh," he says. "That storefront sat empty for so many years, I didn't realize anyone owned it."

It's only seven thirty in the morning and already I've had enough of today. Everything feels so heavy and exhausting. I just want to take a nap.

Elijah stares at his shoes as we turn the corner onto Main Street, and I try not to look at the brown-paper-covered windows in the storefront next to Ron Redd's. "So, can I ask you something?" he says.

I let out a ragged breath. Can I say no? Can I say, *Please just be quiet and let's walk to school without acknowledging each other?*

What about, *You make my head spin when you've only been here a day and a half, Elijah, acting like you don't owe me an explanation about how you disappeared three years ago.* Can I say that?

"Yeah, you can ask me something," I answer through gritted teeth.

He takes a few breaths and adjusts his backpack and then his shirt and then the waistband of his shorts before he finally talks. "Tell me more about Reece," he says to the ground. "I didn't know you... I didn't know there was a Reece."

*Of course you didn't know there was a Reece. The only way you would have known there was a Reece is if you actually tried to call me or text me or even write me a freaking letter and put it in the mailbox.*

"There's not much to tell," I say. "We met online, and then he came to see me, and we just... we just kinda started from there."

This is the most boring version of my relationship with Reece that I could possibly relate to Elijah. When we met online, I was still pretty shaken by my experience with Elijah, and while I really did want to meet someone, I was convinced that everyone was out to hurt me.

One afternoon, after a few weeks of talking, a nice little SUV pulled up in front of our house, and out stepped Reece, his plaid shirt buttoned all the way up his neck and tucked into belted shorts. Sleeves rolled just so to show off his toned arms.

I saw him coming and ran outside. "What are you doing here?"

He tried to hug me, but I pulled away and looked toward the house. "My grandma doesn't really . . . she's not . . . she's . . ." I fumbled.

"She doesn't know you're gay?" Reece asked, eyebrows raised.

I shook my head.

"Then I'm just your friend Reece, okay?" he said, smiling at me. "Introduce me." He nodded toward the house.

The memory of Reece's smile the day that I met him makes my chest ache, but not because I miss *Reece*, really.

Beside me, Elijah clears his throat and the memory evaporates. "Did you . . . were you really close?" he asks, shoving his hands into his pockets.

"I think so," I say. Damn Elijah for bringing it up.

Birdie was so impressed with how polite and clean-cut he was, I don't think it really dawned on her at first what was going on. That first time he came over, Reece whispered in my ear while Birdie was mixing up some sweet tea. "Show me your room."

A new feeling formed in my gut and started to crawl up my neck and down my thighs when his warm breath hit my ear. I showed Reece my room. We kissed for the first time, and that was when I started to forget about Elijah just a little bit. I was scared at first, worried that he might do the same thing Elijah did after we kissed and just disappear, but that didn't happen. He called me that night when he got home and wanted to see me again the next weekend.

"Were you together for a long time? Like boyfriends for a long time?" Elijah stumbles over his words, and I wonder if there's more he wants to ask but doesn't know how.

"A couple of months," I say, feeling a pang of sadness remembering those few months.

I met him during the July before tenth grade, and shortly after homecoming that year, we just kind of fizzled out. He came over less and less until one day we just weren't in each other's orbit anymore. Here and there one of us wouldn't respond to a text or a DM. He'd call, and I'd let it go to voice mail. I'd FaceTime and he wouldn't answer. I don't think anything really went wrong; maybe he just outgrew me. Maybe we outgrew each other. Even though our relationship kind of died on the vine, I never really felt as heartbroken about Reece as I did about Elijah.

One afternoon after he stopped coming by, Birdie asked about him. "Where's Reece been?"

"Busy with school, maybe," I said, but I could feel the heat creeping up my neck.

"Oh," she said. But she put her hand on my back and gave my shoulder a little squeeze. "You gonna be okay?" she asked.

I turned and looked at her. She smiled at me and winked a little bit. We never had one of those conversations like you see on TV where the gay kid comes out to his parents. There was never any *Birdie, I'm gay* on my part or any *I'm so proud of you, Julian. Let's go get some ice cream* on her part. But when she put her hand on my shoulder and asked if I was okay that day, I want to think that was her way of saying, *I know and it's okay.*

After that day, Pastor Ernie and Figg were weekly fixtures at our dining room table.

"Do you ever miss him?" Elijah says, finally turning his head and looking at me. He squints in the sun.

I meet his eye. "Maybe a little bit."

Elijah nods like he knows what I'm talking about. Crenshaw comes into view around the bend on Main Street, and I look at my watch. I don't miss Reece as much as I miss that unspeakable thing that happens when you have someone. That opposite-of-lonely feeling.

I catch sight of Elijah out of the corner of my eye, and his face looks thoughtful but sad. "I understand missing someone," he says.

# · twelve ·

## *ELIJAH*

I have a hard time getting Reece out of my head on my way
to first period. And the image of the way Julian's face softened
when he mentioned his name. It makes me wonder if he ever
thought of me like that. I was such an ass before we left that I
doubt it.

I'm thinking about Julian's father, too, as I make my way to
English class. I never knew that the empty business on Main
Street belonged to Ms. Birdie and Julian's dad. It's obvious he
misses his dad even though he's been gone for ten years now.
My father has been gone for a little over six years, and I don't
exactly miss him. Not like Julian does, anyway.

Camille shows up about halfway through my English class
in her bright pink Powder Puff jersey with PIROUETTE QUEEN on
the back in sparkly silver letters. She hands a yellow slip from

her guidance counselor to Ms. Parliament and plops down at the desk next to mine in the back row. "Schedule changed, and now I've got dance at the end of the day instead of the morning. I guess it was lucky for both of us," she says, smiling.

It feels nice to have a friendly face during first period. Even though it's only the first week of school, it's been pretty rough. I recognize faces and want to wave and say hello, but they don't always recognize me. Or worse, they do recognize me and either pretend they don't see me or give me a dirty look. Sure, some of the guys on the team have been cool to me, but it would be nice to walk through the halls of Crenshaw again with my head up.

I manage to keep my eyes open all through Ms. Parliament's grammar lecture and even take a few notes. Camille waits for me to pack my bag when the bell rings. "Where are you headed next?" she asks.

"I'm supposed to be going to health with the freshmen," I tell her, rolling my eyes. "I never got credit for it in ninth grade, and Ms. Woods says I have to have it to graduate. But right now, I actually have to go see Ms. Woods again. She's put me in a freshman social studies class by accident."

"Oh my god, that's the literal worst," she says. "I've got marketing and then AP Spanish. I'll walk with you," she says, falling in step next to me.

"Marketing," I say. "What's that like?" I ask her, happy to have someone with me in the hallway.

"It's my favorite class!" Camille says. "I've told you my plan, haven't I?"

"I don't think so," I say, hooking my thumbs through my backpack straps.

Camille launches into the details of her fourteen-step business plan that includes going to Coastal Texas for two years, transferring to Texas State to double major in business administration and dance, and eventually moving back to Meridien to open a massive dance studio after a storied dance career somewhere glamorous and far away. "I mean, I want to dance forever, right? But honestly that's not realistic. At some point I'll be old and wrinkly and won't be able to do a triple pirouette anymore or glissade across a huge stage."

"You really think you'll want to move back to Meridien after you live in some cool place like New York or Paris?" I ask her.

Camille shrugs. "I'm happy here," she says. "Doesn't mean I don't want to see the world someday, but it's always nice to come home after an adventure, you know? Someplace where everyone knows you and it's comfortable."

"I agree," I tell her. "Your plan sounds pretty solid."

"It's a dream. I mean, I'm going to get those degrees and open a dance studio here at least. All that stuff that happens in between might be a little bit of a pipe dream, but what's life without a little bit of whimsy, right?" Camille smiles, but it seems a little sad.

I want to ask her what made the light go out of her eyes right then, but it feels too personal. Too pushy. Instead, we walk through the halls, both quiet now. Camille is lost in her thoughts and I'm lost, too, if I'm being honest. I've never given a ton of thought to what I might want to do when high school is over. It's a big decision, and one I've pushed out of my head whenever it taps at me. Julian has had a capital *P* Plan since we were kids, and now even Camille seems to know exactly what she wants. Is it okay not to know? The thought sticks in my gut and I readjust my bag and clear my throat to try to shake it loose.

"You ready for Powder Puff tonight?" I ask Camille, desperate to chase away the gathering cloud above our heads and change the subject before she asks me what *my* plans are after graduation.

Camille brightens again. "We're going to crush those cheerleaders this year," she says. "The Guardettes are ready."

I laugh. I have to admit that I'm looking forward to watching the Guardettes go at it against the cheer squad. Especially if they're all taking it as seriously as Camille is.

"Hey, let me ask you something," I say to her.

"Anything."

"Why do you think Julian is so down on homecoming?"

She rolls her eyes. "Psh. Your guess is as good as mine. I'm sure it has to do with him having to plan the pranks. You know that kind of goofing off is really not in his DNA. I keep trying to get him to lighten up, but he's wound tighter than a tick."

"You think he'll actually do it? Plan the pranks?"

"I think he'll do them his way," Camille says. "Eventually. After a lot of kicking and screaming." She laughs. "Do you think you'll go? To the homecoming dance after the Taylor game?"

"I...I don't think so," I answer.

"Why not? It's a lot of fun! Find yourself a date; you get to wear a garter around school. I know you missed all that stuff freshman year."

I think about Julian's face last night when Camille talked about Reece and the mum he made for Julian. I wonder what that would feel like. Having someone care about me enough to make me a homecoming garter. I wonder what it would feel like to wear it to school, and everyone would know that I had a boyfriend. Someone who cared about me. Someone who would show up for me.

"I *would* like to go," I say. "But I don't know. It still seems pretty far off. I think it might take a while for people to get used to seeing me around again."

"At least think about it." She gives me a half smile. "And hey, the Guardettes are having a fundraising dance this weekend that all of you football players have to come to, anyway. Maybe you'll find yourself a homecoming date." She bumps me with her shoulder.

"This is the most dance-having school in Texas, jeez." I laugh.

"Hey, I know you spent a lot of time in the big city," she jokes, putting air quotes around *big city*. "But spoiler alert: There's not a whole lot else to do out here in the middle of nowhere. Cow tipping? Mailbox baseball? Watch the pumpjacks? Yawn. Hey, did you know that homecoming mums are only a Texas thing?" Camille changes subjects as often as some people change their socks. My head is spinning while I try to keep up.

"No way," I argue.

"Yeah!" She laughs. "Everywhere else in the country, you

just go to homecoming. Mums are this big bushy plant people put on their front porch in the fall. Isn't that weird?"

We laugh together all the way to the guidance office, where Camille splits off and heads toward her marketing class.

Everyone in the guidance office is dressed in either a pink or purple T-shirt in support of the Powder Puff game tonight. Ms. Woods meets me at the door in a bright pink jersey that looks very similar to Camille's. WALTZIN' WOODS is spelled out on the back in glitter.

She sees me eyeing it and twirls around. "I won't tell you how many years old this is, but we played Powder Puff way back in the dark ages, too." She smiles and winks. "What can I do for you, Mr. Vance?"

"I've got a problem with my schedule," I tell her.

"Let's get that fixed, Elijah," she says, perching her red readers at the end of her nose and taking my schedule from me.

She starts typing on her computer, and I look around her office. There are pictures of her with students everywhere you turn. Some are taken at school functions, some right here in her office. On a top shelf in a dusty corner, I spot a picture of Frankie all dressed up in her marching band outfit, smiling away with her arm around Ms. Woods. I didn't notice it yesterday.

"When was that taken?" I point toward it.

"Oh, your sweet big sister. That was her sophomore year at the last football game of the season. Isn't she a cutie with her piccolo?"

"I miss her," I say before I can stop the words.

Ms. Woods removes her glasses from the end of her nose, and they hang on a chain around her neck. "How are things going for you, Elijah?"

"I'm fine," I tell her. I keep the doubts behind my teeth. The way some people looked at me at bingo last night. I heard some of the things they were saying about me. Julian's reaction to seeing me for the first time and later his comments about the pregnant cheerleader. The ache in my gut when I realized just how much I'd missed him. Me, afraid to tell him about Frankie and Coley. Feeling like I take up too much space at Ms. Birdie's house.

She looks at me for a beat longer than is comfortable and then leans back in her swivel chair. "You can always come talk to me," she says. "My door is always open."

"Thank you," I tell her. "That…that means a lot."

She hands me my new schedule with US history right before football at the end of the day. "You can start this schedule tomorrow, okay? Just sit through that freshman class one more day, and tell Mrs. Schad you'll be out of there tomorrow."

"Will do."

"I'm not just here to fix schedules, you know." She smiles.

"I know." I smile back, glad that she's here. I throw one more glance up at the picture of her with Frankie before heading out of the office.

The rest of my school day is a lot better than Tuesday. I notice a few more familiar faces in my classes, and a few of the football players invite me to eat lunch with them. I'm sitting at the end of the table and I'm kind of on the outskirts of most of the conversations, but that doesn't matter. At least I'm not alone.

I feel better by the time seventh period rolls around, and I change my clothes as quickly as I can and run out onto the practice field. I do a few high-knee laps on the sidelines while I wait for Julian and the rest of the team to come outside.

"Short practice today, fellas," Coach Marcus tells us when Julian starts the stretches. "Powder Puff game after this, and I expect all of you on the sidelines if you're not coaching."

A small crowd of pink-and-purple-shirt-clad fans are already gathering in the bleachers. Guess our practice will serve as the warm-up act for the Powder Puff game.

"Defense with Coach Andrews!" Coach Marcus blows his whistle and points to the fifty-yard line after the warm-ups. "Elijah Vance, you're with me."

I jog over to him, carrying my helmet under my arm.

"Yes, Coach?"

"I'd like to try something different with you today," he says. "Okay?"

"You've got to be willing to give it a chance. Keep an open mind. Will you trust me?"

"I trust you," I say, wondering what his plan is. Is he going to make me a kicker or something?

"We've got a little problem with protection," he says, setting his lips in a straight line and crossing his arms over his chest. "How do you feel about offensive line?"

"I've never played offense before," I tell him, which isn't

exactly true. I played both sides of the ball when Julian and Nate and I played peewee ball, but I think we all did.

"I've got to get Julian more protection out there, and I think you're a smart enough guy for the job," he says. "Let's try you out at left tackle today, all right? You watch Martinez for a couple of plays, and then we'll get you in there."

Coach Marcus makes it sound like it's a question, but I know better. The only correct answer here is *Whatever you say, Coach.*

"Yes, sir," I tell him, and strap my helmet under my chin and jog out to where the offensive line is gathered.

Most of the dudes on the line tower over me, but my shoulders are just as wide. Bucky Redd buries a fist in my gut. "Welcome to the o-line, little man." He laughs. The rest of the guys laugh along with him, but I know it's all good fun. Bucky runs me through a few of the plays, and I feel like I've got a good handle on them when Coach calls for a short scrimmage.

"Just keep your eye on the line for these first few plays. You'll pick it up easy, I bet," Bucky says, tightening his helmet under his chin.

The o-line gets down in their stance, and I watch Martinez set up. He's the last one to bend at the waist after watching the defensive setup across from him. He nods to Julian.

"Red 14! Red 14! Hike!" Julian calls, catching the snap from the center and backing up a couple of paces.

Martinez digs in and tries to take out the defense, but the tackle breaks right through the protection, grabs Julian around the waist, and takes him down hard. I hear a loud "oof" as he lands on his side and drops the football.

"Ooh, that's going to leave a mark," Coach Andrews mumbles next to me.

Coach Marcus taps me on the back. "Get in there, Vance. Martinez! You're out!"

Julian is pacing in a circle, panting, when I get out onto the field. He meets my eye, and I can tell he's not okay. I want to ask if I can do something. Get him some ice. Get the trainer. But there's not time before Coach calls the next play.

"Set up!" Coach Marcus yells. "Run Oklahoma hook left!"

Julian stretches his ribs, puffing air through his cheeks. He shakes his limbs loose before he gets in position. Just like Martinez, I check the defensive setup and then get in my stance after giving Julian a nod. My stomach is in knots. Julian's just been smacked hard, and I can't let that happen again. I know what Martinez did wrong, and I'm determined not to take my eyes off the tackle that broke through. A giant mass of a kid that probably has a nickname like Tiny or something else ironic. My heart is beating in my throat when I hear Julian call the play.

"Hike!" he shouts behind me.

I bury my helmet right in Tiny's numbers, and he falls in slow motion like a tower of Jenga blocks. I jump up and make sure Julian's had the chance to make the handoff and step out of the play. He's safe behind me.

"You good?" I ask him as the running back gets tackled a few yards away.

"Yeah," he says, completely out of breath. His hand is on his side and he is grimacing. I know he's lying.

"I'm your left tackle now," I say, standing up a little taller. I don't really know if that's true yet or not. Coach Marcus might decide I'm the worst tackle in history and put me somewhere else after a play or two, but I want to say *something* to Julian. Something so he knows I won't let him get smacked again.

Julian meets my eyes. We stare at each other for a full breath. Finally, he just nods in my direction and puts his mouth guard back in.

I'm laser focused. No one's getting to Julian if I can help it. My entire job as left tackle is to protect him from the defense. It takes a little bit of practice not to want to wrap my arms around the receivers and bury them into the ground after Julian passes the ball, but I start to get used to it. I crush and push as hard as I can to keep the defense from cutting through and sacking Julian while he falls into a nice pocket behind me. It's an easier job than I thought it was going to be as far as reading the plays and anticipating the defensive moves. I don't really have to concern myself with that anymore. Literally my entire job is to hold the defense back from knocking Julian over.

The bleachers are starting to fill up with pink and purple T-shirts, parents with balloons and flowers, and student groups with huge signs on colored butcher paper.

When the dance team and the cheerleaders start to gather at the far end of the field, Coach calls practice and we all head to the locker room. The o-line surrounds me.

"You're a beast out there," Bucky Redd says. "Now all we need is for Julian to throw a few touchdowns and we're golden this weekend."

"That was awesome," I tell him.

"Yeah? It's nice burying the defense, right?" Bucky laughs.

Julian is sitting stiffly on the bench near our lockers, taking deep breaths with his pads still on. "Hey, nice job out there today," he says quietly when I sit down and start untying my cleats.

My cheeks warm. "Thanks. I haven't played offense since our peewee days."

"I got a few good throws in," he says quietly. "I think it's a good fit for you."

I feel like I want to say more to him, but he looks down and starts unbuckling his pads after that. Once he has his jersey off and most of the buckles undone on his shoulder pads, he heads for the shower with just a quick half smile in my direction. He lumbers away awkwardly. Not exactly limping, but not exactly *not* limping, either.

I shower quickly and put on the pink T-shirt Camille threw at me before football practice. In black letters on the front it says COACH. Julian meets me in a matching T-shirt near the field house, where Camille and an army of dance-team girls dressed in highlighter pink are waiting for us. Julian holds the bags with the flags and starts handing them out to the girls.

"Let's stretch a little before we do this," Camille says to her team of warriors in pink. Some of them have painted pink hearts under their eyes. *All* of them are wearing neon pink knee socks. A few of them even have pink tutus on. I don't know how that's going to work with the flag belts, but I don't say anything.

As the girls form a circle on the field and start stretching,

I stand next to Julian and watch the chaos around me. The stands are filled with pink and purple T-shirts, parents with noisemakers, and huge painted signs.

"Are regular football games this well attended?" I laugh.

"This event always draws a huge crowd," he says, folding his arms across his chest and drawing in a quick breath.

"You okay?" I ask.

"I'm good. Just a little sore from that last hit," he says. "I'll be okay."

I know he's not telling me the truth. His voice cracks just a smidge, and the smile he's trying to give me is pinched and forced. But I don't say anything. I don't want to give Julian more of an excuse not to talk to me than he already has.

The girls finish their stretches and nervously size up their purple-clad foes on the other side of the field. Camille is nervously bouncing around the sidelines, reminding her team of the plays and her signals. I want to laugh, but I can see how seriously she's taking her job as team captain.

Bucky, Nate, Darien, and a couple of the other seniors are acting as the referees, and the crowd roars when they run out onto the field in their black-and-white-striped shirts. Nate grabs a microphone from the tech kid who has run out onto the field.

"You look nice, Camille." Bucky pauses on his way past the sideline to smile at our Pirouette Queen. "Good luck out there. I know you'll be awesome."

"Thanks, Bucky," she says, returning his smile.

"Hey, hey, no fraternizing with the refs." Julian blows his whistle near Camille's face and laughs.

Camille whacks him with her flag belt, and her cheeks glow so bright they almost match her neon socks.

"Welcome to the Crenshaw Annual Powder Puff Battle!" Nate is in charge of announcing the game. "The Guardettes, in pink, and the cheer squad, in purple, have been practicing for weeks to bring you this epic matchup tonight. Who are you rooting for, Crenshaw?" He holds the microphone out to the crowd and cups a hand around his ear. The crowd erupts into chants and cheers.

A huge smile spreads across my face. "This is wild," I say to Julian.

"It's a spectacle, all right," he says, but he's smiling, too.

Nate explains the rules to the waiting teams and the crowd, and then there is a coin toss. Camille, her PIROUETTE QUEEN jersey proudly tucked into her pink tutu, calls heads and wins the toss. The Guardettes will have the ball first.

When the dance team huddles, Julian reminds the girls to have fun, and they do a quick cheer before hitting the field with Camille at quarterback.

"I've spent weeks trying to show her how to throw a good spiral that is catchable," Julian says to me, bending at the waist and putting his hands on his knees. He rubs a hand over his ribs, and I see the hint of a wince cross his face. "She still prefers her method of heaving the ball as high in the air as she can and hoping it comes down into a receiver's hands."

I laugh, but this is exactly what Camille does. As unconventional as it looks, her method is actually working quite well, and the dance team takes an early lead.

Julian lets me take over the defensive coaching, and I gather the players around me and give them a few tips about reading the plays and anticipating the movement of the offense before the ball is even in the opposing quarterback's hands. The girls stare at me, unblinking, most of them with pink sparkly stripes or hearts under their eyes.

"And have fun," I remind them with a smile.

The defense all give me hugs on their way onto the field, and I have to laugh. I wonder what would happen if I tried to hug Coach Marcus or Coach Andrews before I headed out on the field before the game on Saturday afternoon.

"A little different than our games, huh?" Julian asks, watching me wish the girls luck.

"Maybe a little." I smile, and he looks down.

The cheerleaders can't hold a candle to the dancers, and Camille's pink team wins the game easily, 28–6. The girls all huddle around me and Julian, jumping up and down and losing pieces of their tutus all over the field. I get wrapped up in their excitement, too, and soon we're all chanting and hopping in the middle of the field. Julian watches from nearby with a smile on his face, but he seems tired or something. Every so often he stretches to his right and rubs his side.

The crowd in the stands joins in the chanting, and pretty soon the cheerleaders join us and everyone is hugging and screaming. This is so different from a regular football game, all I can do is laugh. Girls are congratulating one another with hugs and made-up dances while posing for selfies with their opponents. Moms and friends swarm the field with balloons and flowers.

When the extended revelry finally dies down, the girls head into the locker room and Julian and I are left on the sidelines to collect equipment and clean off the field. There are streamers and silly string and pieces of tutu strewn all over the grass.

"This makes me excited about our first game," Julian says to me as he opens up a big trash bag and starts cleaning the field.

"I'm nervous," I tell him, grabbing a long piece of pink tulle from the grass.

"Been a while since you've been under the lights in front of a crowd," he says.

"You could say that."

Thunder rumbles in the distance, and lightning flashes in the fast-moving clouds above.

Camille is waiting for us by the field house with Bucky, and Darien and Nate are nearby. "We're headed to Burger Barn! Our fearless coaches are coming, too, right?"

I look at Julian, whose face is pale. A line of sweat is forming on his forehead, and he's hunched a little at the waist. "I've got a ton of homework I've got to catch up on, Camille. You go have a blast. You guys kicked some serious ass out there," he says.

"Party pooper," Camille says. "How about you, Elijah? One of these dorks can bring you home after." She gestures to Bucky, Darien, and Nate.

I want to go. I want to do something normal. Something that

a seventeen-year-old kid would do on a Wednesday night with his friends. I glance at Julian again.

" 'S'okay with me," he says. "I'm really just going home to get homework done."

Still, I shake my head. "I'd better take a rain check," I tell Camille. "I've got a few classes to catch up on, too."

Something about the way Julian is standing makes me worry.

"You guys were fantastic tonight. Celebrate hard," I tell her.

I watch the group of them load up into Nate's car and wave goodbye as Nate pulls out of the parking lot.

"You could've gone with them. I wouldn't mind," Julian says, his voice tight behind me.

"Don't think I'm up for a crowd just yet," I say, watching him pull his backpack onto his shoulder, a slight wince on his face. "Thanks for doing this, by the way."

"For doing what?"

I shrug. "Including me."

# · thirteen ·

# *JULIAN*

We manage to make it almost all the way home before the sky opens up and the rain soaks everything. Our shoulders and hair are drenched by the time I get the door unlocked and we get into the house. My ribs are burning again, and I know I'm going to have a massive bruise in the morning if I don't already. I can't believe I managed to get hit in the same exact place twice in one week. What are the odds?

"Man, what a mess," I say when we get through the front door. I grab two towels from the linen closet and throw one at Elijah as I head toward the kitchen. "I'm going to go dry off real quick and then I'll make us something to eat, okay?"

I head toward the bathroom without waiting for an answer. I run my hand over my side on the way down the hallway, and I know I've done some real damage. Just the feel of my wet

T-shirt clinging to my ribs hurts. I close and lock the bath-room door behind me and lift up my shirt. A bright red spot is spreading along my left side. The beginnings of a nasty bruise are already starting to darken the skin near my ribs, on top of the healing bruise I got at practice a couple of nights ago.

I go into my room across the hall, grab a dry T-shirt, and head back into the bathroom. With every step, my side thumps with pain. There's got to be something else in the medicine cabinet that I can take. Ibuprofen isn't going to cut it this time. There's no way I can win this weekend if I can't even walk with-out wincing. The only thing worse than missing the first game would be losing it to a team like the Stephens City Spartans all because of *my* performance.

I dig through the medicine cabinet and stumble upon an almost-full bottle of Tramadol from Birdie's root canal a few months ago. I read the directions on the bottle and pop two in my mouth, following it with a swig of water before throwing the bottle of pills onto my bed and heading back to the kitchen.

Elijah is standing in the kitchen with his wet T-shirt in his hands, the bright yellow towel I offered him earlier slung around his bare shoulders. His hair is loose and tousled, like he just finished rubbing it with the towel.

"Hey, um...do you want a peanut butter sandwich?" I ask him.

"Oh. Um. Sure," he says. "I'll get us some milk."

I set to work on four sandwiches while Elijah pours milk next to me. I want to say something about today, but I'm not sure what. Our conversations this morning about Birdie and my father's property, and later about Reece and knowing what it's like to miss people, are all mixed up in my head.

"You know you can come in here and make yourself something to eat whenever you want to, right?" I say, sliding a paper towel with two fat sandwiches toward him. "You don't have to wait for Birdie or me."

He shrugs. "It just feels weird, you know? It's not my house."

"Birdie doesn't feel that way. She'd probably be thrilled if you came in here and grabbed yourself some leftovers some night. It's really okay," I say.

Elijah swallows hard next to me. I don't know if it's because I put too much peanut butter on the sandwich or something else entirely.

We eat in silence for a few minutes. I watch the moths attack the screen door.

"I'm really sorry that all of this was such a surprise for you," Elijah finally says, his voice thick.

My heart sinks. I want to be angry with him. I want to lash out and tell Elijah that I think the way he left me three years ago was shitty and that showing up on my doorstep now is really making a mess of things. But then I look at him, this big, giant hulk of a guy eating a peanut butter sandwich and trying to be so small. So quiet. So indistinct.

"Thanks for the sandwiches," he says, rolling up his paper towel and throwing it away. He grabs the sponge from the sink and wipes the counter where he was sitting and puts his milk glass in the dishwasher. When he's done, you can't even tell he was sitting there.

"You'll have to make me a sandwich tomorrow," I say to him. "As payment."

He pauses in the kitchen doorway. "Deal."

I clean up my mess in the kitchen and head for my bedroom. I move the Tramadol bottle to the nightstand and lift up the edge of my shirt. I touch my ribs as gently as I can, but they're so tender I can barely get a finger on them. I stretch in the mirror and hope the Tramadol starts working some kind of magic. Seriously, who gets hit twice in the same spot in one week? How bad could my luck be?

I pull out the shoebox I keep under my bed and open the cover. I keep the cash I make mowing lawns and dog sitting and doing odd jobs around Meridien in that box. I probably have a few hundred dollars in there now that I've managed to save over the years. Camille thinks I'm nuts for not putting it in the bank, but I like to have it where I can keep an eye on it.

"What if your house gets broken into? Then it's just gone?" she said to me once.

"What if the bank gets robbed?" I shot back.

She laughed until she couldn't breathe. "Banks are insured, you tree stump. If someone robs the bank, the bank will give you your money back. Jeez."

"I still like to keep it close."

I don't want to tell her that I like to count it every so often. I like the feel of it in my hands and knowing exactly how much is in there anytime I want. I put the bills in stacks and count through them a couple of times before pulling out my phone and looking at used cars online. If I wanted a rusted-out hunk of junk, I could almost buy one now. Maybe in a few more months I'll have enough to buy something that isn't described in the classifieds as "well-loved" or "It even runs!" I could pick Camille up in the mornings and ride to school in style. Maybe we'd even grab a breakfast sandwich at Whataburger before school.

I'm thinking about jalapeño cheddar biscuits when there's a soft knock at the door.

"Come in."

Elijah stands in my door frame. His eyes travel around my room and pause first on the money on the floor and then on the bottle of Tramadol sitting on my nightstand. "I just wanted to check on you," he says. "That hit you took this afternoon wasn't nothing."

"I'm fine," I tell him without meeting his eyes. I shove the money back in the box as quickly as I can and push it back under the bed with my foot.

"I know you're not," Elijah says. "You were always a terrible liar."

"I'll be okay. Just bruised a rib or something. It's nothing." I stretch my head and lean to my right, trying to loosen the slow tightening on my ribs. I know I just tossed two Tramadol in my mouth, but I'm already thinking about taking another pill just so I can go to sleep. My shirt rises up when I stretch, and I drop my arms as quickly as I can.

"Holy hell, Julian!" Elijah takes two long steps into the room and reaches for the hem of my shirt.

"Hey," I say, trying to pull the shirt from his hands. I twist too quickly and flinch.

"That is *not* nothing. Come on, let me take a look at it," Elijah says.

I lift my shirt just enough to give him a peek at the forming bruise. I don't tell him that the red mark extends from my armpit all the way to my hip bone.

"Was this all from today? From that one hit?"

"I took a late hit a couple days ago. Then the hit this afternoon."

"Two in a row? Man, that's some luck." The tips of his fingers gently brush my skin.

"I told you, I'm fine." I yank my shirt down and he pulls his hand back.

"You probably shouldn't be playing with an injury like this. It might just be a bruise, but what if your ribs are broken? Are you going to have the trainer check it out tomorrow?"

"We both know I can't stop playing right now. Our first game is in three days. What would it look like if QB1 was out for the first game? For something as ridiculous as a *bruise*?"

He reaches for the hem of my shirt again, and I meet his eyes. He stares at me, lips pressed together, and I don't pull my shirt from him this time. He lifts it enough to get a good look at the full length of the slowly darkening bruise. His eyes meet mine for just a second before he turns his attention back to my ribs. My skin is warm where his fingers touch. "Does it hurt much?"

"Yeah," I say quietly as his fingers travel along the length of my side.

He drops his hand and looks at me. "You should at least tell Coach Marcus. What if you get hit again in the same spot?"

"Elijah, I *can't*. Scouts are going to start coming to the games soon," I say. "One game could be the difference between a scholarship to college and living under Birdie's roof for the rest of my life." I eye Elijah suspiciously. "You're not going to tell Coach, are you? God, Elijah. You can't!"

He looks at me, then his eyes dart to the bottle on my nightstand for a split second and then back at me. "What is that? What did you take?"

I bite the inside of my lip and avoid his eyes.

"Julian. What did you take." This time it's more of a demand than a question.

I finally nod my head and gesture toward the Tramadol on the nightstand, signaling for him to pick it up. Elijah picks it up and reads the label, his eyes widening.

I sit down on the edge of my bed and hang my head in my hands. "Please don't tell Coach."

Elijah is quiet. He holds the pill bottle in his fist. He puts it in his pocket and lets out a frustrated sigh. Finally, he says, "Does Ms. Birdie have fresh parsley in the fridge?"

"Parsley? The green stuff?"

"Yeah. Go get it for me, and a mug. We can make that bruise go away quicker," he says.

With Birdie out with Pastor Ernie for at least another hour, it's easy for me to rummage around in the refrigerator and find the bag of freshly washed parsley. I bring it back to Elijah, who pulls me into the bathroom and closes the door. He puts the leaves in the mug with just a tiny bit of water and crushes them with the end of his toothbrush. The muscles in his neck flex with each movement. I watch him work. His eyebrows knit in concentration; he studies the concoction he's making in the cup.

"Lift up your shirt again," he says, scooping some of the bright green stuff with his fingers. He sits down on the closed toilet seat and gently paints the red skin on my side with the crushed parsley. "Parsley has vitamin K. It'll help the bruise fade faster. Maybe. Hopefully."

I wince a little as his fingers skate softly over my ribs.

"Sorry," he says, his breath warm on my skin.

He gently pulls my shirt down and offers me a tiny smile. "We can do it again in the morning. Some people say cayenne pepper and Vaseline help, too. Maybe we can try that if this doesn't work."

I nod at him. I want to tell him thank you, but I can't.

He had the chance to turn me in. To tell Birdie I stole her pills. Tell Coach Marcus that I wanted to play hurt and get me in pretty major trouble. Instead, he crushed parsley with the end of his toothbrush.

"I'll see you in the morning," he says, brushing past me and quietly leaving the bathroom.

I don't protest when he leaves with the bottle still in his pocket. I stand and look at myself in the mirror.

He crushed parsley with the end of his toothbrush.

## · fourteen ·

# *ELIJAH*

Tramadol? He's taking *Tramadol*? Jesus H. Christ. I throw it in the top dresser drawer when I get back into the guest room... my room. He's not using that big old brain of his, thinking he can play with an injury like that. I mean, I get it, I guess, but jeez.

Football and grades are all that have ever mattered to Julian, even way back in middle school when nothing but having fun really mattered to anyone else. He's been talking about wanting to see more of the world since we were really little. Would I play with an injury like that if I knew it meant the world would be at my fingertips? If it was the difference between getting to go to school or not?

I don't know.

I lie down in bed and watch the clothesline sway in the

breeze through the open window. I think about Coley. I've talked to Frankie approximately seventeen thousand times since I got here a couple of days ago, but I wonder if she's giving me the real story when we're on the phone.

She says "Everything's fine!" but with a little catch in her voice. It's that super-enthusiastic "Everything's fine!" that you say when everything is clearly *not* fine, but you don't want anyone to worry about you. She says Coley is great and Ma has been great and I just... I don't know if I trust her.

I wonder in the dark if I would continue to play football with hurt ribs if it meant giving Coley and Frankie a better life. If I knew it was the difference between keeping everything the same and possibly having the chance to do something different with my life.

Probably.

I wouldn't have taken the Tramadol, though. I feel better knowing it's in my pocket and not Julian's room. I know first-hand how that kind of stuff can start you down a road you'll never be able pull off of. I watched it happen to my father, and I'll be damned if I'm going to watch it happen to Julian, too. Even though it was just two pills that he took. It's too easy to get caught on that slippery slope. I'm half tempted to flush the rest of the prescription down the toilet, even if Julian does think I'm being overdramatic.

I pull my phone from my nightstand and shuffle through my photo album until my eyes get heavy.

**You awake?** I text Frankie.

She doesn't respond.

**Just thinking about you guys tonight. Today was rough. I'll text you in the morning. Give Coley hugs.** I plug the phone in next to the bed.

I wake up to the sound of Ray Remondo. My bedroom door is open just a crack, and his reminder that it's going to be hot again has reached all the way through the house and tapped me wide awake. Of course it's going to be hot. It's September in Texas.

I check my phone and see that Frankie responded earlier this morning with a picture of her and Coley eating breakfast. I text her back a heart and a smiley face and try not to stare too long at the picture.

I shuffle out of the bedroom and find Julian in the bathroom with the door cracked, looking at his side in the mirror.

I knock lightly and the door swings open.

"How are you feeling?" I ask.

"Still hurts," he says.

The bruise is bright purple and red now. "Oof."

"Maybe...uh...maybe you could do that parsley thing again later?" he asks. I've never heard his voice so shaky.

"I will," I tell him. "Tonight?"

We each get ready for school and head into the living room together. We find Ms. Birdie on the couch in a shower cap and bathrobe, humming and pulling some linen tablecloths out from the chest in the corner.

"Ooh, you smell like Sunday dinner, Julian." She narrows her eyes and waves her hand in front of her nose. "What've you been eating?"

"Must be this new toothpaste," he mumbles. "What's with the tablecloths?"

Ms. Birdie looks at Julian like he has four heads.

"Um...the tablecloths?" He motions, pulling down on the hem of his T-shirt.

"Oh. Oh, yes! The tablecloths. It's Thursday. Team dinner tonight, remember? Can't do it on Saturday because it's an afternoon game, and tomorrow night is out because of the fundraiser dance for the Guardettes. I tell you, I think Crenshaw has got all of you overscheduled. You need time to rest and mentally prepare for these games. That's what I think," she says.

"We better scoot or we're going to be late." Julian nods toward the clock on the wall. We're definitely not going to be late, but I think Julian wants to escape before Ms. Birdie has a chance to sniff him again.

Camille's at the end of the Jacksons' driveway as usual, a pink plastic tiara buried in her curls.

"What the heck is that for?" Julian cackles, shutting the front door behind us.

"I *am* the Powder Puff Queen, am I not? I ought to look like it. Shove it right in Mara Pinkard's ugly face," Camille says, naming the cheer captain.

"This Powder Puff stuff runs deep, huh?" I laugh.

"Almost as deep as the Taylor rivalry," Camille says. "Speaking of which..." She elbows Julian and we both flinch. I hope she didn't catch his bruise.

"I know I need to start thinking about it," Julian complains, shaking his head. "The whole thing is just so, so stupid," he says, throwing back his head and shouting the word *stupid* to the treetops.

"Yeah, we all know your feelings about it, Juls, but that doesn't mean the entire town isn't waiting for you to make your move. You can't let Taylor strike first. You know what that will mean," Camille says.

"What will that mean?" I ask.

Julian lets out a dramatic huff. "Camille, quit being bananas about that stuff. I'm not interested in town superstitions. We've got a better team this year than we've had since we started at Crenshaw. There's no *way* we're losing."

"What will it mean if Taylor strikes first?" I ask again.

"The prank war with Taylor usually starts a few weeks before homecoming, you know. A bunch of little pranks leading up to *The Big One*," she says, holding her arms wide to describe "The Big One."

"I always thought it was just one stupid prank right before homecoming," I interrupt.

"See? Even Elijah thinks the pranks are dumb," Julian says, gently adjusting his backpack. I notice he's not putting a lot of weight on his left side.

Camille ignores Julian. "ANYWAY. It started out years ago as just one prank, but it's kind of grown into a whole thing. There's a superstition that whoever strikes first is going to win the game. And at least for the past four years, that's been completely true." Camille whispers the last sentence for dramatic effect.

"There's a superstition for everything surrounding this Taylor game," Julian says. "Gotta strike first, can't *ever* say we have it in the bag, gotta wear blue socks on game day." He ticks them off on his fingers as we walk. "For the past few years, we haven't had a team that *could* beat Taylor, Camille. That's possibly why we didn't win." He rolls his eyes.

I laugh and my insides warm. This is exactly what this should feel like. Julian and Camille and I are laughing and joking around on our way to school. No one is awkward. No one is excluded from the conversation. Just three friends walking together.

Julian pats his side gently when Camille isn't looking, and I see him take a deep breath and let it out slowly. I know he's hurting, and I wish there was more I could do for him. Parsley is a ridiculous home remedy I saw the internet a million years ago. I don't know if it actually helps, but when I saw that bruise spreading over Julian's ribs, I figured it was worth a try.

Painting it on his skin last night with my fingertips, I'm not going to deny the ache that started to grow in my gut. My face so close to his skin. The intimacy of being tucked into a small space together, whispering.

"Can we please talk about something else? Literally anything," Julian finally says as we pass Crossroads Church in our final stretch toward Crenshaw.

I know what I want to talk about. Homecoming. The dance. I want to ask more questions about Reece. How did he and Julian meet? How close were they? Does Julian miss him? Does he think about him every day? Or even every other day?

"Let's talk about football," Camille suggests.

"Okay, there's a subject I can get behind." Julian laughs.

"So, tell me, do you think you'll be able to break the Taylor curse, even if you don't manage to prank them before they prank us?"

"Oh my god, *Camille*!" Julian says, but he's laughing.

"Okay, okay, I get the point," she says, straightening her crown. "I'm only going to say one more thing. Tonight, at the team dinner, get your shit together. Seriously, Juls. Maybe it's a waste of time to you, but it's not to the rest of the team. Or the boosters or the alumni. They're all looking to you," she says.

"If you actually swear this is the last time you're going to say anything, then yes, I will agree that this is a great big waste of time to me," Julian says.

I can see his point. Pranking shouldn't be the focus at the beginning of the season. Or even the end of the season. Shouldn't we be worried about the actual games? Our plays? Then again, I know how big Meridien is on traditions. Even my dad played football for Meridien for a few years, and I remember him talking fondly about beating Taylor when I was little. I don't have too many great memories of my dad, but any that I do revolve around football.

"Hey, what was all that talk during bingo?" I ask. "Figg said something about something that happened twenty years ago? Does anyone know anything about it? Everyone acted like it was some big secret." My dad graduated around that time.

"There was some massive fight that broke out on the field right before the homecoming game," Camille says. "Someone from Crenshaw started the whole thing, so we ended up having to forfeit the game. It *is* a big secret. Can't find information about it anywhere other than in the heads of all the old-timers around here, and *they're* not talking. And guess what? *That* was a year that Taylor pranked us first."

Julian rolls his eyes so hard I'm afraid they're going to fall out of his head.

We turn the corner into the Crenshaw driveway, and Camille stops short and puts both of her arms out to stop us from going any farther. There on the front lawn in front of Crenshaw is the Taylor High School Titans flag, waving high in the Texas breeze from our flagpole. Underneath, the Guardsmen flag lies in a heap on the ground.

"Well," Camille says flatly. "I guess you don't have to worry about getting them first."

## · fifteen ·

# *JULIAN*

I pulled the flag down as fast as I could and switched it out for ours, but I know it was too late. Most of the school had already seen our flag on the ground. Which meant they knew that Taylor got us first.

I didn't much care. These pranks and superstitions are dumb and nothing but a distraction from the real task at hand, which is beating Taylor at all costs.

Right?

It had been easy to ignore up until the minute Coach Marcus pinned that C to my uniform. It meant a lot that he trusted me to lead the team and keep their eyes on the bigger picture. To the team and to Meridien, it meant that I was in charge.

I balled up the Taylor flag and threw it into my backpack.

"We've got to get them back good now, Cap!" Bucky Redd

shouted to me as soon as I set foot inside the front door of Crenshaw this morning.

"What are we going to do? We can't let *that* go unanswered." Nate cornered me before first period. "You've got to get serious about this."

"I know," I told him. "Back off and let me think. I need peace and quiet to come up with ideas."

For the rest of the morning, I had football players and cheerleaders and Guardettes and band kids all wondering what my next move was going to be. I failed an English quiz because I never did finish the reading the night Elijah showed up in my kitchen. I left my graphing calculator at home, and we had a surprise "checkup" in calculus. My ribs burned every time I sat down at a desk, *and* my favorite pencil broke in fourth period. That was just the straw that broke the camel's back, and by the time lunch rolled around, my head was pounding. I escaped to Figg's classroom with my tray of chicken nuggets and a foil-covered applesauce cup.

"What's up, Julian? Need some quiet?" he asks, setting out his own lunch on his desk, a cardboard carton of Chinese takeout leftovers, complete with a set of wooden chopsticks and a fortune cookie.

"Do you mind?"

"Never. Pull up a desk," he says, tucking a napkin into his shirt to protect his tie and breaking the chopsticks apart with a satisfying click.

I plop into the nearest desk with a sigh and yank the foil

from the applesauce. My head is spinning. And I can't even look forward to the second half of the day.

There are still at least three running plays I can't remember reliably, and our first game is only two days away. My ribs are still buzzing, and I can't guarantee that I'm going to feel 100 percent by Saturday afternoon. And now there's this mess with the flag, and the whole school is looking for me to retaliate, when all I want to do is play football and forget about all the stupid pranks.

Not to mention, I'm still thinking about Birdie and her meeting with Pastor Ernie and wondering what she's up to and why she won't tell me about it.

And of course, there's Elijah.

Elijah, who painted parsley on my ribs last night.

Elijah, who is sleeping in the bedroom next to mine.

Elijah, who basically abandoned me three years ago and seems to have moved past everything that I haven't been able to shake.

"Weight of the world on you?" Figg asks as I sit there in silence.

"You have no idea," I tell him, shoving a spoonful of applesauce in my mouth.

"Want to talk about it? Or is it more of a private weight?"

"You don't want to hear about this stuff," I tell him, trying to sit more upright in the chair. I don't know if I'm ready to unload all this stuff on Figg. I do wonder if he knows anything about Pastor Ernie meeting with Birdie last night, but even if he does, I doubt he'd tell me. He'd probably brush it off with one of those classic Figg "just adult stuff" excuses he uses if he can't talk about something.

"Why don't you try me? My ears still work pretty well, and every so often I have a decent thought or two to lend." He smiles between bites.

"I failed an English quiz," I say.

He laughs. "Call the authorities!"

I cut my eyes at him and smirk.

"Julian, you're allowed to screw up once in a while. What happened?"

"I didn't read the entire assignment, and I walked into the quiz without knowing *anything*."

"Well, that'll do it. What kept you from reading the assignment?"

I hang my head again. "Things just got busy."

"There's a lot going on at your house right now, huh?" Figg comes around the desk and leans against it with his arms crossed.

"Yeah."

"I can understand that."

Figg just watches me as I try to choke down a couple of chicken nuggets. I can feel that he wants to say more, but he's giving me space.

"You know you can come talk to me whenever you need anything, right? My classroom here is always open for you. And Ernie and I would be more than happy to see your face on our doorstep some evening for a Coke and a chat on the porch. No invitation necessary."

"I know."

"I hope you're not just saying that. I really mean it. I know it can't be easy to have Elijah living with you right now."

Even just the mention of his name out loud makes my cheeks burn and my stomach flip. There's a lump in my throat, and it's not from the chicken. Figg has a way of seeing right to the heart of things even if I dance around the details.

"I'm sure having him in your house is probably stirring up some things for you, huh?" he says quietly.

I just nod. I never told him about Elijah and me and what happened in the locker room freshman year. Not in so many words, anyway. I remember him asking me if I was okay after I realized the Vances had moved away, and I lied and told him I was fine. Of course, he didn't believe me, but he never said that. He just invited me to eat lunch in his classroom if I ever needed a break, and that was enough.

"I get that," Figg says. "If you need to talk it through, I'm here."

"Thanks, Figg. That means something," I tell him.

"I won't bring it up again unless you want me to. You know where to find me."

He holds the cardboard box in his palm and sits down on the desk, his legs dangling in front of him.

"Did you see the Taylor flag outside this morning?" I ask, changing the subject. I drag a nugget through the last of the applesauce and toss it in my mouth.

Figg rolls his eyes. "Yep. Guess Taylor struck first this year, huh? Is that on your mind, too?"

"I don't know why we even have to have this stupid prank war." The words burst out of me in a rush. "And why is it all up to me? As if I don't have enough on my plate right now! This whole stupid town is just waiting to see how we're going to retaliate. It's such a waste of time."

Figg laughs and strokes his salt-and-pepper beard. "You sound like your father."

I stop chewing and swallow. It's not the first time someone has said that I sound like him. Or that I remind them of him. I wish I knew what they meant.

"How do you mean?" I ask quietly, covering up the rest of my lunch with a napkin.

"He wasn't too keen on the pranks, either," Figg says. "I remember his senior year, he wanted to do away with the tradition completely. Even started a petition!"

My eyes go wide. "You're kidding."

"Oh yeah. It was a whole thing. Unfortunately, there wasn't another soul on this campus, other than maybe me, that agreed with him, and he got outvoted. Shame what happened that year."

I frown. "Is that the year of the fight? When the game was forfeited?"

"That was the year," Figg says, nodding slowly like he's remembering it all.

"What happened back then, anyway? Everyone always refers to it as a brawl. I'm picturing gladiator-level fighting out on the field." I chuckle.

"You're not too far off," Figg says. "Your Birdie never told you this story?"

"No, sir," I tell him. "She always waves it off when I ask."

"Well, you know your dad was the captain his senior year, too." He looks at me and I nod. Every so often he'd wear his old jersey with the tattered C sewn to the chest. "He was pretty set on taking the high road and not doing any pranks at all. I think that really made Taylor upset, because they love the pranking tradition almost as much as Crenshaw does, right? They decided they were going to pull an *epic* prank at the homecoming game." Figg shakes his head.

"Did they start the fight? Was that the prank?"

"Oh, no. Nothing like that. The pranks can sometimes get out of hand, but they always start out relatively innocuous. The Taylor team had gotten word that one of our players had a pregnant girlfriend." Figg rolls his eyes. "I guess they thought this was something worth calling out, and they came running out of their huddle that night with beach balls shoved under their jerseys. All fifty of them. I honestly don't know how they got past their coaches like that. But of course, everyone in the stands was laughing, and the entire Crenshaw team was embarrassed on behalf of their teammate. When the captains met in the middle for the coin toss, there were words exchanged. And then words became shoving, and shoving turned into a bench-clearing, all-out battle in a matter of seconds. Or, as you put it, a gladiator-level fight." He shrugs. "And of course, we had to forfeit the game."

"Wow," I say, picturing a hundred football players on the field just pounding the crap out of one another. Not a pretty sight.

"Yeah, it wasn't our proudest Guardsmen moment, that's for

sure," Figg says. "And not one that a lot of people in Meridien like to remember. That's probably why your grandmother never talks about it. If it happens to come up, don't you tell her I was the one who spilled the beans. I'll never be invited to dinner again." He laughs.

"I promise I won't throw you under the bus," I say, laughing too.

The bell rings. "I've got a class coming in, Julian. Don't you have history this period? I don't think Mrs. Nguyen would be too happy with me if you're late for one of her fascinating lectures because you've been loitering in the calculus classroom."

I wish lunch were longer. Sometimes it feels like Figg is the only person who *really* understands me. Plus, he's easy to talk to. I slide out from behind the desk and toss my Styrofoam lunch tray in his garbage can.

"Don't be a stranger," Figg tells me as I pack up my things and get ready for the joys of US history.

"I'll see you," I tell him. "And thanks for telling me all of that."

He nods and smiles at me, putting a hand on my shoulder and squeezing.

As I leave the classroom, my head buzzes. My father didn't like the pranks any more than I do. He tried to stop the tradition, too.

The thought buoys me as I walk down the hallway toward history, feeling taller. My father. My *dad*. The guy who played football in college and has a ton of trophies with his name on them outside the Crenshaw gym.

What if something goes too far again? What if the consequences are worse than just a forfeiture of the homecoming game? A ton of my teammates are relying on football for scholarships. If there's a prank that gets out of hand, all that would be on my head.

Something has to change.

# sixteen

# ELIJAH

All anyone can talk about all day long is the Taylor flag hanging in front of the school. I guess I really don't get what the big deal is, but maybe that's because I missed most of the homecoming festivities and buildup when we lived in Meridien before. Frankie loved all the excitement surrounding homecoming, and before her senior year, she would always get all dressed up with her friends and go to the dance. After she got serious with Ty, though, a lot of her so-called friends kind of ditched her. I was at Crenshaw for less than a month before I was suspended, and after that we shipped out to Houston.

I keep my eyes peeled for Julian all morning. I know he was pretty ticked off when he shoved the Taylor flag in his back-pack this morning, but I think he may have been more worried about the flak he was going to get for not being the first to strike rather than angry with whatever Taylor Titan hung the flag up in the first place.

I'm so preoccupied with looking for Julian that I forget to go to my new social studies class after lunch. I get all the way to the old classroom and sit down at my desk before I realize my mistake, and I have to ask Mrs. Schad for a pass to find my new class. I feel like a dolt.

I have to knock on the door to get into the new room. "The counselor changed my schedule," I say, handing the pass to the teacher. "I'm in this class now."

"Welcome, welcome! I'm Mrs. Nguyen. We're just getting ready to do some study questions in small groups. Join wherever you see space," she says, gesturing to the room.

I hate it when teachers say to find a space. Do I sit next to a quiet person? Do I sit in the front? What if the person I choose to sit near doesn't want company? I use a sneakered foot to scratch at my ankle and lose my balance a little bit. A few kids in the front of the room snicker.

I see a hand raise toward the back of the room. It's Julian. "Elijah," he says, pointing to the empty desk next to his. "You can sit here."

My stomach stops bubbling over. "Thanks," I say, settling into the seat and taking out a fresh sheet of notebook paper. "They had me in a freshman geography class. What are we working on?"

"Causes of the Civil War," Julian says, showing me the study guide. "Here, pull your desk up next to mine and then we can share the guide. I'll work on the even numbers and you take the odd. Then we can just share answers."

I scoot my desk up close to his, and he puts the study guide over the tiny crack between the two desks. We work silently for a few minutes, each scratching lengthy answers on our respective pieces of paper. I catch myself looking at Julian's handwriting while I'm supposed to be reading question number five. His *l*'s start with a little flourish, and his *a*'s are round and neat.

"What is it?" he asks, catching me looking at his paper. "Did I get one wrong?"

"Oh, um…no. I think it's good. Your answers, I mean."

We fall back into a comfortable silence. When Julian leans over to read the next question, he's close enough that I can smell his hair. Something minty. His knee touches mine under the desk, and it takes a second before he moves it away. A jolt of heat reaches up my thigh and settles low in my gut.

"I…um…I didn't see you at lunch today," I say, pretending to study the questions in the guide between us.

"Oh. Didn't know you were looking," he says, not looking up from his pencil.

My face burns, and I bite the inside of my cheek.

"I just…I wanted to make sure you were okay after the flag thing this morning."

"I ate lunch in Figg's room. I do that sometimes," he says, still not looking at me.

"Oh."

I let the silence stretch between us while I try to think of something else to say. Julian flips a page in his notebook and keeps writing. I think his answers are going to be a lot more thorough than mine. I can't focus, sitting this close to him. I can almost feel the heat coming off of his knee under the desk. I wonder how much I would have to stretch my leg to accidentally touch his again. I wonder if I did that if I could just leave it there, resting against his knee like it's no big deal. Nothing to see here. Just two dudes touching knees under the desk.

"I'm fine," he says.

"What's that?"

"The flag thing. I'm fine."

"Oh, right. Well, that's good. Have you thought about your next move?'

"Hey, I said I'm fine. I didn't say I wanted to talk about it," Julian says, crossing his legs at the ankle and stretching out in the chair. He pulls his notebook into his lap and continues writing.

I finish the next question and try again.

"Are your ribs feeling okay?"

Julian sighs hard and drops his pencil on the desk. "No. They're really not," he says, clearly not thrilled that he invited me to sit with him.

"Are you going to be able to play this afternoon? What about Saturday? How are you feeling about that?" I press on.

"Elijah, jeez," he whispers harshly. "The questions! Yes, my ribs hurt like mad right now. Yes, I'm still playing today. And Saturday! Can we please just get through this assignment?"

"Sorry, I guess I'm just...I'm worried about you," I say, my cheeks and my neck burning.

Julian's lips are set in a line, but his shoulders release and he relaxes into the chair a little bit. "Yeah."

I try to focus on the next question in the study guide, but the questions swim in front of my eyes and my brain can't make sense of the letters on the page. I start writing, even though I know all my answers are probably wrong because I'm so distracted.

"Thanks," he says so quietly I almost miss it.

He keeps his head in his notebook until the end of the class. When the bell rings, he grabs his bag and bolts out of the classroom without even a glance in my direction. I thought he'd at least wait for me since we're both headed to football practice.

I lope toward the gym, my head filled with Julian. I thought last night that he might be coming around. He at least didn't seem like he was mad at me anymore. And this morning on the way to school, he was friendly. Smiling. Not ignoring me or making angry faces in my direction.

I wish I knew where his head was.

I wish I had the courage to just flat out ask him.

I get dressed for practice and try to put it all out of my head. I've been studying the o-line plays, and I'm feeling pretty confident that I can do this job. It's just tackling, just like being on defense, only now I'm creating a pocket to protect the quarterback rather than trying to mow him down.

Julian is already on the field, tossing a few passes to Nate and Darien when I make it out of the locker room. What did he do, sprint all the way to the gym after history? Or do I just walk that slowly?

The breeze has picked up since this morning, and wide bands of clouds float across the field during afternoon practice.

It feels less humid than it did earlier in the week, but there's another kind of heaviness in the air. Those wide clouds are thick with rain, and you can feel the electricity that comes before a big thunderstorm hanging above the football field.

"Let's get in a short scrimmage this afternoon, boys. I don't know how long this weather is going to cooperate," Coach Marcus says after warm-ups. "And I know I've got to get you out of here in time to get ready for the dinner tonight."

Coach puts the backup QB, Corey, in for the first few plays. Martinez sits and I get the start. I make a few tackles, and I'm starting to learn how to anticipate the defense. Corey manages to get off a few good passes without being tackled, so I'll consider that a win.

"Julian! You're in for Corey! Elijah, you stay right there," Coach Marcus shouts after a few plays. "Let's work on those running plays."

Julian calls the play, and the center hikes the ball right away. I plow right into the defense and take down the first guy I come into contact with. I look up from where I land and see that Julian has handed the ball off to the running back, who is making his way downfield quick. The defense is just chasing. There's a tiny ache in my chest. I know I could have caught him.

I guess there was a little bit more glory on defense. On offense, the quarterback gets all the credit.

"Nice play, 87!" Coach calls to me. "More blocks like that and Alabama will be knocking on your door!"

I raise my hand in thanks to Coach Marcus and set up again, watching how the defense sets their feet. Just from the way they're standing, I know just how they're going to try to sack Julian. In a split second, I change my stance before the play is called. I position myself exactly where I need to, to keep that defensive end off of him.

"Blue 42! Blue 42! Hike!" Julian calls, and the defensive end takes off.

I put my body between Julian and the incoming defense, but my timing is off. The defense just scoots around me and makes a dive at Julian's shins. I see him about to topple over, and I change course and dive toward him instead, my hands outstretched. I can feel Julian about to fall on my arms, and I make them as strong as I can to try and break his fall.

"Shit, I'm so sorry," I tell him when we both hit the ground. "Your ribs! Did you get hurt? Holy shit, Julian, I'm so sorry."

Julian laughs. "I'm okay," he says. "It's football, Elijah. I'm going to fall down. You can't apologize every time you miss a tackle. Besides, you're not the only guy who's supposed to be protecting me out there."

"You better get your head screwed on straight, Julian!" Coach Marcus starts to scream. "You're broadcasting the play to the whole damn world before you even set up! I know I taught you better than that! Taylor would be all over you in a heartbeat!" He goes on and on while we set up again.

I watch Julian bend at his side and put his palm on his rib a couple of times before he calls the play, and I know it had to have hurt, even though the defense took him out at the shins.

"Don't listen to Coach," I say to Julian before I get in position.

"I'm not," he says, a defiant smirk on his lips.

"That one was on me. I misjudged. It won't happen again," I say, digging my fingertips into the grass and facing off against the defense.

We're able to pull off only one more play before thunder rumbles in the distance and lightning starts to flicker in the dark clouds. Coach Marcus blows two short blasts on his whistle and points toward the field house. "That's all we can do today, boys! Elijah! Uniform fee by Monday! Julian! Come on over here, son," he says.

Julian jogs to Coach Marcus, and I hear him yelling again while Julian looks down at the ground. Part of me wants to go over there and take the heat for that sack. I know it was my fault. I knew I'd misjudged it before the defense even got their arms around Julian's legs.

Luckily, the sky opens up and Coach can't continue to rip Julian up one side and down the other in the middle of a Texas gullywasher. We make it into the locker room just seconds after the fat raindrops start to fall from the heavy clouds. I wait for Julian after practice near the football trophy case. Inside, trophies are crammed in so tightly that you can barely see the lettering on most of them. On the back wall of the case are framed team photos taken at the end of each season going all the way back to the late 1970s, when the school was built. I marvel at some of the haircuts back then until my eyes fall onto the pictures from twenty years ago. I lean in close to see if I can find my father in any of the photos. Once I find the right year, spotting him in the crowd is easy. His white-blond hair sticks out, and his wide smile is recognizable to me even through the dusty, smudged glass of the trophy case. I trace the names at the bottom of the picture. E. Vance is standing right next to J. Jackson.

Julian's father.

I glance back up at the picture.

One blond-haired and one dark brown–haired kid stare back at me. The two boys stand shoulder to shoulder, smiling widely for the photographer. Both the same height. I follow down the line of pictures and find them together for three years in a row, standing side by side. Their senior year, I only find Julian's father.

"Hey," I call to Julian when he finally comes out of the locker room, his hand holding onto his ribs. "Come look at these pictures."

He drops his hand and stands next to me. "Man, look at these haircuts." He laughs.

"Tell me about it. But look, it's our dads." I point to the three pictures of them together. "Did you know they played together?"

"Huh," Julian says, the laughter in his voice fading. "Look at that."

"Do you think they were friends?"

"I don't know," he says, his palm pressed to the trophy case.

His left hand travels to his ribs again, and his eyebrows pinch in the middle of his forehead. "I never really paid too much attention to these pictures before."

He stares for a long time at the case and the pictures inside. I wish I had the courage to ask him what he's thinking.

"Hey, let's get you home. You look like you're hurting," I say instead.

We don't talk all the way back to Julian's house. The rain that was falling earlier has slowed to barely a drizzle, and steam rises from the blacktop as we make our way down Main Street.

Ms. Birdie is bopping around the kitchen when we get to the house, stacking plastic containers full of food on the counters. "Oh, I'm so glad you're home, boys. I need a hand getting the car packed for the team dinner. Go get cleaned up, and then maybe one of you can grab the steam-pan sets from the shed," she says, throwing a dish towel over her shoulder. Under her breath, she grumbles, "I've got to keep this pasta warm, and I know Pastor Ernie isn't going to have what I need in the church kitchen."

"I can do that for you, Ms. Birdie," I tell her as she disappears down the hallway. I quickly open the spice cabinet and grab the blue container of cayenne pepper.

I follow Julian toward his bedroom and glance behind me to make sure Ms. Birdie is safely back in the kitchen before quietly closing the door behind me.

"Have you taken some ibuprofen or something yet tonight?" I ask him quietly. "Ice? Heat? Anything?"

"I iced it right before practice and took a couple of ibuprofen right after practice. Nothing is really helping tonight," he says, his lips twisting.

"We can try this if you want," I say, showing him the purloined cayenne. "I just need some hand lotion or Vaseline or something to make a cream."

He grabs a bottle of dry skin lotion from the bathroom and hands it to me. I shake a generous amount of the pepper into my hand and use my finger to mix in the lotion until I have a dark rusty cream in my palm.

"I hope this works," I say as I sit in the desk chair while Julian lifts his shirt.

"Me too," he says.

The bruise is dark purple today, stretching across his ribs.

"I really wish you weren't so stubborn about playing through this," I say as I gently put the lotion onto the bruise.

"I already told you why I'm doing it," he answers, his voice tight. "So don't try to talk me out of it."

"I know, I just—"

"I know. Just don't worry about it, okay?" he snaps.

My stomach flips a little.

He winces. "Sorry. I'm sorry. You're trying to help. I just...I don't need anyone worrying about me. I got this," he says.

"You're not taking anything again, are you?"

"I said I got this."

I finish spreading the lotion on his side and gently pull his shirt down again. "That should feel better in a little bit. I'll keep the pepper in case you need it again later," I say, standing up and putting the shaker in my pocket.

I turn to leave the room, and Julian reaches out and grabs my elbow. "'lijah," he says.

I turn to him, but he doesn't move his hand from my arm.

"I shouldn't have snapped at you." His fingers flex lightly on my arm, and I get goose bumps.

I watch his face for a full three seconds before I gently pull my arm back. "I told Ms. Birdie I would get the pans from the shed."

My stomach is all mixed up when I leave Julian's room. I'm thinking about those pictures in the trophy case, Julian's knee almost touching mine in history this afternoon, the way he snapped at me just now when I was only trying to help.

It's dark and dingy in the shed, with boxes stacked to the ceiling and assorted other knickknacks lying around. Behind a box marked JEFFREY in bright blue marker are the steam pans Ms. Birdie needs. I move the box to the floor to get to them. The box isn't sealed shut, and I catch sight of a newspaper clipping from the *Meridien Register* on top.

## LOCAL LINEMAN DIES IN TRAGIC ACCIDENT

With three pans in my hand, I hold back the flap and pull the clipping from the box. The article is about Jeffrey Jackson, Julian's dad.

"Mr. Jackson played football at Coastal Texas Community College before moving back to Meridien and securing a job as a lineman with Gulf Electric. He knew the risks but enjoyed serving his community, explains Eleanor Jackson, Jeffrey's mother." Below the article, there's a picture of Mr. Jackson with a young Julian on his shoulders, taken outside of Hartwig Field at Crenshaw. Mr. Jackson holds a football in his hands, and Julian is wearing a tiny Guardsmen jersey with the number one on it. "Mr. Jackson and his mother recently purchased the abandoned property at 4859 Main Street in Meridien, with plans to open a youth community center in the future. Ms. Eleanor Jackson had no comment on how that project will now proceed without him. Arrangements for Mr. Jackson are being handled by the Crossroads Church of Meridien," it reads underneath.

Buried under the article in the box are the same pictures I found in the trophy case this afternoon. Even in the darkness of the shed, I can spot my father and Julian's, smiling next to each other. There are a few other pictures, too. Candid shots. In the first one I pick up, my father and Jeffrey Jackson stand with their arms thrown over each other's shoulders on the football field, sweat pouring down their faces as they smile widely.

Another newspaper clipping flutters in the slight breeze coming through the open shed door.

## HIGH SCHOOL ATHLETES LEND A HAND WITH LOCAL CHARITY

Beneath the headline is a picture of my father and Jeffrey, together again. This time, they're loading stacks of wrapped Christmas presents into the back of a pickup truck.

"Elijah? Did you find the pans?"

I hear Julian's voice calling me from the backyard. I close up the box as quickly as I can and carry the pans outside.

"Got 'em right here," I say, my voice shaking. Not only would Julian string me up by my toenails if he thought I was snooping in his father's things, but something isn't sitting right with me. If they were friends, how come neither Julian nor I knew about it? Or did Julian know and maybe I'm the only one who didn't? It doesn't make any sense.

"Elijah!" I hear Ms. Birdie call from inside.

We follow her voice to the guest room. My room. Whatever.

"Yes, ma'am?" I ask. Julian is right behind me.

Ms. Birdie is standing by the nightstand with the bottle of Tramadol in her hand.

My stomach sinks to my knees.

"Have you been in my medicine cabinet?" she asks, a hint of disbelief in her voice. "I found these in the guest-room drawer when I was looking for more tablecloths."

"No, ma'am. I…uh…I don't know how…" I swallow hard, very aware of Julian behind me.

"I took them, Birdie," he says, scooting by me and walking into the room.

My shoulders relax. The boulder that was forming in my gut eases just a little bit. He's going to tell Ms. Birdie about his ribs, about the bruise. She'll talk some sense into him.

"You took them?"

"When I was cleaning the bathroom the other day. I meant to throw them out, and I got distracted and didn't. I threw them in there without thinking," Julian says. "See, they're almost expired." I notice Julian's pulse pounding at the side of his neck.

Ms. Birdie turns the pills over in her hand and looks at the label. "Oh, I see that," she says.

"I should flush them down the toilet, right?" Julian says, taking the bottle from her hand. "Sorry I left them out like that."

"That's not like you," she says. "You've been under too much pressure lately." She sighs and shakes her head. "Come on now, boys. Let's get all of this stuff in the car." She walks out with a stack of white tablecloths in her arms.

Julian and I are alone. "Why didn't you tell her the truth?"

Julian shakes his head. "I only took them once. I'm going to flush them, I promise. But I can't tell her about my ribs. She'll make me sit the game out."

*Exactly* is what I want to say, but don't.

"She believed my story, though. It's okay," Julian says. "You're not in trouble."

I turn to him. "She still thought it was me. She immediately thought I was the one who took the pills." I can tell by the look on Julian's face that he doesn't see the same problem with this as I do.

"Because they were in your room," he says slowly.

"You don't understand," I say, hurt. "I'm always the one who gets accused first. It doesn't matter what she thinks of me—whether they were in my room or not, she would have always assumed it was me."

"I do understand," Julian protests. "I told her I put them in there accidentally, and she believed me. You don't have anything to worry about. I promise."

I don't think I'll ever be able to explain in a way that he'd understand. I heard what everyone said about me at bingo. I know what they all really think of me. I thought maybe Ms. Birdie was the exception to that, but apparently I was wrong.

Julian will never understand what it's like to always be the first one accused when something goes wrong.

I saw the way people used to look at me and Frankie out of the corner of their eyes when we lived here before. I thought maybe disappearing for a few years would help that. I thought people would have had time to form a new opinion. Or at least be open to getting to know me, rather than thinking of me only as Eric Vance's no-good son. A screwup, just like his father.

And I know that during those weird middle school years, all those snap judgments might have been justified. I wonder if I had never broken that window, or if word hadn't gotten around that I was breaking into the office to steal money, I could've just been Elijah the football player. Or Elijah, Coley's uncle.

Or Elijah, Julian's boyfriend.

I wonder what that would feel like.

## · seventeen ·

# *JULIAN*

"Come sit with us!" Nate calls to Elijah as we all carry our plates, piled high with Birdie's spaghetti, to a table near the front of the Crossroads Church multipurpose room.

Elijah just waves at Nate and offers up a completely fake smile before sitting down at a table near the back. By himself.

"What's eating him?" Bucky asks, tucking a napkin into his shirt collar.

"Eh, who knows? Maybe he just wants to be alone," I say.

But maybe I do know.

I don't understand what the big deal was about Birdie and the pills. She believed my little white lie, and Elijah didn't get into any trouble. But apparently he's still upset enough about it to spend the team dinner at a table by himself.

"Hey, should we all dress the same for the Guardettes' dance tomorrow night?" Darien asks, interrupting my thoughts.

Nate snorts. "Are we in seventh grade and someone forgot to tell me?"

"Oh, come on, I just thought it would be fun. You know all the girls are going to wear matching outfits," Darien laughs. "Besides, I have no idea how I'm supposed to dress for an '80s dance. I don't want to look stupid all by myself."

"Have you heard of Google?" Nate laughs again. "Jeez, Murphy. Are you sure you didn't get knocked around a little too hard in that tackle drill this afternoon?"

We all tease Darien mercilessly, making sure to give him as much wrong outfit information as possible for tomorrow's '80s dance.

"Slicked-back hair, white T-shirt, black leather jacket," Bucky says.

"Bell-bottoms, gold chains, and a flowered shirt unbuttoned to your navel. I have at least three you can borrow," I tell him with as straight a face as I can manage.

"You guys can go to hell." Darien laughs. "I'll just ask my dad."

Bucky begins regaling us with a story about the cows getting out of the gate of his family's farm during a thunderstorm a couple of weeks ago. It apparently took four neighbors to corral Bessie in the middle of Old Barn Road while thunder rumbled and the street started to flood.

We're all cracking up loudly over our plates of pasta and salad when I catch a glimpse of Elijah sitting alone across the room, watching us. My chest aches watching him watch us.

Team dinners always feel like they stretch on for hours and hours, but that's probably only because Birdie volunteers me as a one-man cleanup crew when it's all over. Scrubbing out those giant pans caked with red sauce in the church kitchen takes forever, but at least this time, Elijah is here helping to wipe down the tables. By the time we load the washed pans and tablecloths back into the trunk of Birdie's car, I'm exhausted.

Elijah doesn't speak to anyone on the way home other than to say, "It was good, thank you," when Birdie asks him if he enjoyed his first varsity team dinner.

Part of me wants to knock on his door after Birdie goes to bed. As angry as I've been, I still didn't like to see him looking that dejected.

But instead of knocking on his door, I lie on my bed staring at my ceiling, thinking of all the things I'd like to ask him.

*Hey, remember when we kissed? That was kind of important to me. Apparently it wasn't to you?*

Nope, that wasn't going to work.

*You basically ripped my heart out when you rejected me and then disappeared without saying goodbye. Are we just never going to talk about it?*

Mmm...probably not the best choice, either.

Maybe I could just write it down.

*Dear Elijah, You broke my heart.*

*Dear Elijah, I loved you.*

*Dear Elijah, Was it more important to me than it
was to you?*

I fall asleep drafting letters in my head that I know I'll never
write.

• • •

On Friday morning, Elijah's bedroom door is wide open, and I
don't see him in the kitchen.

"Where's Elijah?" I ask Birdie.

"He left a note that said he was grabbing some extra time in
the weight room. He didn't tell you?" she asks.

"No. I guess he just forgot," I say, checking my backpack for
my homework and supplies.

I spend the rest of the day looking for him, but I don't see
him until sixth-period history.

He slides into the room just as the bell rings and chooses a
desk a few feet from mine. The back of the classroom is empty
except for the two of us.

"Hey," I call to him as Mrs. Nguyen straightens papers on
her desk and waits for the class to settle.

"Hey," he says, not lifting his head from the crook of his arm
while he writes in his notebook.

"You okay? I haven't seen you all day," I whisper across to
him.

"Doing fine," he answers, flashing me the quickest and fak-
est smile I've ever seen.

I decide to ignore it. "Camille wants us to help her out tonight at the '80s dance. She's handling the ticket table from six to seven. You up for it?" I ask him.

He lowers his eyes back to his notebook. "I kind of forgot about the dance, to tell you the truth."

"The whole football team *has* to go," I remind him. "Coach Marcus's rules."

"I know," he tells me. "It's just...I'm not feeling so hot...."

Mrs. Nguyen taps her dry-erase marker on her desk, cutting our conversation short. I try not to think too much about Elijah and focus on my schoolwork, but it's pretty useless. I keep stealing glances in his direction all through class. He doesn't look sick. Just sad.

He doesn't wait for me after class, and nongame Fridays are always spent in the weight room instead of on the field. He spends the entire two hours at the pull-up bar and ignoring everyone around him. I watch him while I'm lifting with Darien and Nate, but I don't talk to him. It's clear he needs space.

I don't want to admit it, but my gut somehow misses him. I'm so mixed up. One minute I hate him for abandoning me, and the next, when he's looking at me or putting ground-up parsley on my skin or even just *smiling*, I can't deny that there's still something there. At least on my end, that is.

It's not until I'm getting myself ready for the '80s dance that there's a soft knock on my door.

"Julian?"

I open the door and see Elijah standing there, gripping the

door frame with one hand. "Hey," he says, shoving a hand into his pocket.

"Hey. I didn't see you after the weight room."

"Just came back here when I was done." He shrugs, looking at the floor.

"Aren't you going to get ready for the dance?"

"I don't think I'm going to go," he says, setting his jaw.

"How come?" I sit back down on my bed and go back to trying to tight-roll my jeans. I feel like I'm cutting my circulation off in my ankles. How did kids in the '80s even do this every day?

"I'm still not feeling that great." He shrugs. He looks like he wants to come into the room, but he hesitates at the door, biting his lip. I see his fingers grip the door frame tighter. I look at him there, in a Crenshaw football T-shirt and gym shorts, his socks slouched around his ankles.

I can't pinpoint *how* I know, but I know he's lying. I study his face, pinched and sad-looking as he stands in my doorway. "I can let you borrow something to wear if you want," I tell him, even though we are nowhere near the same size. Elijah's shoulders are much broader than mine. "Do you have any pants with you?"

"Just the khakis I wore last night," he says, letting go of the door frame and hesitantly coming into my room.

"Those will work. Let's just find you a shirt, then. I think we wear the same size shoes, too." I open my closet and pull out a bright green polo shirt that's always been too big for me to wear. "Try this on." I throw the shirt to him.

He yanks off his T-shirt and I watch his abs tense. I catch his eye, and the corner of his mouth turns up. "Thanks for this," he says.

He pulls the polo over his head, and it's pretty snug around his chest. His biceps are stretching the fabric a little bit, too. "How does it look?" he asks, looking down at the shirt and smoothing it over his stomach.

"Here, let me just," I stand in front of him and pop the collar of the shirt up. "Much more '80s," I say, straightening the shoulders. A piece of Elijah's hair falls from behind his ear. I tuck it back into place without thinking.

"Oh," he says, his cheeks turning pink. He says it so softly, it's almost more of a sweet sigh.

*Oh.* My hand lingers near his collar, a warm feeling spreading through my gut and up my spine. I meet his eyes. His lips part and he looks back at me. "Thank you," he says.

I clear my throat. "I'll find you some shoes." I turn quickly back to the closet.

Birdie wants to take our picture on the front porch. I've given Elijah a pair of sunglasses, and I'm wearing identical ones. "Don't you look like two peas in a pod!" Birdie exclaims, pointing her phone at us. "Let me give you a ride to the school. You don't need to be sweating all over those outfits, walking up there."

I'm thankful that Elijah is sitting in the back seat instead of me, because I'm not sure my stomach could handle staring at the back of his head right now. I'm still imagining what his hair felt like in my fingers a few minutes ago.

Birdie turns onto Main Street, and her Bluetooth picks up her phone. Barry Manilow bellows through the car at an alarming volume.

"Oh, I just love this song," Birdie says, singing along.

My face burns. I don't know why I'm suddenly very aware of Elijah. What does he think of Barry Manilow blasting through the open windows while we drive to Crenshaw? Does he think I'm a huge loser, needing my grandmother to chauffeur me around? Why do I even care?

I catch sight of him in the rearview mirror. He's mouthing the words along with Barry and Birdie.

"...if you wanna believe it can be daybreak..."

He sees me watching him, and a shy smile spreads across his face.

"You know this song?" I ask.

He shrugs. "Maybe."

"Don't stop singing on account of me," I tell him, only half joking.

"Come on, Ms. Birdie, let's bring it home," he says, raising his eyebrows at me and leaning forward in his seat.

"Come on and let it shine, shine, shine, all around the world!" Birdie lets her falsetto fly, and I can barely hear Elijah, but I know he's singing along with her.

Birdie laughs. "Julian never sings Barry with me," she says, glancing at Elijah in the mirror. "We might have to keep you around, Mr. Elijah."

Birdie pulls the car into the circle drive by the gym doors. A few kids are milling around in the parking lot, and I spot

Camille near the door. She's wearing pink leg warmers over her jeans and a rainbow-colored sweatshirt with the neck cut out. Her hair is pulled into a high side ponytail.

"You look amazing!" she squeals when she sees Elijah step out of the car. "I'm so glad you decided to come." She hugs him tight around the neck.

"What about me? Don't *I* look amazing?" I ask, my arms outspread.

Camille laughs. "Yes, Juls. You look just like the pictures of my dad in middle school that I found in the attic this summer."

"Well, I can't tell if that's a compliment or not." I scratch my head and she bumps me with her hip.

"You have fun and be safe walking home, now!" Birdie says through the open window.

"Yes, ma'am," Elijah answers. "Thank you for the ride."

"And thank *you* for singing with me!" She waves her arm out the window as she drives away.

"You're helping me with ticket duty, right?" Camille asks.

"That's why we're early." I smile at her.

I straighten the collar of my shirt and turn to look at Elijah. His collar is still popped, and he's managed to keep his khakis tight-rolled better than my jeans. On his feet are a pair of my old docksiders and no socks. He looks like a high school kid straight out of one of those movies they play on cable on Saturday mornings. The ones Birdie always claims were my father's favorites.

We stay outside with Camille until the tallest and loudest pickup truck I've ever seen pulls into the parking lot. Bucky jumps down from the driver's seat and a handful of football players spill out of the passenger door. Bucky enthusiastically volunteers to help Camille at the ticket table, and Elijah and I follow Nate and Darien inside. The gym has been transformed into a spectacle of neon and black lights. Everyone is literally glowing. A loud song with a heavy bass line is playing on the speakers, and a big group of kids are bouncing around in the middle of the gym floor under a huge spinning disco ball.

"Wow, the Guardettes sure know how to put on a party," Elijah says, taking in the room.

Nate and Darien spot a group of cheerleaders near one of the speakers and leave Elijah and me alone near the door.

"Do you want me to ask the DJ to play some Barry Manilow?" I joke, elbowing him playfully.

"Knock it off," he says, an embarrassed smile on his full lips. "My uncle Jacob used to play Barry Manilow all the time. We lived with him for a little while when we first moved to Houston." His smile fades just a little bit.

I want to ask him about his time in Houston. I want to know where he was, what he was doing.

I want to ask him what made his smile fade just then.

Instead, I study the way the bottom of his nose curves gently into his top lip. My eyes travel up his face. The juxtaposition of his sad eyes under the spinning disco ball and neon flashing colors makes it very hard for me to keep looking at him.

"You want something to eat?" I ask.

He nods, and we wander over to the food table together.

"Ugh, look what the cat dragged in. Watch your wallets," I

hear someone say as we squeeze by a group of marching-band kids on our way to the chip bowl. The rest of the group titters behind their hands.

"Who said that?" I turn and face them.

They all look at me silently, eyebrows raised. No one admits to anything.

"You can all go to hell," I say to them.

"Watch your mouth, Julian." Evan separates himself from the rest of his group.

"Screw you, Evan," I say, taking a step toward him. My gut tightens. Just looking at his smug little face pisses me off.

"That's not necessary," Elijah whispers next to me, putting his hand on the crook of my elbow.

"Come on, who made that comment? So big and bad until someone calls you out. Was it you?" I pull my arm away from Elijah and put my finger in Evan's face.

Evan just chuckles and rolls his eyes at me.

"Hey, please don't make a scene," Elijah says quietly. "It's really okay."

"Maybe you need to learn some manners," I say, jutting my chin toward Evan.

"Let's just go dance," Elijah says, pulling on my elbow a little bit. "Please."

His *please* is more of a demand than a polite request.

I walk away, even though it's the last thing I want to do. The music pounds through the speakers, and Elijah and I join a whole crowd of kids on the dance floor.

"I can't *stand* that guy," I tell Elijah, looking back toward Evan and his cronies.

"He's not worth getting into a fight with, though," he says.

"How can you just let him say stuff like that and brush it off? Doesn't it make you mad? Those stupid rumors are bullshit," I tell him.

Elijah just shakes his head. "That's been going on my whole life, Julian. You're just noticing now?"

I turn to glare at him. "What do you mean?"

"It's the same thing that happened with Ms. Birdie yesterday. And at bingo," he says. "Why do you think I was upset earlier about the pills?"

I clamp my mouth shut before finally admitting a lame "Oh."

A little bit of guilt starts to chew at my insides. My dad was really well-liked in Meridien. So is Birdie. I don't really carry any of the burdens that Elijah does, mostly just because of his last name. Maybe he was right earlier—I really *don't* understand.

"Hey, let's have fun," he says. "Don't worry about Evan or any of that stuff. I'm rocking this shirt and these sunglasses, and I'm not letting them go to waste."

An old Wham! song comes over the speakers, and Elijah starts moving his hips and his feet in time with the music. A bunch of kids bounce around us in a big group, and the lights flash and pop. I try to copy Elijah's moves. I am *not* a natural dancer.

He notices and starts to do more intense steps. He's laughing, and I'm laughing when the song ends. Someone bumps into me, and I lurch forward just a half step toward Elijah.

"Oh," he says, just an inch away from me. I look at the bright disco lights reflected in his dark eyes. The fine sheen of sweat on his forehead, the small dark blond curl that he tucks behind his ear. His face is so close to mine. He swallows, and his Adam's apple bobs in his throat.

There's a growing buzz in my head that reaches down to my fingers. I feel it in my bones and in my lips and in my intestines and in my cheeks.

"Isn't this the best?" Camille and Bucky come up behind me just as the next song starts pounding through the speakers. She grabs my shoulders and spins me around, Elijah disappearing from my vision. I look for him, but he's disappeared into a mass of our dancing friends. My stomach is still buzzing, and I don't answer Camille. Slowly the feeling starts to come back to my fingers, and I spot Elijah dancing just a few feet away. I meet his eye through the crowd, and he gives me a tiny private smile.

Bucky stays close by and starts doing some country steps in his scuffed cowboy boots. To Bucky, "dressing up" includes shaving, jeans without holes, and his nicest belt buckle. I watch Elijah try to learn Bucky's moves while Camille and I goof around doing ballet positions in time with the music. Well, Camille does ballet positions. I try desperately to keep up.

Eventually, Nate and Darien and a few of the cheerleaders join the group, and we just widen the circle. We're having a blast, sweating our asses off in the decorated gym. Elijah is opposite me in the circle, and I watch the disco ball throw dancing white light across his cheeks. His whole face is smiling, and it's the first time I've seen that since he got back to Meridien.

The DJ puts on a slow song, and all around us, our friends are coupling up. I watch Camille wrap her arms around Bucky's neck, and I raise my eyebrows in Elijah's direction. He mirrors my expression.

"Want to go outside?" he asks.

It's dark in the circle drive outside the gym, with a few students standing here and there laughing. Elijah sits down on the concrete planter. I sit down next to him.

"So, Bucky and Camille?" Elijah says with a chuckle.

"Bucky's been waiting in the wings for years." I laugh. "Maybe he figured tonight was finally the night he was going to stop *thinking* about it and just go for it. Good for him."

"She looks pretty happy, too," Elijah says.

"She deserves to be," I answer. "In the past, she hasn't exactly had the best luck in the romance department."

Elijah doesn't answer, and the crickets and bullfrogs fill the silence between us.

"I'm surprised no one has asked me about Taylor tonight," I finally say.

I hear Elijah swallow hard next to me. "The night is still young."

I chuckle. "I suppose that's true. You feel ready for the game against Stephens City tomorrow?" I ask.

"Yeah," he answers.

I hear a catch in his voice. It's something I remember about Elijah, that when he's this quiet for this long, he's working up the courage to say something or ask something. I let the darkness fill the space around us, knowing that he'll spill whatever he's got in his head when he's darn good and ready. I just need to give him the space.

My breathing falls into the rhythm of the night noises around me, and I can almost forget Elijah is sitting next to me. He's so quiet and still. Behind us, muffled voices and music seep through the gym doors and spill out into the driveway.

"Our dads were friends," he finally says into the darkness.

I turn my head to him. "What do you mean?"

"I found some pictures of them together in the shed last night when I got the pans for Ms. Birdie. Completely by accident," he says. "You didn't... you've never seen those pictures?"

"No. I didn't..." I shake my head. "I knew Birdie had a box of his things in the shed, but I never looked through them. I couldn't really... I just never did. I don't remember him having any pictures of people other than family up in our house."

"I don't know if they were real close or anything, but they were definitely buddies. Football buddies," he says.

"I wonder why no one ever told us," I say. I try to wrap my head around it. My father was a football hero in Meridien. The only thing I know about Eric Vance is that he's been in jail since just before Elijah and I started middle school.

Elijah is quiet after that. The crickets and bullfrogs seem even louder when we're not talking.

"I'd never hurt you on purpose, you know," Elijah says.

I turn to look at him in the dark. His face looks sad.

"That day in the locker room," he says, looking down at his lap. "Things were complicated for me at home and... I didn't mean..."

He lets out a heavy sigh and runs his hands through his hair before looking back up at me.

"I screwed up," he says, reaching his hand across the concrete planter and finding my fingers. He loops his pinkie around mine.

"I thought you hated me," I say.

"Not even close," he answers without turning his head.

"You didn't even say goodbye."

Elijah shakes his head. "I couldn't."

"But that doesn't even make any sense. Why couldn't you talk to me? What did I do? You just...disappeared, Elijah. And I spent all these years just wondering what happened to you!"

Inside the gym, the music stops, and we hear the DJ on the microphone telling everyone to drive home safely. Elijah lets go of my pinkie as groups of kids spill out of the gym and into the parking lot.

Bucky and Camille come out holding hands. Darien and Nate are with them. I want to tell them to go back inside. All of them. I want to finish talking to Elijah, but I know he's going to clam up now that everyone else is here.

I don't have all the answers yet. What if I never do?

I thought he hated me.

*Not even close.* His words just a minute ago replay in my head and turn my insides to Jell-O.

"Can I drive you guys home?" Bucky asks while we all stand outside the gym. He grips Camille's hand tight.

Elijah hangs back away from the group.

"We're going to walk, thanks," I tell Bucky, hoping to get a few more minutes alone with Elijah.

"I'm going to walk with them!" Camille says, dropping Bucky's hand.

"Wait...are you sure?" he says, looking lost without his hand in hers.

"Yeah, are you sure?" I say. I know Elijah won't talk if Camille is with us.

"Yeah, I'll see you tomorrow." She smiles and stands on her tiptoes to give Bucky a kiss on the cheek.

"But..."

"Bye, Bucky," she says.

He walks backward into the parking lot with Darien and Nate. He doesn't take his eyes off of Camille.

"So *that's* new," I say to her.

She shrugs one shoulder and smiles all sly. "He's nice."

"He's been pining for you since kindergarten. Since when did you start thinking of him as *nice*?" I use air quotes.

"Since tonight, I guess." She smiles again, never taking her eyes off of Bucky walking backward through the parking lot.

Elijah slides up next to us while the other three climb into Bucky's truck. "Must be the belt buckle," he says.

We laugh until we can't breathe.

## · eighteen ·

# *ELIJAH*

We watch Bucky's truck pull out of the parking lot and wave as it turns onto the road in front of the school, random laughs still erupting from all three of us.

"What happened in there, anyway?" Camille turns and asks Julian. "I heard you almost got into it with someone?"

"Ugh, it was just that asshole Evan. Running his mouth again," Julian says.

I hope he doesn't tell Camille the details. It's not a big deal, and I just want to forget about it.

"Best thing I ever did was kick that kid to the curb last year," she says, shaking her head.

"You're telling me." Julian laughs.

We walk for a block and a half in silence, and Main Street is starting to come into view just past Crossroads Church.

"Want to grab a burger?" Julian asks.

"Always up for Burger Barn," Camille says.

"Sure," I say even though all I have is a five-dollar bill in my pocket. I can at least sit with them. Maybe have a Coke or something.

We go inside this time, piling into a turquoise booth under the buzzing fluorescent lights. Menus are already on the table, but no one even glances at them. I look across the table at Julian and catch his eye while Camille digs in her purse beside me. He smiles with one side of his mouth, and I try to smile back.

I'm still hiding the big thing from him. Coley.

I probably would have told him if Camille and everyone hadn't come outside at the dance. It was on the tip of my tongue. I would have just apologized later and explained myself. Frankie would understand. Maybe.

But then there were Camille and Bucky holding hands and Nate and Darien and the whole school spilling out into the parking lot, and the moment was gone.

I'll tell him. I will.

I have to.

He thought I hated him, and I can't let him continue to think that.

"Cheese fries?" Julian says when Camille pulls her head out of her purse.

"Cheese fries are always the correct answer," Camille says. She turns to me in the booth. "Cheese fries?" she asks.

"Oh, um...nothing for me," I say, pretending to be completely engrossed in the end of my fingernail.

"Nonsense," Camille says in a fake British accent. "There's a rule. Cheese fries before every home game. It's the only way you'll win. Duh."

"I don't have any—"

"Hi!" The server, a pretty sophomore girl with a high ponytail and a nametag that says MERRI in block letters comes over just then with a tray full of sodas and sets one down in front of each of us. "Daddy says y'all better win tomorrow afternoon." Her voice shakes, and she nods toward the kitchen. A tall man with a hairnet stands flipping burgers at a huge grill. "Dinner's on him tonight."

"Thank you, Mr. Brannigan." Julian raises his soda glass toward the kitchen. "First touchdown has your name written all over it."

Mr. Brannigan salutes Julian with his spatula.

Camille leans across the sticky table and whispers, "We never pay at Burger Barn the night before a game. Julian's like a local celebrity. And I'm guessing after tomorrow, you will be, too."

"I don't know about all that." I laugh.

"What? Are you nervous about tomorrow or something?" Julian asks, peeling the paper from a straw. His eyes are soft. He's looking at me differently than he did at the beginning of the week.

I stretch my legs out under the table and let my foot rest against Julian's ankle. He doesn't move. "Maybe a little. I haven't been out on the field *in a game* since eighth grade," I remind him, meeting his eyes. He moves his foot a little so that his shoe strokes my ankle lightly. "I was gone before our first game freshman year. That's a long time to go without touching a football. Or wearing cleats or strapping on pads or any of that stuff." The more I talk about it, the more my stomach ties itself in intricate knots.

Or maybe that's because of the feel of Julian's foot on my skin.

"You'll be amazing," Camille says. "Once you get out there and hear the crowd cheering, you'll fall right back into it."

I'm pretty sure that's not how it's going to go, but I appreciate Camille's optimism. In my head, there's a lot more sweating, vomiting, and dizziness involved.

Merri brings a big platter of cheese fries and three small plates to the table. "Careful, they're hot," she says, speaking only to Julian.

"Thanks, Merri," Julian says, smiling at her. Her cheeks turn three shades of pink, and she can't look him in the eye.

Camille waits until Merri turns and heads back toward the kitchen before she whispers, "Should we tell her you're gay or just, I don't know, let her stumble upon that massive heartbreak all on her own?"

"Knock it off." Julian rolls his eyes, but I laugh out loud.

"Oh! Someone who appreciates my jokes! You're my new best friend, Elijah," Camille says, throwing her arm around my neck and pulling me close for a big, noisy kiss on the cheek.

Julian makes a face while he drags a fat French fry through the cheese sauce pooling on the giant plate in front of us. "Not that either of you care, but I have come to a decision about the Taylor prank," he announces.

Camille sits up super straight in the booth. "When? Just now? Ooh, tell me tell me! Wait. Don't say anything until I'm properly hydrated." She takes a massive sip of her cherry Coke and makes a big show of dabbing the corners of her mouth with a napkin and then folding her hands in front of her.

I can't stop laughing. She clearly gets a kick out of giving Julian the business.

"Okay. I am ready. Lay it on me," she says.

"I have decided to do nothing," he says.

"Wait. What?" Camille's face drops.

"Yep. You heard me. See, Figg told me that my dad actually wanted to do nothing when it was his senior year. He even tried to get a petition signed to bring down the entire thing! So, in his memory, I'm. Doing. *Nothing.*" Julian leans back in the booth and folds his hands behind his head, smiling. He shuffles his feet beneath the table, and he's no longer touching my ankle.

Camille looks at me, and I can see what she's thinking. This is probably not going to end well for Julian. Not at all. The team will be pissed; the alumni will be pissed. The only one who won't be pissed is Julian.

"Think about it, though!" He sits up in the booth again and puts both fists on the table. "Taylor will be so distracted at the game, wondering why we haven't made a move yet and worrying that something big will be coming in the middle of the game, that they'll be completely psyched out! Only *we* will know that a prank isn't going to happen. It's an ingenious plan, actually." He leans back, a self-satisfied smirk on his face. "The prank is that there *is* no prank! I'm pretty proud of it."

"I don't think that's how it's going to go down," Camille says, suddenly very serious.

"Well, I've already made up my mind. The town's insistence on stupid traditions that mean absolutely nothing is not worth me getting in trouble. Or getting anyone else in trouble, for that matter. I'm noping out of it. The end." He grabs another fry.

Camille and I share another look.

"So, when do you plan on telling the team about your grand idea?" Camille asks.

"Before the game tomorrow," Julian says. "I want to make sure our heads are in the right place. We need to think about what it's going to take to beat Stephens City, not worry about the Taylor Titans and whether or not they're going to fill our weight room with Ping-Pong balls or something."

"Uh…I'm going to ask you to please, please not tell the team before the game," Camille says.

I nod my head in agreement. All that's going to do is paint a great big target on Julian's back.

"Why are you so against all of this? I mean, I get it, it really pulls focus from playing football, but why are you so adamant about breaking this tradition?" I ask Julian.

"I've been doing some reading," he says.

"Reading?" Camille raises her eyebrows.

"Twenty years ago, the big brawl resulted in us forfeiting the game. Ten years ago, the Crenshaw quarterback slips in the parking lot after spraying shaving cream all over the Taylor bleachers and breaks his arm *the night before* Crenshaw's first game. He's out for the season. Loses his scholarship. *Five* years ago, six seniors get suspended for stealing the bronze statue in front of Taylor. One of them *got arrested*. Boom, scholarship gone. Are you noticing a pattern here?" Julian says.

"Oh, good lord, Juls," Camille says. "You don't have to do anything that serious! Filling a locker room with Ping-Pong balls is not exactly the same as *stealing a statue*! Look, this is something the guys have been looking forward to since freshman year. Please rethink it."

"I'm serious. This prank crap ends here," he says. "I'll tell them after the game, but this is the end of it."

Camille looks at me and raises her eyebrows.

This is absolutely not the end of it.

## · nineteen ·

# *JULIAN*

The Stephens City bus pulls up outside of our field house just after ten. We've been out on the field for over an hour already, doing some light passing drills and just getting the feel of the grass under our feet. We all pause to watch the players file off the bus and into the visiting locker room. I don't see any surprise monster-sized players, and my stomach starts to settle.

I grab a bag of footballs and jog over to the target, ready for some easy accuracy drills. I get into a smooth rhythm, being sure to match my inhale and exhale with the pull back and release of the ball. I visualize the waiting hands of my receivers as I drop ball after ball through the targets from twenty to thirty yards out. Before our warm-up ends, I back up to fifty yards out and continue to make easy, relatively accurate throws.

My arm feels pretty good, and there's just a little bit of stinging in my ribs. Elijah whipped up more cayenne pepper ointment before Birdie woke up this morning, and I've taped them up, too, just in case. I'm hoping my offensive line can do its job this afternoon and I don't get sacked. Another couple of days of not getting punched in the ribs, and I can probably quit worrying about it at all.

Coach blows his whistle three times to signal us into the locker room to change and get ready for the game. By the time I clean up my passes and roll the target back toward the field house, the rest of the team is already in the locker room getting ready.

Elijah is sitting on a bench with his game jersey in his fists, looking positively green. His leg shakes up and down, and it looks like he's trying to take deep breaths.

"You okay?" I ask him, throwing my practice clothes into my locker.

"Nervous," he says.

"You know what to do," I tell him. "You've got this."

He tries to smile at me, but it looks like he's going to throw up instead. "I haven't played in a game in over three years."

I sit down on the bench next to him. "Coach wouldn't put you in if he didn't think you could do this," I tell him. "You know this new position. I know I've got great protection with you in front of me. You've got this."

"Okay," he says, the green look on his face not fading.

"Elijah," I say.

He finally turns to look at me. "Yeah?"

"Just don't think too much," I tell him.

He nods and his shoulders relax just a tiny bit.

Pastor Ernie comes into the locker room, and we all take a knee and put a hand on the shoulder of the guy in front of us. Pastor Ernie talks about keeping the spirit of the brotherhood fresh in our minds, and I can feel the guy behind me squeeze my shoulder just a little bit. I pass it on and squeeze the shoulder in front of me, and Coach Andrews and Coach Marcus take over.

Their speeches are decidedly louder than Pastor Ernie's, and we do our usual pregame chant. I catch Elijah's eye when we're on our way out of the locker room and nod at him.

He nods back. I can see his pulse pounding in his neck, and sweat is already forming above his lip, but he does look a little bit less green.

We run through the banner the cheerleaders made for us and out onto the field and get our first good look at the Stephens City Spartans. In green jerseys and silver pants, their uniforms are sharp, but they don't look any bigger or tougher than we do. I take my place on the fifty-yard line and call the coin toss, shaking hands with the Stephens City captain. I know in less than five minutes that captain is going to be standing across from me, ready to tackle me to the ground, but we wish each other luck anyway.

As I run back to the sideline to watch the opening kickoff, I spot Birdie in the stands. Right on the fifty-yard line with her blue-and-white pom-poms and her glittery GUARDSMAN GRANDMA T-shirt. "Go, Julian!" she yells from the stands, waving frantically at me. I raise my hand and give her a quick wave to let her know I know she's there.

The kickoff is a good one, and our receivers bring it up to the forty-yard line for me. I run out onto the field, pulling on my helmet. It's the best feeling, pulling that helmet over my head. One minute I can hear the crowd cheering and chanting, coaches yelling, and the announcer over the loudspeaker. The next, most of the sounds are muffled. My eyes are focused, and all I can see is the field, the goalposts, and my teammates beside me.

Coach calls for a simple running play, and I set up behind my center. Elijah is in front of me, just to the left. I watch him dig his cleats into the grass and face off against the Spartan defense. I hope my pep talk did him some good.

And then the game really begins.

"Green 16! Green 16! Hike!" I yell, and the center places the ball perfectly into my waiting hands. I back up a few steps, keeping on the balls of my feet, and hand the ball off to Will, my most reliable running back, and step out of the play. Elijah and Bucky and the rest of the o-line shut down the Spartan defense pretty effectively, and Will gains a good twelve yards before being taken down just past the fifty-yard line.

I settle into the game pretty easily after that first handoff, and I keep the momentum going with a few more running plays before Coach calls for a long passing play. I take a look at Nate and my freshman wide receiver. "I'm going to the right with this one," I tell Nate.

He nods, and the freshman looks more nervous than I've

ever seen anyone look. Including Elijah before the game. The freshman shoves his mouth guard in and bites down hard.

"Set!" I yell, and watch my team fall into their stances.

"Blue 42! Blue 42! Hike!" I yell over my mouth guard, and my center hits me with a perfect snap. I catch sight of Elijah fighting hard, and I know I have only a few seconds to set up and let the pass out before I'm taken down. The Spartan defense is catching on to our style of play, and they're learning quickly how to get past Bucky and Elijah and the rest of the o-line.

But Elijah holds on.

Meanwhile, my freshman has taken off downfield and is nearing the ten-yard line when he pivots right and turns to look right at me. I let the ball go, and it falls perfectly into his waiting arms. He pivots again and runs as fast as I've ever seen him run right into the end zone. I end the first possession without even a tiny grass stain on my white pants.

I pound my fist on Elijah's shoulder pads on our way off the field. "See? See? You got this, 87! You got this!" I shout in his face.

His smile is so wide I feel like it might crack his face right open.

Our defense does its job perfectly, and the Spartans never even gain enough yardage for a first down on their first possession. I barely have time to catch my breath before it's time for us to take the field again.

Elijah is the last to set up, checking out the pattern of the defense before nodding at me and getting into position.

"Set!" he yells.

"Red 15! Red 15! Hike!" I yell, and Elijah goes to work, clearing the defense and giving me a nice deep pocket to work with. I see Nate hustling downfield. Out of the corner of my eye, I notice the left tackle digging in and heading in my direction, and everything starts to happen in slow motion. Elijah is wrestling with the middle linebacker, and the rest of the o-line is fighting hard to keep the other defensive players at bay. With that tackle coming at me, I know I have to make a quick decision.

I wasn't planning on letting a long bomb go so quickly after the last one, but I can see that Nate is a perfect option right now. Out of nowhere, Elijah flies in front of me and takes the tackle out at the knees just as he reaches out to grab my shins. I can feel the tackle's glove brush my right leg right before Elijah pulls him down onto the turf.

I let the ball go just like my father taught me, fingers between the laces and pointer finger on the seam. The ball rolls off my fingers, and it's one of those passes that I just know is going to look beautiful when I watch the playback later. Everything about it feels right as it spirals out of my hand and drops perfectly into Nate's arms. He pivots and runs right into the end zone. *Again.*

There isn't a green jersey anywhere near him. Nate spikes the ball, and the Crenshaw bleachers go absolutely wild. I can see Birdie on her feet, screaming and waving a glittery poster with the number eighty-seven, Elijah's number, emblazoned on it.

Elijah catches me on our way off the field and gives my pads a hearty punch. "Yeah! Yeah! That's how you do it," he yells, his face full of pure joy.

The entire first half of the game goes like that. I feel like I'm on fire, and nothing can stop any of us from marching into the end zone over and over again. We head toward the fieldhouse with a score of 24–3 as the Guardettes and the band take the field behind us.

All the Guardsmen are whooping and hollering at the top of our lungs when we get into the privacy of our own locker room. Most of the players bump pads with Elijah or bump his knuckles when they walk by him.

"Nice work out there. You tired yet?" I ask him, sitting down next to him on the bench and pulling off my sweaty helmet.

"Heck, no," he says. "I can do this all day long."

"Let's hear it for our Iron Man," Coach Marcus calls, standing in the middle of the locker room and pointing at Elijah. The team yells so loud I know the Spartans can hear it in their locker room.

"Let's keep our heads in the game. We all know how quickly things can go south in the second half," Coach Marcus tells us.

He pulls Elijah aside as the rest of us run back out onto the field. I hesitate, wanting to wait for him, but in the end, I don't. I take a deep breath and pull my helmet back on, ready to get back out on the field and score some more points. I pat the tape on my ribs to make sure it's secure and take a deep breath. As long as I don't get hit on my left side, I'm good. My ribs are only sore when I touch them, and the adrenaline is pumping so hard I can barely feel them when I'm on the field.

And as long as I've got Elijah in front of me when I'm making plays, I know I'm not going to go down.

## · twenty ·

## *ELIJAH*

**Iron Man. That's what Coach Marcus called me at halftime. I** *feel* like Iron Man, too, digging into the grass before every play and watching the eyeballs of every defensive player that's in front of me. I know their moves before they do. I can feel my muscles tighten and pulse before every snap, and my body knows exactly where it needs to go before my brain does. I never figured protecting the quarterback would have come to me so easily, although I'm sure it doesn't hurt that it's Julian I'm taking care of back there.

The game ends with a score of 59–27 in favor of the Crenshaw County Guardsmen. We dump a full bucket of ice water on Coach Marcus before running back to the field house.

Bucky hooks his phone up to a speaker and plays our hype song as soon as we get into the locker room and keeps it going at full volume until the coaches get there. The atmosphere is electric, and guys keep coming up to me to congratulate me. They're all calling me Iron Man.

I am soaking it up.

"Beach night, boys! Bring your tents and meet us at marker forty-eight!" Bucky yells to the full locker room while we're all getting dressed.

I throw on my clothes as quickly as I can and meet Julian outside the locker room. I can't wipe the smile off of my face.

"Feels good, right?" Julian smiles when he sees me.

"Aw, man…" is all I can manage to say.

Julian gives me a high five and claps me on the back. "That was an epic block you made at the end of the first quarter. I thought for sure I was going down."

"I saw that tackle coming at you out of the corner of my eye, and I just dove for him. The only thing I was thinking about was your ribs." I laugh. "Man, it felt good to take him down. How are you feeling? Hurting?"

"Not so bad right now," he says, touching his side with his fingertips. "Can't promise it's not going to be sore from all of those long passes I let fly when all this adrenaline wears off."

"Well, we know how to take care of that now, right?" I laugh a little.

He cocks his head to the side and gives me a shy smile.

We start walking toward home when Bucky yells from the gym doors. "Y'all need a ride tonight? I got room in the truck."

"Yeah, that'd be good," Julian tells him. "Just got to talk to Birdie and pack up some stuff. What time are you coming by?"

"I've got to grab Darien first, then we'll swing by your house around five thirty," Bucky says.

"You all right with that? Riding with Bucky down to Port A?" Julian asks as we turn out of the school driveway.

Port Aransas postgame camping nights. I heard about them when I was a freshman but never got the chance to go. To be honest, I'm more than a little excited to be included. I wonder, but only for a second, if they would've asked me even if I hadn't made that great block. Little thoughts like that creep in when I least expect them.

"Hell yeah, I'm all right with it," I say, shaking off the thought and falling in step next to Julian.

We hightail it home, and Ms. Birdie has a feast of sandwiches and chips and potato salad and sodas waiting for us. Pastor Ernie and Figg are there, too, both wearing Crenshaw Booster Club T-shirts.

"To the champions!" Pastor Ernie says as he pours ginger ale into a glass and holds it high in the air for a toast.

"Let's not get ahead of ourselves," Julian laughs. "It's only the first game of the season."

"The two of you keep up the show you had going this afternoon, and we're headed for quite a season," Figg says, holding a ham-salad sandwich in one hand and a Coke in the other.

"Hey, Birdie, is it okay if we head out for the night? The team is going down to Port A for the postgame campout," Julian asks.

"Oh, Port A campouts," Figg says. "I remember those!"

Pastor Ernie laughs. "Way back in the Stone Age, Thomas?"

"Hey, it's a tradition! If you camp out in Port A after your first victory of the season, you're guaranteed another victory in your second game," Figg says.

Julian rolls his eyes. "More tradition. More superstition. Does it *ever* end?"

Ms. Birdie tut-tuts. "Meridien is steeped in them, Julian. None more important than the Taylor game, though. You keep your eyes on that prize. It's coming up sooner than you think. Oh, and yes, you and Elijah may go to Port Aransas. Is that sweet Brian Redd picking you up?"

"Yes, ma'am," Julian says, a smirk pulling on his lip. Probably for the same reason I'm laughing; no one would ever refer to Bucky as "that sweet Brian" other than Ms. Birdie.

"Hey, I didn't know you played football at Crenshaw, Mr. Figg," I say, grabbing a second sandwich. Skipping breakfast this morning was probably a mistake, but I had been way too nervous to think about chewing and swallowing.

"Class of nineteen, uh…never mind all that," Figg says, laughing. "I'll never tell."

"Thomas was the kicker," Pastor Ernie says, grabbing Figg's hand and giving it a squeeze. "I was the equipment manager."

"You two knew each other in high school?" Julian asks.

Pastor Ernie and Figg share a look. "Not exactly," Figg says, smiling.

"We found each other again after a lot of years away from Meridien," Pastor Ernie says. "It wasn't until then that it dawned on us that we graduated just a few years apart."

"Did you guys have the Taylor prank tradition way back then, too?" I ask them.

Pastor Ernie starts to laugh. A big hearty sound from his belly. "Oh, sweet Elijah," he says. "It was the highlight of the season even 'way back then,' as you so kindly put it. Though we probably weren't quite as creative as some of you boys are now."

I can see Julian's face starting to pinch. "Hey, we better get packed if we're going to be ready when Bucky gets here," he says to me.

We walk down the hallway together toward our rooms, and I can see the muscles in Julian's neck and back are flexed and tight.

"You okay?" I ask him.

"If I have to hear one more word about how *steeped in tradition* Crenshaw is, or the Taylor prank is *the most important thing in the world*"—he rolls his eyes—"I'm seriously going to hurt someone."

"Can I ask you something without you flying off the handle?"

"I can't exactly promise that until I know what you're going to ask, can I?" Julian chuckles.

"How come it bothers you so much? All the tradition?" I ask, standing in Julian's doorway while he pulls a few pairs of shorts from his dresser.

Julian shakes his head. "You know how much pressure it is? To not only win the games, but to pull off pranks, lead the team, get a scholarship. And all of that with the eyes of the entire town on me. My dad..." He shakes his head again and goes back to his dresser.

I walk into the room and sit down on the bed. "Your dad what?"

"My dad was good at everything." His voice catches. "Birdie tells me all the time about what a good quarterback he was, that he got straight As, that the whole town loved him. He was some kind of hero around here. How am I supposed to live up to all of that?"

"I don't know that anyone expects you to be exactly like your dad," I say. As soon as the words are out of my mouth, I realize what I've said. That's exactly what everyone seems to expect from me.

Julian ignores my comment. "When Figg told me how my dad tried so hard to get rid of the prank tradition, I thought, *YES!* Here's something I can actually do that he didn't manage to do first. Or do better. I just...I just want to think he'd be proud of me if he was still around," Julian says. "And seeing all the trouble the pranks have caused...I want to think he'd be proud of me trying to do something different."

My stomach still churns around the realization of how alike Julian and I actually are. "I think he'd be proud," I tell him.

Julian lets out a long sigh. "Thanks, man. Let's get our stuff packed up. I need to tell the team tonight that we're not doing a prank. We've got football games to win, and if Coach Marcus expects us to do that, we're going to have to keep our heads in the game. Stephens City was like peewee stuff compared to what we've got coming up."

"Are you sure tonight is the best time to break the news?"

"We're all going to be together. The quicker I can get

everyone's attention off the pranks, the quicker we can focus on actual football." He clamps his mouth shut and focuses on packing his bag.

I stuff my own black duffel with an extra pair of shorts and my bathing suit. I honestly don't know what else to throw in for a campout. Or if I'll even need another pair of shorts. I've never done anything like this before. Or had friends to do this kind of thing *with*.

I meet Julian in the living room.

"I've got two sleeping bags and a tent, and I threw a package of hot dogs in a cooler. Probably need a few water bottles and some sodas and maybe a bag of chips," he says, heading for the kitchen. "Maybe we can talk Bucky into grabbing some dough-nuts and kolaches on the way down."

Ms. Birdie and Pastor Ernie and Figg have moved to the back patio, where they're sitting on the wicker furniture and reminiscing about their favorite Crenshaw memories. I wonder if every game day will be like this, with the house filled with laughter and food and just a warm feeling. I stand in the living room and soak it up.

Bucky's truck pulls up in front of Ms. Birdie's driveway, the engine rumbling loud enough to shake the front screen door.

"We're out of here, Birdie!" Julian shouts toward the back door, swinging his bags over his shoulder and tossing one of the sleeping bags to me.

"Be safe, boys! See you tomorrow! Love you both!" she hollers back, all three of them waving through the door.

"Love you, Birdie!" Julian yells, ushering me out the door.

I need the step to get into the sprawling back seat of Bucky's Ford. Julian climbs in beside me, throwing the bags between us on the worn bench seat. Ms. Birdie's entire car could probably fit into the cab of Bucky's truck.

"So, tell us about this new development, loverboy," Julian says to Bucky as he buckles his seat belt. "You finally got Camille to look twice at you, huh?"

"Hey, sometimes things just naturally happen," Bucky says, the tips of his ears turning pink.

"Sure. Natural. Like you haven't been dreaming about being with Camille since kindergarten." Darien backhands Bucky on the shoulder.

"Exactly! I gave Camille space. Let things simmer. It all came together exactly like it should have," Bucky says. He's laughing, but his whole face lights up when he says the name *Camille*. We're teasing the shit out of him, but I can tell that he really cares about her a lot.

It makes me smile to think of the two of them together. Somehow, they just work.

Julian talks Bucky into stopping for doughnuts, and we're on our way after that. We take off down the highway, windows open and Bucky's new stereo pumping out a steady playlist of Crenshaw's best hype songs. Bucky, Darien, Julian, and I all sing loudly, our voices fighting with the wind at highway speeds, and we're all laughing like maniacs by the time we pull off the road and into the sand, headed for beach marker forty-eight.

Nate and a few other guys have got a good bonfire started by the time we pull the truck up next to the dunes and grab the gear from the back.

"I'm sleeping back here," Bucky announces, standing in the bed of the truck and rolling out an air mattress. "Everyone else, find your own spot."

"Let's get this tent set up before it gets dark," Julian tells me. "I'm no good with this kind of stuff, and trying to do it in the dark would make it even worse."

I pull everything out of the ripstop bag and have it set up in no time, without any help from Julian. As smart as he is, he sure doesn't have a whole lot of mechanical aptitude.

"How'd you do that?" he asks, standing next to the setup, scratching his head.

"Easy. There's really only one way to put it up." I laugh.

"Well, I'm glad you're here. Otherwise I'd be sleeping in the sand tonight," he says, clapping me on the shoulder and heading for the fire with the package of hot dogs he brought. "Hot dogs on the fire, I can handle. Thankfully. Want some?"

He hands me a long fork, and I thread a couple of hot dogs onto it and hold it over the glowing coals. I glance around at the team goofing off in the sand, splashing one another in the water and just talking by the fire. Everyone is smiling. Everyone is having a good time. My chest almost aches.

I have this feeling that I really missed this, but how can you miss something you never had before?

I pull my phone from my pocket and take a picture of my hot dogs hanging over the fire and text it to Frankie. She texts back a picture of Coley, fresh from her bath, wet curls springing from her head. It's been only a couple of days, but she looks older somehow.

"Who's that kid?" Julian is peering over my shoulder.

I click the power button and shove the phone back into my pocket as quickly as I can. "A cousin," I mumble.

I feel like an ass for chickening out of telling him about Frankie and Coley at the dance last night, but his words about the pregnant cheerleader still sting. Maybe I'll tell him tonight later on, when there aren't fifty other guys listening in. One thing's for sure, I don't want to leave it for Frankie to tell him when she gets here. Maybe if he has some time to get used to it, he'll be nice to Frankie and not judgmental. I know that would kill her.

"Hey, gather round here, Guardsmen," Julian yells over the crashing waves and the conversations around us. "I've got some news for you."

"Taylor praaaaaaank!" someone yells, and everyone laughs.

The team moves closer to where Julian is, and I try to back away. I have no idea how they're all going to take this news, and I really don't want to be a part of it at all. I wish Camille were here to stop it. Or at least ease the tension that's sure to follow this announcement.

"Actually, it *is* about the Taylor prank," Julian says, and everything falls silent, the air full of anticipation. The only noise is from the rolling ocean and the logs popping in the fire.

Julian hesitates for a beat too long. "What's going on, Cap?" Bucky says.

"Well," Julian starts. "I think we're not doing a prank this year."

"Wait, what?" Darien yells from the other side of the fire.

"Listen," Julian goes on. "Not playing a prank is the *ultimate* prank! Taylor will be so distracted at the game, waiting for us to make our move, that they won't be able to concentrate on playing actual football. They'll constantly be looking over their shoulders, wondering what's coming. We'll tan their hides at homecoming. Pretty much a guaranteed victory! That's what we all want in the end, right?" Julian really tries to sell it. He stands up on a boulder and holds his arms out like he's giving an epic before-game pep talk.

"That doesn't make a whole lot of sense, dude," someone says.

A bunch of mumbles flutter through the crowd, but no one outwardly disagrees with Julian. I think they all respect him too much for that. But the mood of the team kind of falls flat, with no one sure how to respond.

Julian watches our teammates give one another sideways glances and lowers his arms. His face falls a little bit.

"We beat Stephens City!" I yell suddenly, raising my arms high in the air, and the team turns toward me and cheers. I may want no part in this discussion, but I can't leave Julian hanging like that. "Bucky, turn that music up!"

Bucky starts the hype song again, and the guys start grabbing one another's shoulders and jumping around in the sand, singing along. I grab onto Darien and Nate and add my voice to the celebration and then motion with my chin for Julian to come, too. He steps down from his boulder and joins in, but his face isn't as triumphant as it was a little bit ago.

This probably won't be the last conversation we have about the prank. Not by a long shot.

## · twenty-one ·

# *JULIAN*

Eventually, the sun starts to dip behind the dunes, and someone turns the music down to a manageable volume. We all stick by the fire, though, toasting marshmallows and talking about the game. Someone brings out a case of beer, but I don't really notice anyone drinking it.

Bucky plops down in the sand next to me and Elijah, and pretty soon Nate and Darien join us.

"Tell us you're joking, Cap," Nate says. He's holding a Coke in his hand and has a wary smile plastered on his face.

"I'm *definitely* not joking," I tell them. "This tradition ends here."

"Listen, we all know this isn't exactly your area of expertise," Bucky says. "How about if *we* come up with the prank, and all you have to do is help us carry it out?" The rest of the group nods in agreement.

I glance over at Elijah. He's sitting in the sand with his knees drawn up to his chest and his arms wrapped around his legs. He doesn't nod along with the rest of the group, but he still looks at me expectantly.

"Look, we really just need to focus on the games coming up, guys," I say, trying to reason with them. "Every single one of us has got something to lose this year. Scholarships, all-conference status, ammunition for why you're the best sibling. It's just too risky! What if someone gets hurt? Or suspended or arrested? What if one prank ended your entire football career?"

Nate groans. "Come on, Cap. It doesn't have to be something that could get us in trouble. Can you at least consider it?"

"My dad will never let me live it down if we don't do *something*," Bucky says. Bucky's dad and even his grandfather have almost made a career out of reliving their Crenshaw Guardsmen glory days.

"Not to mention what Taylor will say about us," Darien says, throwing a rock out toward the ocean. "How are we going to look them in the face after the flag incident if we don't at least try and retaliate?"

"Yeah, what about that?" Bucky asks. "What if they show up to homecoming with something epic planned and make us look ridiculous? You're so sure that we'll throw *them* off *their* game, but they could just as easily do it to us by catching us off guard," he reasons.

"You owe it to us to at least think about it," Nate says, poking at the fire with a long stick. It pops and crackles as sparks float up into the dark September sky. "A good captain is supposed to listen to his team, not rule with an iron fist."

I glance at Elijah again. His eyes reflect the bright flames, and he nods almost imperceptibly in my direction.

I let out a long breath. "I don't know yet, guys. I can't just make up my mind right now."

Bucky turns to me. "So, you'll at least *think* about it?"

My lips pull into a straight line. "Yeah."

We all watch the fire crackle in silence for a few minutes, the heaviness of the conversation putting a damper on the earlier celebratory feelings.

"Can we talk about my epic block again?" Elijah says, breaking the tension.

Everyone starts laughing, and Darien pelts Elijah with a marshmallow. Elijah jumps up and drops a handful of dried seaweed on Darien's head, and that starts a massive game of chase up and down the beach, all of us flinging dried seaweed at one another and dodging marshmallow bombs.

The game ends when we run out of marshmallows, and everyone retreats back to the shrinking fire or to their tents or pickup beds. Elijah and I stay by the fire until the last dying embers finally turn black. I pour a bucket of sea water on top of them before dragging myself into the tent Elijah pitched earlier. I'm still grateful he was there to help with the tent; otherwise I'd be sleeping in the sand using a rock for a pillow. I've never been any good at putting up tents or putting together

IKEA furniture or anything like that. I can see too many possibilities.

"Well, that didn't exactly go over well," I say to Elijah, lying down on top of my sleeping bag.

"I think maybe everyone's just a little disappointed. I mean, it's a thing the whole team looks forward to. I understand that you think it's a distraction, and I agree, but, um...maybe not everyone else does," Elijah says, his voice quiet but insistent in the dark.

I know he's right, but I can't let it go. "It's just way too easy for things that start out small and harmless to grow into something that you can't control. We've got to try to at least get a regional title. That's the only way I'm going to get a scholarship. I need everything to line up just right if I have any chance at getting out of here."

"Did your dad get a scholarship?" Elijah whispers in the dark.

My gut sinks. "No."

"He made the most out of it, though, didn't he? Why are you so hell-bent on leaving Meridien? Leaving Texas?"

I roll over to face him. "Why *aren't* you so hell-bent on leaving Texas? I mean, there's so much more out there. Didn't living in Houston make you want to see more of the world?"

I can feel Elijah shrug next to me.

I don't understand why someone wouldn't want to get away from here, even just for a few years, to see something else. I know my dad was happy here, and so many other people are, too. But I want to see *all* the oceans, not just the Gulf of Mexico.

I want to taste food from all over the world. I want to see snow thick enough to ski in and ice strong enough to skate on. I want to know how small I look next to a giant sequoia tree. I want to know what the leaves look like in New England in October. I don't know what "purple mountain majesty" even *means*.

I've seen pictures of all that stuff, but I want to know what it *feels* like. I want a reason to wear a scarf and winter boots. To put on mittens and roll myself a snowman taller than me. I've soaked up enough Texas to last me a lifetime. *Show me something else, world.*

Sometimes I feel that so deeply I want to scream it as loud as I can.

"Don't you ever think about leaving Texas? Even a little bit?" I ask.

"Not exactly," Elijah says. "Everyone I love is here."

I frown. "It's not like you could never come back," I say. "I just want to see more. At least for a little while."

"Texas is home," he says softly. "I'm not sure what else I need."

I listen to the waves rolling onto the shore. The hushed, sleepy voices of some of my teammates just outside the tent wash over me as my eyelids start to droop.

"What even happened at that game twenty years ago?" Elijah asks into the dark. "Why did Crenshaw get into a fight with the Taylor kids, anyway?"

"Figg told me they caught wind that one of the football players' girlfriends had gotten pregnant," I say, my voice thick with the weight of the day. "Taylor showed up with beach balls stuffed under their jerseys, and the Crenshaw kids just went nuts. Bench-clearing brawl, he said."

Elijah sits up on his sleeping bag next to me. "Seriously?"

"That's what Figg said," I yawn.

"And it was twenty years ago. When your dad was a senior," he says. "Which means my dad was a senior."

"Uh-huh," I yawn again, louder this time.

Elijah is quiet for a moment. Then, "I think that might have been my mom and dad." His voice is small.

Now my eyes are open all the way. *"What?"*

"I know my parents were still in high school when Frankie came along," he says. "I mean, how many other football players would have had pregnant girlfriends at homecoming exactly twenty years ago? Meridien isn't quite a metropolis with a million people."

"I didn't know that about Frankie." My brain flips through the math, and I sit up in my sleeping bag. In the dimly lit tent, I can see Elijah's face is a mask of worry, and I hear his breath start to quicken.

"What if it was *my* father that started that fight? What if it was his fault that Crenshaw had to forfeit? No wonder he wasn't in the football team picture his senior year. He probably got kicked off the team. It's no wonder the whole town hates his guts. It's no wonder they hate mine just for being a Vance." All of a sudden, he's unzipping his sleeping bag and pulling his legs out of it, crawling to the door.

"Hey, hey, hey," I say, trying to pull him back. "Calm down! Figg said the whole *team* was involved in that fight. Even if it was your mom that was pregnant—"

"It was, I know it was," Elijah says.

"Okay. Even if it was, the whole Crenshaw team was sticking up for your mom and dad. They were all angry that Taylor was being so awful. It wasn't your father's fault that Crenshaw had to forfeit that year," I tell him. I can hear his breathing slow in the dark. "Or at least it wasn't *only* his fault."

Elijah lies back down on top of his sleeping bag this time, and I lower my head onto my pillow, too. I'm curled on my side, watching the fuzzy outline of his profile in the dark tent.

"Hey, Julian?" Elijah says into the dark. "I gotta tell you something else."

"Okay."

"And I'm going to need you to just…listen without judgment, okay?" he says, his voice unsteady.

I frown, but I try not to let it show in my voice. "Yeah, of course."

"Part of the reason we left Meridien three years ago was because of Frankie," he says, suddenly quiet again.

I sit up. "What happened? Was she sick or something? Did she have to go to a different school?"

"She had a baby." The words rush out of him like he can't contain them any longer. "I have a niece, okay? Her name is Coley and she's almost two and a half, and she's the most important thing in my world right now, and I just…I don't care if that makes you think Frankie is irresponsible and she's ruined her life." His voice picks up strength. "She's not! She's not *any* of those stereotypical things people think about teen moms!

She's this amazing mother. And I couldn't even imagine what my life would be like right now without Coley in it."

"Wow," I say, letting his words settle around me. "Frankie's a mom."

He finally breathes, but it comes out all shaky like he's about to break into a million tiny pieces.

"Hey," I say, reaching across the tent for his hand. "I don't think she's ruined her life. Why would you say that?"

"Dani Patrick. Those horrible things you said about her." His voice catches, and even in the dark I know he's crying.

My gut flip-flops. I did say awful things. I called her irresponsible and said she was ending her life before it even began. Ugh.

*Way to stick your foot in it, Julian.*

I sit up and cross my legs on my sleeping bag. "Hey, come here." I hold my arms open, and Elijah leans forward and lets me hug him. Eventually he lets go and sits across from me, our knees touching. I hold on to both of his hands.

"Hey," I say after we sit in complete silence for a few beats.

"What?" Elijah says, his entire body stiffening across from me.

I don't even have anything to say. I know what I said about Dani, and I know what that must have sounded like to Elijah.

"I'm sorry?" I say.

"Are you really? It doesn't sound like it," Elijah answers.

"I just…I didn't know that Frankie had a baby." I know I sound pathetic, but I really don't know how to apologize for any of this.

Elijah shakes his head. "But it's obvious what you think of people who have kids when they're young. Sometimes shit happens, Julian. To Dani Patrick. To Frankie. To my own parents! It doesn't make any sense, and maybe it's not the choice you would make if you found yourself in the same situation, but...it doesn't make the people it happens to *less than*. Don't do that."

I hang my head and squeeze his hands in mine. "I don't want to hurt you. I really didn't mean to."

"Frankie didn't want me to tell anyone," Elijah says. "She said she didn't want people gossiping about her before she even gets here. But I couldn't let you think I just left and didn't say anything because of something *you* did. It wasn't you. Frankie told me she was pregnant the day before we...in the locker room."

"When I kissed you."

"When *I* kissed *you*," Elijah says.

A smile pulls on my cheeks.

"I had to take care of her. I was fourteen, I could only focus on one catastrophe at a time. I...I broke the window to steal the car wash money to try to take care of her. Frankie needed to see a doctor and she hadn't told my mom yet, so everything was just a mess. That day you found me, thinking about crawling through that broken window to steal that money, was probably one of the worst days of my life," Elijah says. "I felt like I was backed into a corner, and I didn't have the smarts to do anything else. All I knew was that I needed money to take care of my family, and that was the best way I could think of at the time to get it. So stupid." He shakes his head and lowers his chin to his chest.

I put my hand gently under his chin until he raises his eyes to meet mine. "You can't be mad at your fourteen-year-old self, Elijah. It sounds like you've done a pretty good job taking care of everyone since then," I say.

We stay quiet for a long time. Eventually, Elijah curls up on his side on top of his sleeping bag with his back to me. His breathing slows, and I'm pretty sure he's fallen asleep. I lie on my side, watching his ribs rhythmically rise and fall. The coming sunrise paints the inside of the tent with a warm purple light. It illuminates the curve of his neck, his earlobe, his shoulder.

I'm close enough that he can probably feel my warm breath on his back. My fingers ache with the nearness of him. I scoot closer, curve my body the way his is curved. Knees tucked up, right arm curled under my head. I breathe in his skin, his hair, his body. I lie behind him, aching to reach out and make the connection. My skin touching his. My knees tucked behind his. My lips on his neck.

Instead, I lie perfectly still, my fingertips a hair's breadth from his lower back, hoping he'll inch my way sometime before the sun fully rises.

## · twenty-two ·

# *ELIJAH*

I wake up to the dulcet tones of Bucky's truck rumbling. It feels like the entire beach is shaking. The sun is beating through the thin tent material, and I'm covered in sweat. Julian is already up and out.

"Good morning, sunshine," Nate jokes when I finally crawl out of the tent. "It's almost noon!"

I glance down the beach and see most of the guys bobbing around in the ocean. Throwing a football back and forth and making these spectacularly dramatic catches in the water, creating the biggest splashes they can. I blink the sleep from my eyes and see Julian in thigh-deep water, making the passes. The sky is the kind of impossible blue you can see only near the beach. I yank off my T-shirt and join the rest of the team.

I dive under the first wave that hits me. Instant relief from the heat. I push my hair back from my face and see Julian watching me. He nods and raises his eyebrows. I know he's asking if I'm okay. I nod back at him and join the crew of receivers. Julian tosses the ball to us over and over, each one of us making a catch more spectacular than the last. When it's my turn, I try to do a diving backflip and catch the ball with both feet out of the water. It doesn't go so well for me, and the ball whacks me right on the forehead. I stand up in the water, laughing.

"Hey, you look better than Darien out there!" someone yells, and everyone laughs.

"Not cool, man," Darien says, stepping forward for his turn at a catch. He leaps backward, legs splayed out like a starfish, landing with a tremendous splash and an audible *kerplunk*. But somehow he still manages to keep the ball in his hands. "Beat that!" he yells when he surfaces. "Beat that, you defensive toads!"

Plenty of ribbing and dunking and chest puffing ensues, the entire group of us laughing and tackling one another in the shallow water.

Someone suggests a race, and pretty soon we're all running full speed down the beach in the sand, all of us trying to beat the pants off the guy next to us. Darien smokes everyone, of course, and some of the bigger defensive guys are still huffing and puffing back near the tents when the rest of us reach the crumbling jetty about two hundred yards away.

"Who was the genius who suggested that?" Julian laughs, coughing. He pulls on the hem of his tank top. He hasn't taken it off since we got here, even when we were all goofing off in the water. I'm sure it's because he doesn't want anyone to see his bruise.

"High knees all the way back! Come on, you lazy asses!" Darien yells in a perfect imitation of Coach Marcus.

Most of the guys run ahead, following Darien like he's some crazed pied piper, their knees pumping all the way up to their chests.

I hang back with Julian. "Your ribs okay?"

"A little sore, but not any worse than yesterday," he says.

We walk through the wet sand where the water splashes over our feet. I stop every few feet and pick up shells and shove them into my pocket. I don't know what I'm going to do with all of them when I get back to the tent, but I like the feel of them, warm in my pocket.

"I'm glad you told me about Frankie and Coley," Julian says as we get closer to the tents.

The words *I'm glad I told you, too* sit right on the edge of my tongue, but I can't get them out. Instead, I try to smile and I know it's crooked.

"It will be good to see Frankie again," he says to me. "And I'm excited to meet Coley."

"I miss them both," I tell him quietly, squeezing the shells in my pocket tightly.

We stay at the beach until almost three in the afternoon. Sunburned and sandy, we pile back into Bucky's truck for the trek home. It's way quieter than the trip out.

"Guess none of us went to church this morning," Bucky laughs, his voice gravelly.

"The entire back three rows of pews were probably empty." Julian laughs, too. "Pastor Ernie will forgive us. We had our own kind of church this morning."

I rest my head against the seat. We did have our own kind of church this morning, didn't we? I let that really unfamiliar feeling settle in my bones.

"Hey, Cap," Bucky says, turning the volume on the radio down. "You thought some more about that prank?"

"I can't make a decision about it right now," Julian protests. "You gotta give me more time than just overnight."

"I really hope you think about what we're saying," Bucky says, scratching at his head with a sunburned arm. "This prank war has been going on for so many years.... We can't be the class that ruins it. Or the lame team that got caught with their pants down because Taylor surprised us and we didn't retaliate. We'll never hear the end of it!"

"Bucky's right, man," Darien says. "My dad asks me every day what we're doing to get Taylor. I can't tell him we're doing *nothing.* You know what kind of flak I'm going to get for that at Thanksgiving when both of my grandfathers and all of my uncles are here visiting?"

I watch this conversation unfold all around me, but I don't add anything. I don't feel like I have as much at stake as the rest of the guys.

Julian is quiet for a long time, sitting next to me and staring out the window. "Did you know my dad tried to start a petition his senior year to stop the prank war with Taylor?" he finally says.

"No," Bucky answers, turning the radio off completely. "I didn't know that."

No one says another word all the way back to Rudy Street. I don't think anyone knows how to respond to Julian talking about his father.

"Catch you later, Elijah," Bucky says to me when he drops us off at the top of Ms. Birdie's driveway. Julian grabs his gear and hops out of the truck without saying goodbye to anyone.

"Thanks for the ride, Bucky," I say, waving to him and Darien as they drive back toward Main Street.

I catch Julian on the porch and stop him before he goes inside. "Hey, what's going on?"

Julian looks at me, his eyes full. "I don't think the guys understand how important this is to *me*. I've heard what they're saying about their fathers and grandfathers, but what about my father? Knowing that he was working to try to stop it?"

"There's got to be a way to do both," I say. "Give the guys what they're looking for and honor what your dad was trying to do."

Julian shakes his head, looking defeated. "If you have some brilliant plan, feel free to key me in."

He pulls the front door open and tosses the camping gear into the hallway near the washing machine. I follow him, throwing my bag of extra shorts I never used onto my bed. We find Ms. Birdie in the backyard, pulling at weeds in the flower beds with a huge straw hat on her head.

"Hey, Birdie. We're home," Julian says, going out the screen door and letting it slam behind him. I stay on the patio.

"We missed you boys at church this morning," she says with her eyebrows raised. "I hope you all had a nice little moment of silent prayer at the beach."

Julian chuckles and gives her a hug. "I bet Pastor Ernie will forgive us just this once."

"Professor Robles-Garcia has invited us to a potluck at her house tonight, boys. You ought to get your homework finished if you've got any. We're heading out of here around five thirty," she tells us. "How are you doing there, sweet Elijah?" She waves at me on the porch.

"I'm good, Ms. Birdie. Sorry about church this morning." I wave.

"Oh." She fusses at me. "Julian knows I'm just giving him the business. We'll say an extra prayer over our dinner tonight. The Good Lord knows you don't have to be in a church building on a Sunday morning to be a good person. And the Good Lord also knows that there are plenty of people with their behinds in those pews every Sunday morning that are *not* good people."

Two hours later, we're unloading casserole dishes from the trunk of Ms. Birdie's Corolla. Buttermilk pie, banana pudding with vanilla wafers, and a massive bowl of spinach salad with feta cheese and blueberries from last summer's garden. Ms. Birdie has got bags and bags of them in the freezer. My mouth is watering just watching all the food coming into the house.

Camille meets us at the front door. "Hi, hello, and welcome. Now that that's out of the way, come with me." She grabs

Julian's elbow and pulls him down the hallway toward her room. I follow behind.

"I've gotten sixteen texts this afternoon, boys," she says, closing the door behind us and whisper-shouting. She holds her pink phone in her hand. "Sixteen! All from angry football boys who want *me* to do something about *you*." She pokes her finger into Julian's chest.

"What are you talking about?" Julian asks.

"This prank thing! It's out of control! They all think you're ignoring them, and apparently they think *I* have some kind of control over what goes on in that empty vessel above your neck—"

"Hey, now," Julian says, putting his hands up.

"AND," Camille continues, ignoring him, "they're asking for my help. So, this is me. Helping them." She folds her arms across her chest and taps her foot. "Park it."

Julian sits on the edge of her bed, and I take the desk chair. Camille paces the wood floor in front of her dresser, steam practically coming out of her ears. "One day! One day I didn't see you, and you've gone and gotten the entire football team upset with you. Do I have to hold your hand? Is that it? Do I have to tell you exactly how to act? You're the captain, for crying out loud! You're sailing this ship! You're not supposed to be pissing people off!"

Camille isn't exactly talking *to* Julian. Or to me, either. She's kind of talking to the air. I glance at Julian, and he just raises his eyebrows at me.

"Hey, calm down and let me tell you what happened," Julian says, patting the bed next to him.

Camille considers him for a minute and ultimately sits down next to him with a great big huff. She keeps her arms folded.

Julian launches into a long explanation of the things he learned from Figg, and the reason he thinks it's better if we just sidestep the whole prank war this year. Camille looks at me when he finishes his lengthy diatribe.

"And what do you think?" she asks.

I blink at her. "Me?"

"Um. Yes. You."

"Well, I mean...I can see both sides of this, really."

"Oh, good lord." Camille hangs her head in her hands. "It's a prank, boys. *A prank.* I'm not asking you to go into battle against Taylor. How can you not see that *not* pulling a prank is what started the mess with your fathers in the first place? How are you *so* clueless that you can't see that? Taylor will just keep escalating and at some point, at *some point*, they're going to do something you can't ignore. Or that the team can't ignore. And then there will be *hurt feelings* because y'all are *toddlers* who cannot handle your emotions and boom...brawl on the football field again. Homecoming canceled." Camille stands up again, pulling at her hair from the roots. "I swear to y'all if my homecoming is canceled my senior year? You are *not* going to want to be around me. I've got my garter for...for whoever I'm taking all planned out. I've ordered a red dress with more sequins on the bodice than all the dresses in the entire Miss Texas pageant.

If you can't guarantee me that I'm going to be marching in the homecoming parade with my sparkliest Guardettes outfit on or accepting my homecoming queen crown and sash on Hartwig Field four weeks from now, then you better just get on out of my room right now because I am about to blow."

"Whoa," I whisper under my breath.

"Homecoming is not going to be *canceled*, Camille. There's no reason for all the drama," Julian says, sighing loudly. "You're letting your imagination get out of hand."

"Okay, maybe. But can't you see that this isn't just about you?" she says to Julian, sitting back down next to him.

Julian hangs his head. "It's supposed to be about football."

"It's supposed to be about tradition!" she almost yells, jumping up again. "What makes you think homecoming is only about football? That's a pretty narrow vision, don't you think? The entire school gets involved! Everyone wears mums and garters! There's a dance! A parade! A king and queen! The alumni have a huge bonfire! Sure, there's a football game, but this is about so much more than that, Julian. It's about so much more than just you!"

Camille is completely out of breath, and her face is bright red.

Julian gets to his feet. "But if I'm the one who is supposed to make the decision about what we do, then I'm the one who is going to have to take the fall for it when it all goes to hell! That's probably the reason my dad didn't want to do all of this, either!" he yells back.

"Hey, hey, let's all just calm down a little bit," I say, trying to ease the tension between the two of them. It doesn't work.

"Who says it's going to all go to hell?" Camille shoots back. "This is supposed to be fun, Julian. Fun! Taylor hanging their flag on our flagpole is hardly revolutionary stuff," she says. "Not exactly going to start World War Three with that, are they?"

"Camille's right," I say quietly.

"I thought you were on my side," he says, angry. "I've already told you both that things don't always go off without a hitch during these pranks. I'm sure Taylor didn't come to the game twenty years ago prepared for WrestleMania SmackDown, either. People have gotten hurt; some guys lost scholarships. I don't have the luxury of taking those chances. And I don't want to get anyone else on the team in trouble, either."

"I *am* on your side," I tell him. "But I'm also on the team's side. No one is expecting you to have some brilliant plan of attack that involves doing something that's going to get you into hot water with the administration or get you kicked out of school. It's okay to plan something harmless. Something small. I think that would be enough to get the team and the alumni off your back. Show them that you do care about what they think. That maybe their traditions aren't so bad." I shrug.

The room falls silent after that.

The memory of the newspaper clipping that I saw in the shed drifts through my head. The picture of Julian's dad and my father loading wrapped Christmas presents into a pickup truck. "What if we did some kind of community service? As a team? After the prank. Give the guys what they want, without getting too out of hand, and still find a way you can honor your dad."

Julian looks up at me.

"Hey, that's not a bad idea," Camille says quietly, bumping Julian gently with her shoulder.

"I could think about that," Julian says.

I can hear a crowd gathering outside the door in Camille's kitchen. I know eventually we're all going to have to come out of the bedroom, but it doesn't look like Julian ever wants to leave.

"We better show our faces before my mother comes looking for us," Camille says.

Julian agrees, but he's the last one to get up and follow us through the door and into the fray. We join the party in the kitchen and on the back patio. Pastor Ernie and Figg are there, and they both give me high fives. There are some faces I recognize from bingo, including Mr. Cooper and Ms. Brownie and a few team members and their families. There are plenty of people I don't recognize, too. I try to stay either close to Julian and Camille or alone in a corner.

The food is spread out on several tables on the patio. Professor Robles-Garcia made *pernil* with *arroz con gandules*, and a huge platter of tostones with an avocado cream sauce that I could eat by the spoonful. Figg tells me that Pastor Ernie made the gumbo with crab legs and he brought the lentils and flatbread, so I make sure I take heaping helpings of both. Before I know it, I'm carrying a plate and a bowl, both piled high with so much food I barely know where to start.

I find a quiet spot outside at a wooden picnic table, and Julian and Camille eventually join me.

"You know you can take more than one trip through the food line, right?" Julian says, dipping a chicken skewer in tzatziki sauce.

"I'm afraid I'll miss something. And I'll probably take at least one more trip." I laugh.

"Yeah, you didn't even hit the dessert table," Camille says, peering at my plate.

Neither Camille nor Julian says anything else about the prank for the rest of the evening. The three of us help Professor Robles-Garcia clean up the food tables, and I use that time to take small bites of all the plates I didn't try the first time around. By the time I get to serving myself a second one of Ms. Brownie's blondies (I know, right?), I'm glad I've worn elastic-waist shorts.

Everyone is quiet on the way home. Ms. Birdie's banana-pudding bowl was scraped clean, but we've still got a few slices of buttermilk pie and some salad in the trunk. Not to mention the leftovers Professor Robles-Garcia put into Ziploc bags for us.

"I hope that's not a weekly thing," I say, leaning back on the headrest. "I don't think my gut can handle it."

Ms. Birdie laughs. "You'll learn to pace yourself next time."

Julian and I help Ms. Birdie bring the dishes in, and then she grabs a paperback and settles into her La-Z-Boy. I let Julian take his shower first, and I sit down with Ms. Birdie in the living room. The creeping realization that tomorrow is Monday started to sneak up on me on the way home from Camille's, and I've had a nervous flutter in my chest ever since.

Between the excitement about the game and then the campout and *then* the dinner at Camille's, Monday was the last thing on my mind. I know I have to give Coach Marcus the uniform fee tomorrow, and I don't have enough left in my wallet to cover it. I don't have a choice but to ask Ms. Birdie for it, and just the thought of having to do that is making me nauseous.

"Ms. Birdie? Can I ask you a favor?" I say, my stomach in knots.

"What is it, sweetheart?" she asks, putting a bright bookmark in her book and lowering her reading glasses.

"I have to pay Coach Marcus the uniform fee tomorrow, and I don't have enough to cover it," I say, embarrassed. I don't know what else to do, though. I'm afraid if I don't give him the fee, he'll bench me until Ma and Frankie get here and I can pay.

"Oh, Elijah, why didn't you just ask me? Of course, you can borrow. I'll settle it up with your ma when she gets here. You wipe that worry off your face now," she says, standing up.

She disappears down the hall, and I hear her rummaging around somewhere. She returns with three folded twenty-dollar bills, handing them to me.

"Thank you. I'm sorry I had to ask. I'll make sure I tell Ma that I borrowed, and maybe she can send it in the mail, and you won't have to wait for her to get here to pay you back."

"Oh, hush now," Ms. Birdie says. "I can wait until she's here. Don't you worry about that. You just keep doing what you're doing on that field and we're going to have us a season, aren't we?" She laughs.

"Thank you," I tell her again, tucking the money into my pocket.

"Don't you keep worrying about it. Focus on that o-line." She winks.

Julian is still in the bathroom, so I go to my room and text Frankie.

**I have never eaten so much in my life**

Frankie answers with a vomit face emoji. **Ooh! We had soup from a can. Tell me every single detail.**

I explain the dishes with as many adjectives as I can while Frankie texts me back drooling emojis and hearts.

**Coley misses you. She keeps asking for Uncalijah to read Knuffle Bunny and her pigeon books,** she texts.

**The school library has a few of those books on the shelves. What if I record myself reading one or two and then you can show her on your phone?** I answer.

**That would be perfect! She'll be so excited!** Frankie texts back.

I don't tell her that I broke the news about Coley to Julian. I don't think she'll stay mad about it forever or anything; I just need to think of a way to tell her gently. When I hear Julian finish in the bathroom, I tell Frankie good night and text her a picture of me blowing a kiss. She texts one back.

Once I finish washing my face and brushing my teeth, I notice that Julian's door is already shut and lie down on my bed. I have just leaned over and clicked the lamp off when there's a soft knock on the door. So soft that I'm not sure I even heard it correctly the first time.

There's a second knock, a little louder this time. "Come in?"

Julian pushes my door open and whispers, "Hey," leaning against the door frame. "Can I come in?"

I sit up in bed but don't turn the light on. "Of course."

Julian closes the door behind him and sits down on the edge of the bed. Other than the backyard lights peeking through the curtains, the room is dark.

"What's up? You okay? Is it your ribs again?" I ask, the nearness of him making my heart race a little bit.

"No, I'm feeling better. Since the cayenne and the parsley." He chuckles softly. "I feel like a pot roast."

I laugh.

"I just...I wanted to say that I'm sorry again. And thank you...for telling me about Frankie and Coley. Do you have any pictures of her?"

My heart slows down a little, and I grab for my phone on the nightstand. My hand brushes Julian's, and he grabs it and holds on. I pull up the pictures with my other hand and show him Coley.

"She's everything to me. I can't even remember what things were like before she was born," I tell him. The dark stillness settles between us.

"She's so adorable," he says, turning his body sideways on the bed but never letting go of my hand. He's facing me now, the glow of the phone between us on the bedspread.

"Do you really think we can manage to pull off a prank without getting in trouble?" he says into the quiet.

"I think we probably can," I tell him. "Camille is on board with helping now, and she's pretty smart about stuff like that. Social things. Keeping everyone happy."

"She is," he says, hanging his head. "I think you are, too."

I laugh a little, wanting to brush it off, but instead I let the compliment settle in my bones like warm syrup.

"Hey, 'lijah?" Julian whispers.

"Yeah?" I whisper back.

"Thanks for knowing how important it is that I make my dad proud," he says.

"Yeah," I say, lacing my fingers through his and squeezing.

"I want you to know that it meant something to me. That moment in the locker room all those years ago. You meant something to me. It...it never stopped meaning something," he says, his voice whisper-quiet in the shrinking space between us on the bed.

I lean forward and put my lips on his. My hand finds the waistband of his shorts and I rest my fingers there on his hip while my other hand still holds on to his. He puts his other hand around my back, just above my waist.

He breaks away first, leaning his forehead on mine in the dark quiet of my room.

"It never stopped meaning something to me, either," I tell him.

## · twenty-three ·

# *JULIAN*

**I don't sleep much.** The feel of Elijah's lips on mine lingered when I finally left his room to go to bed. I ended up staring at the ceiling for hours, wondering about Coley. Wondering about Frankie. Wondering why he kept his secrets for so long.

I feel like I've barely fallen asleep when my alarm goes off in the morning. I slap around on my nightstand for my phone and eventually pull myself out of bed and get dressed.

"I've got another meeting with Pastor Ernie this morning," Ms. Birdie says, dressed and frantically searching for her keys. "You boys want a ride to school today?"

"Another meeting on Main Street?"

Birdie looks at me with kind eyes and puts her hand on the side of my face. "Julian, I promise everything is going to be okay," she says. "I'm sorry about the building, but I really do think this is best."

"It was important to Dad," I say, feeling a strength from somewhere outside of myself. I stand up taller.

"I know it was. It's very important to me, too," she says, stroking my cheek with her thumb before planting a kiss on the side of my head. "Trust your old Birdie, okay?"

"I do," I tell her, even though I don't fully feel it yet. I wish I had more control over what was going to happen to the old place. All I can do is hope Birdie keeps it. But is that selfish of me? It's not like I'm going to be around here forever to help her take care of it. A creeping sense of guilt starts to build in my stomach, but I squash it down quickly. *Birdie will do what's best*, I tell myself.

"I think we'll walk," I tell Birdie. I want a few extra minutes alone with Elijah before we walk to school with Camille.

She meets us at the end of the driveway as usual. The sun is already beating down, and all three of us are hot before we even make it up to Main Street. Elijah's shoulder bumps into mine, and we share a secret smile. I bump him back gently.

"Hey, wait a minute." Camille stops us as we turn the corner onto Main.

"What's up?" Elijah asks.

"I should be asking the two of you that. Is there something going on here? I've got instincts about this kind of stuff," she says, giving both of us serious side-eye.

I share a look with Elijah. The corner of his mouth turns up very slightly, and I can feel the tips of my ears start to burn.

"What's going on with the two of you?"

I look over at him again, and we both stifle a laugh. I reach for his hand and loop his pinkie in mine. I look Camille in the eye and say, "Oh, nothing."

She looks down at our hands. "All right, then." She laughs. "I like this kind of nothing. The two of you have been fighting this *nothing* for way too long. I'm happy to see that nothing is happening, finally."

We walk the rest of the way to school like that, our pinkies linked together. We talk about the prank and try to come up with a few simple ideas that won't get anyone into trouble, but none of them sound good enough.

"We'll think of something. Write them down or text them to me if you have any ideas during the day," I say as we turn into the Crenshaw driveway.

I spend almost the entire day thinking about the prank. How can I do something that will make the guys happy, and make sure we're not letting down all the dads and uncles and grandpas, while still keeping our asses out of trouble? We don't need whatever we do blasted across the internet for the whole world to judge.

And I'm not going to lie, kissing Elijah is taking up a huge amount of my brain, too. If I think about it hard enough, I can almost feel his lips on mine again. I know I have to try to push it out of my head so I can get through the school day without failing every single class, but all I want to do is daydream about it and plan when I can kiss him again. I'm finding secret hiding spots in every hallway I'm walking in, and inevitably my thoughts turn back to kissing Elijah. Over and over and over again in one of those secret spots.

I spend so much brainpower thinking about both these things that I miss turning in my homework assignment in calculus and have to backtrack during lunch to find Figg.

"Hey, I'm glad you're here. I forgot to ask you last night if you could come over after practice this afternoon and cut the front grass. We're looking a little shaggy at Casa de Ernie and Figg." He laughs, pulling leftovers from last night's potluck from his blue lunch box.

"Absolutely," I say. "And, hey, I'm sorry I spaced out in class. Here's my homework."

"That's not like you to forget to turn things in. You doing okay? You seemed okay yesterday," Figg says, digging a spoon out of his box and tucking a napkin into his shirt collar.

I just shake my head and grind my teeth. I don't know if I can talk about all this with Figg again. He always has outstanding advice, but sometimes I feel like I lean on him too much. "Eh, you don't want to hear about all of this stuff."

"I wouldn't ask if I didn't care about it, Julian," he says, chuckling. "You know you can talk to me. Always got time for you."

"It's still this prank business," I say, sitting down and pulling a bag of granola bites and a yogurt from my bag.

"Oh? I thought I heard that you were going to try to stop that from happening this year?"

"Pressure from the guys," I say. "Not to mention Camille. I guess a bunch of the guys went to her to complain about me when I tried to stop it all. I don't want the team to hate me. Especially over something so ridiculous."

"Can I ask you something?"

"Of course."

Figg exhales through his nose like he's thinking of the perfect words to use. "Why were you fighting it so hard? These pranks...why didn't you want to participate?"

I take a deep breath and prop myself up against a desk at the front of the room. I lower my backpack to the floor because I know this is going to be a longer conversation than I anticipated having with Figg this afternoon.

"I just want him to be proud, you know?" I say, mostly to the floor.

"Your dad?"

"Yeah. He was this great stand-up guy that everyone loved, and here's me...I'm just kind of...I don't know."

"Hey, look at me," Figg says.

I raise my eyes to meet his.

"Don't put him on a pedestal. He was a regular guy just like me. Just like you. I know he would be damn proud of you right now. Prank or no prank. Damn proud," Figg says quietly.

"I don't want do anything that might get anyone in trouble. Imagine if I planned a prank and someone got hurt? Or someone lost a scholarship or got blackballed from all-conference or something? Or what if it's *me*? What if some college scout gets wind of some dumb prank I pulled and won't come give me a look after that?" The words tumble out into the air between Figg and me.

"Hey, whoa, slow down," Figg says quietly, coming around to the other side of his desk and sitting on top of it.

"Things can get out of control really quickly. I don't want to take chances. Not with the guys and not with myself...not with any of it," I tell him, finally taking a deep breath.

"You're right. Sometimes things can get out of control without that ever being anyone's intention. But things can get out of control even when you're doing something mundane, Julian. That's just the way life goes sometimes. You can't control everything. And sometimes it's how you recover from those kinds of things that teaches you the most about yourself. About how much you can handle. About your ability to lead," Figg says. "Does that make sense?"

I nod. It does. It doesn't mean I'm exactly thrilled to go out and plan two hundred pranks now, but I can see Figg's point.

"How are things with Elijah? Feeling a little more settled now?" he asks.

My cheeks burn, and I feel like the tips of my ears are on fire. "Things are definitely better," I say, unable to keep a smile from pulling on my cheeks.

Figg raises his eyebrows. "Well, that's nice to hear," he says, giving me a side-eyed look.

"Hey, can I ask you a question? Just between us?" I ask.

"Absolutely. Shoot."

"Was it...when those Taylor guys stuffed beach balls up their jerseys, was it because of Eric Vance? And Elijah's mom? Was she pregnant with Frankie?"

Figg hangs his head. "Your grandmother is going to kill

me for talking about this with you, but yes. It was Eric Vance the Taylor team was trying to get to. He was a real threat to them that year. A cornerback that was leading the league in interceptions."

"Elijah was right," I say. "He said it's no wonder the entire town hates his dad and him by extension, since he made Crenshaw have to forfeit."

"Well," Figg says, bracing his feet on the floor. "That's not exactly how it happened."

"But Elijah said his dad apparently got kicked off the team his senior year because of the fight during the homecoming game. Why else would a guy leading the league in interceptions suddenly disappear from the roster?" I groan in frustration. "I just don't know why everyone is so hush-hush about it. I've tried finding articles about it in old issues of the *Register*; I've asked Birdie about it. Short of bribing Mr. Cooper and demanding he tell me all the details, I don't know where else to turn."

Figg takes a deep breath through his nose and folds his hands over his stomach. I know this is something teachers do before they give you some kind of crappy news. Like *You've failed the final and there's no way you're going to pass my class* or *We are reading* The Odyssey *in its original Greek and an essay is due on the author's purpose next week.*

"Meridien is very proud of their football," Figg says. "No one wanted to be the guy who wrote the scathing article about the Guardsmen and published it in the *Register*. Likely find a flaming bag of dog poop on their front porch after doing something like that." He chuckles, only half joking. Then his expression turns serious. "But it wasn't Eric Vance that started arguing with the Taylor team. He was trying to get the team to ignore what was happening. He insisted, actually, that they keep their heads in the game," Figg says quietly. Then he sighs. "Your father and Eric were friends. Really close friends. And when that Taylor team came out onto our field, clearly trying to make a laughingstock out of Jeffrey Jackson's best friend…well, it didn't exactly go over really well. It was your dad that started that fight. He was sticking up for his friend."

My stomach is in knots. My *dad* was the one who started the fight? With everything I've ever known or heard about him, he doesn't seem like the guy who would start a massive fight, especially at the homecoming game in front of the entire town.

"Then why did Elijah's dad stop playing football?"

Figg takes another deep breath and meets my eye. "It was complicated, really. From what I understand, Eric took the fall for your dad. Told him that he was probably going to have to quit playing football after his senior season anyway because he had a baby on the way and a girlfriend that he loved, and he wanted to do the right thing and take care of them. He knew your father had a chance at college scholarships and whatnot. So instead of going to the coach and telling him the real story, Eric Vance insisted that the fight started with him, that he was the one who started the verbal argument *and* threw the first punch. That was all the coach needed to hear, and Eric was made an example of and kicked off the team."

"Whoa," I say, trying to pull all the pieces of this wild story together. "So, Eric suffered the consequences even though *my dad* was the one that started everything? The coach didn't even blink?"

"It was easier for everyone to believe it was Eric's fault," Figg says, hanging his head. "He was a decent kid, but he always seemed to be around whenever there was trouble. Had a real knack for finding himself in the middle of it even when it had nothing to do with him. Taking the fall for your dad was a really selfless thing for him to do."

"So how come you knew about it back then and never said anything?" I can't quite keep the heat out of my voice. "You just let Eric Vance suffer the consequences and never turned my dad in?"

"Oh, Julian, I had no idea what really happened back then. I was a brand-new teacher and had zero instincts about anything. I took everything at face value." He laughs. "It wasn't until years later, after you were born, that Jeffrey came to me and told me the whole story over a beer. I was as dumbfounded as you are right now. No one in a million years would have suspected Jeffrey was capable of starting something like that. But when they messed with the bull, embarrassed one of his friends, someone he considered family back then, they got the horns."

Figg looks like he wants to say more, but he bites his lip. I let the information settle in my chest. It feels heavy and out of place. For years, I've heard about my father being a hometown hero. A football star who came back to Meridien and was ready to use his skills to do some good in the community. A guy who really loved his town and wanted to make a difference. A guy who caused a bench-clearing brawl doesn't really fit the narrative I've been fed my entire life.

"I don't remember Eric Vance and my dad ever even talking when I was a little kid, never mind being friends. What happened if they were close enough to consider each other family?"

Figg sets his lips in a straight line. "I think it's something your father struggled with for a lot of years," he says quietly. "I'm only telling you this because I think you're mature enough to handle it, but I think Jeffrey carried a lot of guilt for letting Eric take the heat for something he did. They drifted apart, like friends sometimes do when they take different paths."

The bell rings, signaling the end of lunch, and I hurriedly pack up my things and throw away my garbage. My head is swimming with all this new information, and I'm not quite sure what to do with it all.

"Hey, Julian," Figg calls to me before I walk out the door.

"Yeah?"

"I'm sorry you had to find out about this from me," he says, looking truly sad.

"It's okay," I say, turning on my heel and heading toward Mrs. Nguyen's class. "Thanks for letting me talk."

*Is* it okay? I don't know that I actually believe that. Maybe it borders on okay. Maybe it's okay's next-door neighbor. Or across-the-street neighbor. Yeah, that seems more like it.

I've always seen my father as this pillar of strength and perfection. Even at seven, I wanted to be exactly like him. Even now, ten years later, I want to be exactly like him. I want to achieve things and go to college and make a difference. To think that maybe those things might not have happened for him if it weren't for Eric Vance kind of throws me for a loop.

I wear the same guilt my father probably carried around for the rest of the afternoon.

## · twenty-four ·

# *ELIJAH*

Julian is distracted. He's been throwing long bombs that are way off the mark all afternoon, and he's been sacked twice by that monster freshman who now thinks he's hot shit because he's taken the quarterback out. I'm doing everything I can to keep this giant kid off of him, but Julian's not doing himself any favors. He keeps calling one play and executing another. He's got his o-line so confused, we don't know who we're supposed to be paying attention to.

Coach Marcus blows his whistle so hard, I wonder if he's trying to spit it right at Julian's head. I watch him pull Julian to the side and give him a real reaming about a half hour before practice ends. Coach Andrews takes the o-line to the end zone for gap-blocking drills, so I don't have a chance to catch up to Julian and ask if he's okay.

Come to think of it, he was quiet in history, too. Mrs. Nguyen lectured for the entire class period, so there really wasn't a lot of time for talking, but Julian didn't look like himself, anyway. He held his chin in his hand and had his notebook out to take notes but didn't write even one word down while she was talking. In fact, I think it's the first time that I took more notes than he did.

I hurried to practice after class so that I could give Coach Marcus the sixty dollars for the uniform fee, and Julian was dawdling like he wanted to talk to Mrs. Nguyen, so I didn't wait to walk with him. When he finally got to the locker room, he looked tired, so I chalked it up to the Monday blues even though that didn't exactly feel right, either.

Our kiss has been on my mind since it happened last night, keeping me up most of the night with butterflies in my stomach. It didn't seem like Julian regretted it. I know I certainly didn't.

For once, everything felt like it was falling into place. Football was going great, school wasn't terrible, and even living at Ms. Birdie's was starting to feel a little more comfortable. Holding onto Julian's pinkie on the way to school this morning felt exactly right, too.

I watch Julian out of the corner of my eye as we get dressed after practice. I try to push the growing worry out of my gut while I wait by the trophy case for Julian to be ready to go home.

"I've got to cut the grass at Figg and Pastor Ernie's place this afternoon," he says, finally coming out of the locker room. "Figg cornered me at lunch." He smiles a little.

"Okay," I say, studying his face.

He hands me his key to the front door. "Just in case Birdie isn't home before you get there. She was meeting with Pastor Ernie again today, remember?"

"I remember. Hey, Julian?" I ask, something really niggling in my gut. "Are we okay?"

"Of course," he says, flashing me the world's weakest smile. "I'll be home in an hour or so, okay?" He glances down the hall and then leans in to give me a quick kiss on the lips. He tries to smile at me, but it never reaches his eyes.

"Okay," I say, as he wanders down the hall toward Figg's classroom.

I hold the key in my fist and start to walk toward Ms. Birdie's in the five o'clock heat. My neck is burning by the time I reach Main Street, which doesn't bode well for the rest of my walk. What I wouldn't give for a massive thunderstorm right now.

"Elijah! Wait up!" I hear Camille's voice behind me.

I turn and wait for her and she runs to catch up.

"Hot enough for you?" she says, out of breath from running.

Why do people in Texas always feel like they have to talk about the weather? It's hot. It's always hot. Sometimes it's surface-of-the-sun hot, and sometimes it's just equator hot or desert hot, but it's always hot. Always.

"Fire-breathing-dragon hot," I tell Camille.

"Has Julian come up with any ingenious plans yet?" she asks, falling in step beside me as we plod down Main Street toward home.

"Not that he's mentioned to me," I tell her. "He seems a little off today."

"He seemed okay walking to school this morning, holding your hand." She bumps me with her shoulder.

My cheeks burn and my stomach flip-flops.

"What was in my mother's tostones?" She laughs.

I shrug and hope Camille changes the subject because right now I feel like I want to keep it all to myself. That kiss we shared on Sunday night, and the little ones that followed as we sat on my bed and talked, it feels like something I want to keep close to me for the time being, like it's fragile enough to need to be protected.

"So I was thinking about something, Elijah." She takes a deep breath.

"Yeah, what's that?"

"I think you and I should have something in our back pocket in case Julian craps out of this prank thing," she says. "I told Julian a long time ago that I wasn't going to help him come up with anything because it had to come from him, but I'm beginning to think he's going to need a little, um...*help*."

"You think he's going to back out?"

"I think I know Julian. And I think I wouldn't put it past him to get cold feet and start worrying, *again*, that he's going to somehow get in trouble," she says. "And that's where you and I come in. If we already have some kind of plan in place, he'll be less likely to back out of it. Even if he doesn't do the prank himself, he'll at least have to let it happen, if the wheels have already started turning."

"So, I guess we ought to start brainstorming, right?" I say.

"Blue food coloring in their ice-bath tubs?" she says. "A ton of those plastic ball-pit balls in their locker room? A singing telegram or a mariachi band in the middle of their afternoon practice? It's got to be something good, but nothing that will make Julian turn tail and run."

"I agree." I try to think of other options. "How about a flash mob performance of the Crenshaw fight song at their next home game?"

"Ooh, that's a good one, but I think it might be too hard to coordinate," Camille says, tapping her lip as we near Rudy Street.

"I'll keep thinking," I say as we pause at the top of the street.

"We got this. Even if Julian doesn't, we'll make it happen," she says, hugging me. "Bye, 'lijah."

"See you in the morning," I tell her.

Ms. Birdie isn't home yet, so I use the key to let myself into the empty house. I leave my bags on the floor of my room and head into the kitchen. There are plenty of leftovers from last night's feast at Camille's, and I help myself to a plateful of tostones and a small bowl of Pastor Ernie's gumbo. What is it about gumbo that makes it so much more delicious the next day? I cut myself a tiny sliver of Ms. Birdie's buttermilk pie and eat it while I wait for the microwave.

Once the food is warm, I set it down at the table and call Frankie on speakerphone.

"How's my favorite brother?" she answers.

"I'm your only brother," I say, laughing.

"Then you didn't have much competition! Seriously, how are things?"

"Pretty good," I tell her.

"Oh, I hear something in your voice. What's going on?"

"What?" I ask innocently. "Nothing going on here." I don't even know if I want to tell Frankie about Julian. Not yet. It feels too new.

"How's things with Julian? Is he still acting like you've got the plague?" she asks.

"Oh, things have definitely gotten better in the past couple of days," I say, my heart skipping.

I do tell her all about our game on Saturday and the campout that I already texted her about. I tell her more about the potluck at Camille's house and how Julian has finally decided that pulling a prank on Taylor is probably not going to get him a black mark on his permanent record.

"How's my Coley?" I ask her.

"She misses her Uncalijah, but she's doing okay. She did the cutest thing the other day. She stood up on one of the moving boxes and started shouting 'Ladies and gentlemen' over and over again like she was a circus ringmaster. I think I got a video of it. I'll text it to you tonight," she says.

I hear the front door opening, so I tell Frankie I need to get going and that I'll call her soon. She promises to text me the video of Coley and hangs up. I'm washing my dishes at the sink when Julian comes into the kitchen. He leans against the counter next to me, sweaty and smelling like freshly cut grass.

"I am beat," he says. "I got tossed on the ground in practice today more than I used to when we played peewee ball."

"How are you feeling?" I ask him.

He winces a little bit. "Honestly? The bruise is going away, but my ribs are burning again."

"Do you need an ice pack? Or how about I get you some more parsley?" I turn to him and let my fingers gently touch his arm.

His eyes meet mine and he gives me a crooked smile. "Parsley sounds good," he says. "Let me get cleaned up first, okay?"

"Sounds like a plan. I'll get it ready," I say, drying my dishes and putting them away.

Julian walks toward the shower, and I have to take a deep breath. Being that close to him in an empty house stirred something in my gut, and now all I want to do is grab him and kiss him right here in the kitchen. I'm going to need to calm myself down a little bit. Grinding the parsley will help.

I hear the shower turn on and I get to work, using the back of a spoon this time instead of the end of my toothbrush. Once I have a good paste, I bring the bowl down the hall with me. The shower has already stopped, and I hear Julian shuffling around in his room. I knock on the door, the bowl of parsley paste in my hand. "You ready for me yet?"

He doesn't answer, so I push the door open a smidge.

He's sitting on the bed, hair still dripping from the shower. I sit next to him, the bowl of parsley balanced in my hand. "You okay?"

He looks over at me, his eyes sad and dark. "I've got to tell you something and I don't know how," he says.

## · twenty five ·

# *JULIAN*

Elijah's face goes pale as soon as the words are out of my mouth. He sets the bowl of parsley down on the floor. "Just say it."

"Figg told me what happened twenty years ago," I start, shifting uncomfortably on the bed.

"Yeah, you already told me about that," he says. "My dad got the whole team in trouble, and they had to forfeit the game."

Words tumble around in my gut, and I don't know how to pull them out and put them in the right order. My damn ribs burn. "That's not...that's not exactly how it actually happened," I finally say, haltingly.

Elijah stands up and wipes his hands on his shorts, kicking the bowl with the parsley in it. A hunk of mashed parsley lands on my carpet. "Oh, shit." He crouches down and tries to clean it up with the corner of his T-shirt.

I sit down on the floor with him and grab his wrists. "Hey, don't worry about that right now," I say, moving my head so that he's looking me in the eye.

He picks his chin up. "Hi," I say when his eyes land on mine.

"Hi," he says back, looking worried.

"It wasn't your father's fault that the game was forfeited. He didn't start the fight," I say, my stomach whirling.

Elijah frowns. "He didn't? I thought... I thought it was my parents the Taylor Titans were making fun of with those beach balls," he says. My hands don't leave his wrists, and he twists his hands and holds onto my wrists, too.

"It was," I tell him. "But it wasn't your father that started the fight. He actually... um... he actually tried to stop the fight."

Elijah pulls his hands from my grip and stands up. "Wait... what? Who started it, then? Why?"

"It was actually *my* father," I say, looking down. "He and your dad were friends, and he couldn't handle the Taylor team making fun of him like that."

I explain everything while Elijah stands very still, braced against my dresser. The whole time I'm talking, he never looks up from the floor.

"Even Figg didn't know the real truth until after we were born," I finally say.

Still Elijah doesn't talk.

He leans against my dresser, bracing himself on his hands, and looks at the floor. His breathing is measured and even, but his eyes dart around wildly, like he's trying to make sense of this huge puzzle.

"You okay?" I ask.

Slowly, he raises his head and looks at me. "No. Not even a little bit." He turns and leaves my room and goes into the guest room. A second later, I hear the door slam.

I wait a moment before following. "Hey." I knock on the door softly. "Can I come in?"

"Go away," he says, his voice muffled behind the door.

"I'm sorry," I say. "I know it might come as a bit of a shock, but...but why are you so mad?" I ask.

The door swings wide open. "Why am I so *mad*? Are you *kidding* me?"

I open my mouth to respond, but he doesn't stop to let me speak.

"All it would have taken was for your father to have told the truth and maybe...maybe *everything* would have been different!" he yells. The door closes in my face again.

I knock again. "What do you mean, everything?"

"I mean everything!" his voice yells behind the door. It swings open one more time. "Everything, Julian. Think about it." I watch him from the doorway as he paces in front of the window. "I'll tell you what *I'm* thinking. I'm thinking that most of the shitty decisions my father made came after he stopped playing football. I'm thinking that I don't remember many good things about him, but most of the good things we did share revolved around playing football, or listening to him tell me stories about Guardsmen football. I'm thinking that if he had never stopped playing football, things may have looked very different for Eric Vance." Elijah's voice shakes with anger. "For me. For Frankie. For my mom. Even for Coley."

That earlier niggling guilt intensifies, and I feel like I'm going to be sick.

"And now, here you are telling me that the only reason he stopped playing football is because he took the fall for someone *else*? Because he was being a good friend? Sorry, you just tilted my world, Julian. In more ways than one. You're going to have to forgive me if it takes me a minute to process all of this," he says, walking toward me until I back up into the hallway. He slams the door again, and I hear the lock click into place.

I stare at the door, my nose just inches from it, and finally lean my forehead against the wood.

"'lijah," I say. "Please let me in."

"Go away. I don't want to talk to anyone," he answers.

Out in the living room, the front door opens.

"I'm home, boys!" Birdie calls. I hear the crinkling of several plastic bags, and her keys jingle as she takes them out of the lock.

I leave Elijah in his room, behind the locked door, and try to fix my face as I walk into the living room.

"Let me get some of those, Birdie," I say, pulling several grocery bags from her arms.

"Oh, Julian," she says, balancing the rest of the bags. "We were looking like Mother Hubbard's kitchen this morning. Come on, help me put some of this away."

I unload several bags' worth of canned goods and frozen

vegetables while Birdie washes fruit in the sink. She hums while she works.

"Where's Elijah? Doing some homework?" she asks between hums.

"He's...he's not feeling well," I lie, my gut twisting. "He went to bed early. I think he pushed himself a little too hard at practice or something. It was a hot one out there today."

"You can say that again. I'm ready for the cold snap, I'll tell you what," she says, dropping apples into a bowl on the counter and starting on the grapes and clementines.

When I finish putting all the other groceries away, I join Birdie at the sink. "How was your meeting?" I ask her.

Birdie stops humming. "Let's go on and sit down for a minute," she says.

Turning off the water, she wanders out into the living room and settles into her La-Z-Boy. I sit on the couch, my legs folded underneath me.

"Pastor Ernie is going to buy me out," she says.

"Wait a minute, you're selling?" My heart races, and a lump forms in my throat faster than I can stop it. "You're actually selling it?"

"Shhh, it's going to be okay, Julian," she says. "Just listen for a minute, son. Pastor Ernie wants to follow exactly what your father's plans were for the place. He's going to do everything exactly how Jeffrey wanted to do it." Her voice cracks when she says my father's name.

My heart slows and the lump starts to dissolve. I blink and a few tears escape. "So why are you stepping back? Why are you selling it?"

"It just makes more sense like this. I've got a college education to think about, don't I?" She smiles and holds her hand out to me. I reach out and let her squeeze my hand. "Mr. Figg is probably going to retire in the next couple of years, and he'll take over running the business. I'm going to help, of course. Pastor Ernie and I have already discussed my role as director," she says. "Your father would be so proud of you, Julian, even if we're not the ones who own the center."

I let my hand drop, and that guilt comes sneaking back into my chest.

"Birdie," I say. I want to tell her everything. That I know my dad was the one who was responsible for the Crenshaw forfeit. That I know Eric Vance took the heat for it and I made the mistake of telling Elijah. That everything I thought I knew about my father has come crumbling down around me and I don't even know who I am right now. But what good would it do? I don't think it will make me feel any better, and sometimes talking about my father makes Birdie's eyes look sad. I don't want to be the reason she looks sad.

"What is it, my sunshine? You look like you've got the whole world on your shoulders tonight," she says, her voice soft.

"I...I think I'm going to go to bed early," I say.

"Okay, then." She stands up from her chair and holds her arms open for a hug. I fall into her, and she smooths the hair on the back of my head. "Everything's going to be okay, Julian. I promise," she says.

I lie awake in my bed way past the time Birdie turns out the lights in the living room and the house falls silent. I turn Elijah's words over and over at the same time that Figg's story about the Taylor forfeit tumbles around in my brain.

They were friends, Elijah said. Figg admitted it, too. What happened? I grab a flashlight from my nightstand and throw on my heavy black rain boots.

The shed is creepy at night. It's creepy enough during the day, with cobwebs stretching across the corners and the musty smell of old stuff permeating the wooden walls and floor. But at night, it's like something out of a horror movie. I keep the flashlight as close to the ground as possible, so I don't accidentally shine it into Elijah's bedroom, which has the only window that faces the backyard. It doesn't take long for me to find what I'm looking for. A large cardboard box with the name JEFFREY written in bright blue marker on the side teeters on top of a bunch of Rubbermaid bins and old Christmas decorations.

I pull the heavy box down carefully and bring it inside, clicking off my flashlight first. I walk carefully through the house, knowing one wrong step on a squeaky floorboard will wake everyone.

In the safety of my room, I click on the desk lamp and open the box. On top are several newspaper articles about my father's accident. I flip past those and see his football team pictures. Just like the ones Elijah pointed out to me outside the locker room in the trophy case. Then, an article from the *Meridien Register*. My father and Eric Vance smiling broadly for the camera, loading wrapped Christmas presents into the back of a pickup truck. The headline boasts:

## HIGH SCHOOL ATHLETES LEND A HAND WITH LOCAL CHARITY

Beneath it is a story about Jeffrey and Eric as high school juniors, volunteering their time to collect toys for a shelter a few miles away from Meridien. "The two boys have made it a habit to volunteer all over Crenshaw County," the article states. I put the clipping to the side and pull out the next stack of pictures and memorabilia. Snapshots of football players goofing around on the beach during a campout. Programs from several football games. Newspaper clippings from homecoming parades. If you look past the haircuts, these pictures and articles could easily be about my class of Guardsmen.

Eric Vance shows up in almost all the pictures and articles that feature my father. When I reach the section of pictures and papers from their senior year in high school, my father is alone.

## JEFFREY JACKSON SIGNS LETTER OF INTENT TO PLAY FOOTBALL AT COASTAL TEXAS COMMUNITY COLLEGE

## LOCAL ATHLETE JEFFREY JACKSON NOMINATED FOR GOVERNOR'S SERVICE AWARD

## JEFFREY JACKSON AWARDED FIRST TEAM ALL-STATE
## QUARTERBACK POSITION

Underneath all that is a picture of Eric and my father in shorts and Crenshaw T-shirts. My father smiles widely with his arm around Eric, who is holding a tiny bundle in his arms wrapped in a pink blanket.

I lean back against the bed, and my hand brushes against the forgotten bowl of parsley paste on the floor. Gently, I lift my T-shirt and paint it on my ribs myself.

# twenty-six

# ELIJAH

I wake up way before my alarm goes off. In fact, the sky is still dark when I open my eyes. I try to close them again, try to quiet my head and go back to sleep, but there's no way that's going to happen. I glance at my phone. It's only about an hour before I'm supposed to be awake anyway. Screw it.

I get dressed and throw some extra clothes and toiletries into my backpack and sneak quietly out of the house. I pull my backpack straps as tight as I can and do some stretches in the dark in the driveway before I take off running toward school. I know the weight room at Crenshaw opens at six for anyone who needs to lift in the morning instead of after school. That's the plan I have in my head as I take off, working up a good sweat as I run down Main Street.

Frankie would probably say I'm running from something.

Thoughts in my own head. The expectation of a ton of people here in Meridien that I'm just a screwup. The thought that I'm always going to make the wrong choice. The fact that all these perceptions are possibly based on a giant lie my father told to protect his best friend twenty years ago.

Did I screw up in the past? Absolutely. I own that shit. I know breaking the window and thinking about taking that car wash money was wrong. It doesn't matter what my reasoning was; it still wasn't a good choice. I know my dad's reputation didn't help anyone's opinion of me, but it was my stupid choice that got me in trouble. Not my dad's.

But what if Jeffrey Jackson had taken responsibility for his own actions?

How would things be different right now if my father hadn't stepped out in front of the entire town and admitted guilt for something he didn't do? The whole thing makes me so incredibly angry I just want to scream. And why is Julian so clueless?

I don't think anyone has ever truly understood, except maybe Frankie, what it was like to grow up in the shadow of Eric Vance's mistakes in a town this small. In Houston, I was invisible. But here? There was no escaping that reputation.

Julian had the memory of Jeffrey Jackson behind him, a great big shining beacon of perfection. A single dad raising his perfect quarterback son. Football heroes, both of them. Both of them trying to lead Meridien to what they've always dreamed about: Texas football glory. Will Meridien ever make it to a state title? Probably not, but that doesn't keep the town from pinning their hopes on the shoulders of their current Golden Boy. This year it's Julian. Twenty years ago, it was his father.

I wonder what life would have looked like for me if, twenty years ago, Meridien had pinned its hopes on Eric Vance instead.

Everything could have been so different.

The sun is barely starting to peek over the horizon as I run up the Crenshaw driveway and right into the gym doors. The weight room is empty, but I can see Coach Marcus in his office, shuffling through paperwork. He raises his hand to me, and I wave back, eager to get to the leg-press machine and load it up with as much weight as I can stand. The only way for me to get rid of all this crap inside me is to sweat it out.

I get almost an hour of time with the weights before a couple of the other guys start trickling in. Nate and I spot each other doing bench presses without talking. I wonder if he's escaping his own head, too. Whatever he's doing, he at least doesn't talk too much other than to ask if I need more weight.

Yes. The answer is always yes. Put as much weight on me as you can, and I will always lift it.

"You okay, Elijah?" Coach stops me on my way to the shower. "You were here awfully early."

"I've got a lot on my mind, Coach. Needed to burn a little bit of that off," I say, somehow knowing Coach Marcus will probably understand without asking too many questions.

"I get that," he says. "I'm here before six every morning except Fridays if you need me, yeah? A little extra weight-room time is never a bad thing, especially with St. John's coming up at the end of the week. Taylor is right around the corner."

"Yes, sir." I nod at him. "Thank you."

"Hey, you're doing an outstanding job," he tells me, clapping me on the shoulder. "Don't let anyone tell you differently."

I head to the shower. Sore, but feeling a lot more settled than I was before the sunrise. I stand under the steam, knowing the only thing I can do today is keep to myself. I don't even want to talk to Julian.

I probably *especially* don't want to talk to Julian.

I wish he could comfort me. I wish he could say that he's sorry about what happened with our dads and magically it would make all these shit feelings disappear, but I don't think it would.

All through first period, Camille keeps whispering my name and trying to pass me notes. I keep my head down and eventually put my earbuds in to get my reading done. She finally gives up, and I race out of the classroom as the bell is still ringing.

At lunch, I get to the football table first and take out a brown bag with a peanut butter sandwich and some fruit. Julian sits down next to me.

"Can we talk?"

"I can't talk to you right now," I say.

"Later? Can we talk later?" he asks under his breath as the rest of the guys sit down with their lunch trays.

"I don't even know what to say right now," I tell him, and I turn away from him, toward the rest of the team.

"Well, the pigs got out last night," Bucky says loudly as he pulls the skin from an orange.

The rest of the guys laugh because they know an Epic Bucky Story is about to follow.

"My dad and I had just gotten the pen closed when we realized that someone had left the opposite gate wide open. That 'someone' was probably me, but let's just not talk about that little piece of the story. Do you know how hard it is to wrangle three dozen little baby squealers when your boots are covered in pig shit and it just rained a couple days ago? Good gravy." He shakes his head and yawns loudly. "Then their mama is madder than a wet hen while we're chasing the piglets through the yard, thinking we're trying to make bacon out of 'em."

The whole table is in tears while Bucky talks about the piglets, and even I let a laugh or two escape. He talks through almost the entire lunch period, which means I never have to turn my head to look at Julian.

It doesn't mean I'm not thinking about him, though.

My strategy for history class is more of the same. Keep my earbuds in, keep my head down, get my work done. Luckily, Mrs. Nguyen only assigns silent reading and some study questions for the class period. I sit in the back corner of the room and completely ignore Julian's attempts to get my attention.

I can't run away in the locker room, though, and Julian corners me while I'm tightening my pads for practice.

"Why are you so pissed at me?" he asks, out of breath and sounding exasperated.

I look up at him.

"If anyone should be pissed, it's me!" he says when I don't respond. "Everything I ever thought I knew about my own father is basically a lie." He considers that statement and then shakes his head a little bit. "Okay, maybe not everything, but some of the most important stuff."

"Yeah? And how's that feel?"

Julian just blinks.

"And how do you think it would feel to be told that, just kidding, it wasn't your father's fault the football team fell from grace twenty years ago! Whoopsie! The whole town hates you because of it, but nope—it actually wasn't his fault! As a matter of fact, things could have turned out *very* differently if his best friend hadn't been a big liar. Do you know how much shit Frankie and I have had to go through just because we're Eric Vance's kids? Maybe things wouldn't have turned out any different. Maybe my dad would've still made the same choices and screwed up anyway. But what if he hadn't? What if that football game was the tipping point?"

Julian's shoulders fall and his eyes search my face. He reaches his hand out and touches my elbow. "The whole town doesn't *hate* you—"

I yank my arm back. "Don't touch me."

"Elijah." His voice is soft. "Nobody hates you. And nobody judges you because they think your dad got in a fight—"

"I gotta go," I say to him, strapping my helmet under my chin and running toward the field. I can't handle looking at him anymore or talking to anyone. I just have to put my head down and make it through this practice.

I stand in back of the pack for warm-ups and don't meet Julian's eyes at all. I'm here to play football and go to school.

Sure, I'm sleeping one room away from Julian, but that's not forever. Eventually, Ma and Frankie and Coley will be here, and I will be able to move out of that house and I'll only have to see Julian at practice. I can do anything for a couple of weeks.

## · twenty-seven ·

# *JULIAN*

I wait until Birdie goes to bed before I knock on Elijah's door. Honestly, I don't expect him to answer, but I feel like I need to try.

The door opens slowly, and Elijah stands there in pajama pants, his hair still wet from a shower and dripping on his bare shoulders. "What?" he says, sounding tired.

"Can I come in and sit down?"

He doesn't answer. Only rolls his eyes and sits back down on the bed in the dark room.

I take that as a reluctant yes and follow him in, closing the door before I sit down with my feet folded underneath me at the foot of the bed.

"I just...I wanted to say I'm sorry," I tell him, a sliver of light pouring in from the backyard floodlights, illuminating his profile.

"Do you even get why I'm so angry?" he asks, turning his head to face me.

"Look, Elijah. I don't know that I'll ever understand exactly what it's like to be you. Or what it was like to grow up as a Vance in Meridien, but I *do* know what it's like for everyone to judge you based on the ideas they have about your family," I tell him. I don't feel like I'm explaining myself really well, but it's the best I can do right now.

"It's different when they expect you to be amazing," he says quietly.

"Maybe, yeah. But do you know how much pressure that is?" I ask. "I feel like everyone's eyes are on me all the time, and if I don't do something amazing, I won't be living up to my dad's legacy or some bullshit. It's exhausting," I tell him. My voice gets quieter. "It also feels like the entire town knows my father better than I do. I hardly remember anything about him anymore. Not memories that are just mine, anyway. It feels like everything I know about him has been told to me by someone else."

"I guess we're the same in that," Elijah says quietly.

We don't talk for the next few minutes, and I get lost in my own thoughts while I listen to the rhythmic pattern of Elijah's breathing and the out-of-balance ceiling fan above the bed.

"Anyway, I'm sorry," I say again.

Elijah stays quiet for so long I worry that he's fallen asleep.

"You okay?" I ask.

"Just processing," he says.

"Can I…give you a hug or something?" I move forward on the bed, and I can see his face more clearly in the muted light flooding in from the window.

"I don't think I want that right now," he says, the light touching his bare shoulders. His back hunches, and a hint of sadness touches his eyes.

"Oh." My stomach sinks.

"I'm sorry, too, though," he says. "I guess I never considered what it would feel like to grow up as a Jackson. Night, Julian."

He lies down with his back to me.

"Night," I say, leaving his room.

I lie awake, blinking in the dark for hours. *Things will get better*, I tell myself. *You apologized. He apologized. His feelings are hurt just like yours are, but it's going to be okay. Give him time. That was a big blow you hit him with. It's going to be okay.*

Now if I can only get myself to actually believe that.

I must have eventually drifted off to sleep because my alarm jolts me awake just as the sun is coming up. I smell breakfast cooking in the kitchen, and I wander out of my room to see Elijah and Birdie having cups of coffee while just-baked muffins cool on the counter.

"Good morning, sunshine," Birdie says when she sees me.

Even Elijah turns and offers me a real smile. "Morning," he says.

The knots in my gut ease, and I smile back. "Hey. I thought I smelled something delicious," I say, helping myself to a corn muffin and sitting down next to Elijah.

The three of us sit and have breakfast together, Birdie sharing some of Pastor Ernie's plans for the Main Street Community Center with us. "There will be a childcare center with a huge playground in the empty lot next to the building," she says. "That's the eventual plan, anyway. It might take Pastor a little while to raise enough funds for that. Oh, it's just going to be the jewel of the town when it's done," she says.

"I'm so happy for you, Birdie. I'm glad you still get to be a part of it all," I tell her before going to get ready for school. And I almost mean it.

"Your father would have loved this," she whispers when she hugs me.

Elijah and I walk to school alone this morning. The Guardettes have started their early morning practices today in preparation for the big homecoming halftime show in three weeks. He still doesn't talk much, but I don't feel the same anger radiating off him that I did yesterday.

"Were you listening yesterday when Bucky was telling that story about his pigs?" I laugh, remembering it as Crenshaw comes into view in the morning sun.

"Yeah," he says with a soft laugh. "The guys were cracking up. I thought Nate was going to wet his pants."

I laugh with him. "I can't believe he—" And then I stop.

You know how sometimes brilliant ideas take months of planning and thinking over, and other times a brilliant idea hits you out of nowhere, like a lightning bolt?

"Oh my god," I say, stopping at the bottom of the Crenshaw driveway. "I just had the most amazing idea for the prank."

"*What?* Tell me," Elijah says, finally sounding more like himself.

"I can't. I have to talk to Bucky first," I say, jogging up the driveway toward the gym doors. "I'll see you later!"

"Bucky?" Elijah sputters. "But—"

"Tell all the guys to meet me at the lunch table today!" I yell back at him, laughing all the way to the front doors.

After I share my brilliant plan with Bucky and he assures me that both he and his dad will be on board, I have a hard time keeping my mouth shut until lunchtime. The plan is just too good to keep quiet for long, and I'm finally starting to understand why this prank is so important to everyone.

I draw out the suspense until the whole team is gathered around our lunch table.

"What's happening with the prank, Cap?" Nate asks. "We've been waiting all day to hear this."

I glance around to make sure Coach Marcus or Coach Andrews isn't nosily poking around the cafeteria. "I had this idea this morning," I say, and a murmur runs through the team. "Greased. Pigs."

"Wait, what the hell are you talking about?" Darien asks, and everyone laughs.

Bucky breaks into loud laughter, and the soccer team, at the next table, glances over at us.

"Hey, shh," I warn him. "We've got to keep this quiet. Piglets. Bucky's family has got a ton of them, right? I got the idea after Bucky told us that story about the piglets getting loose yesterday.

We're going to grease up some of those piglets and let them loose on the Taylor field on Thursday morning. Early...like pre-*dawn* early. They're impossible to catch when they're covered in Crisco. They'll spend their entire morning practice chasing pigs instead of getting ready for their Friday night game," I say.

"Oh my god." Someone laughs. "They'll be slipping in pig shit through their entire morning practice."

"Exactly," I say.

The team chatters and the laughter gets louder. Loud enough for some of the cafeteria monitors to start wandering our way.

"Hush, now," I tell them. "I have one condition! This year, we're starting a new tradition." I look at Elijah, and he nods his head once and offers a small smile. "For every prank we pull, we're also doing some community service."

The team groans.

"Now, hear me out," I say. "Once we finish the pigs, we're going to help Pastor Ernie with a new project he's got going. We're clearing that vacant lot next to Ron Redd's because he and Figg are going to be building a playground there soon. I expect us to help out when it comes time for that, too."

The guys all nod and agree with me. "I think we can handle that. Good call, Cap," Nate says, patting me on the back.

• • •

It's Thursday morning, and about half the team is gathered at Bucky's farm, helping to load squealy pink piglets into a cage in the back of Bucky's truck.

Bucky's dad is there, too, helping corral the little animals while we load them.

"Yes, sir, this is going to be a good one," Mr. Redd says, laughing while we bring pig after pig to the truck.

"And there's no chance these guys are going to tear up the field, right?" I ask Mr. Redd. "We just want to inconvenience them, not ruin them."

"Aw, no. These little porkers aren't going to do anything to that big old field," he says. "Not unless someone throws some feed down and they start digging for it. You're going to be just fine. It's prank season.... Taylor's expecting you!" He laughs out loud.

Elijah has been quiet and a little withdrawn this week. He's still speaking to me, but he won't let me hold his hand or touch him. It's almost like he's lost in thought a lot. I'm giving him as much space as he wants, but I miss him so much.

"I'm glad you're doing this with me," I told him on our way out of the house this morning.

"I'm doing it for the team." He smiled, climbing into Bucky's truck for the ride back out to the Redd barn.

We decided earlier that after the team helped load the animals at Bucky's farm, Bucky, Nate, Darien, Elijah, and I would be the ones to deliver the piglets. A mess of pickups driving onto the Taylor field before the sun comes up might cause a bit of a ruckus, and that was the last thing we wanted. We didn't need to give Taylor a warning about what we were trying to do.

The drive out to Taylor takes about thirty minutes. "Did

you remember the Crisco, Darien?" I ask, my leg shaking from nerves.

"Got it right here, Cap." He points to a few grocery bags at his feet. "Quit worrying. This is going to go off without a hitch."

For some reason, that fails to make me less nervous about all of this. It was a fantastic idea when it first hit me, and it's still a great idea, but I can't shake the feeling that I'm about to get in trouble for something. Or get the rest of the guys in trouble.

I guess it's harder to quiet that old worried Julian than I thought it was going to be. As we get closer to the school, my stomach just keeps flipping and flipping. I hold my head in my hands to keep the dizzy feeling at bay.

"Hey," Elijah says next to me. "It's going to be fine." He smiles, then reaches across my lap and links his pinkie through mine.

The darkened football field is covered in dew when Bucky pulls the truck right up to the chain link fence. Elijah and Darien hop the fence with Crisco and settle down to wait for the rest of us to lower piglets from the bed of the truck.

Bucky sticks a yard sign right by the gate that reads PIGLETS COURTESY OF CRENSHAW COUNTY HIGH SCHOOL AND REDD FAMILY FARM at the insistence of his father. "I want my piglets back," his father told us this morning, laughing. "At least this way I know someone will return 'em to me."

I hand the first one over.

"Slippery little sucker." Darien laughs as he holds the

squirming piglet while Elijah slathers it in Crisco. The two of them are laughing like hyenas while the rest of us watch from the bed of the truck.

"Let him go, let him go!" Elijah exclaims after he's sufficiently covered it in grease.

None of us can breathe because we're laughing so hard at the first little pig loose on the big field. The little guy takes off like he's been held hostage for months instead of just for a few minutes in the back of a pickup truck.

We continue our piglet bucket brigade until the field is hopping with tiny pink porkers. I'm lowering the last one into Elijah's waiting arms while Darien jumps back over to wipe the Crisco from his arms when we hear someone yell from the Taylor field house.

"Hey! What are you doing out there! Hey, you!" the voice calls, and we see a man running from the equipment shed toward the field.

Elijah quickly drops the last pig and hops over the fence and into the back of the pickup just as we see a camera flash go off. Bucky throws the truck into drive and takes off through the grass toward the road, Elijah holding on for dear life in the open bed of the truck.

Bucky finally pulls over about a half mile from the highway, and we let Elijah get into the back seat.

"Holy shit, I didn't think I was going to make it," he says, out of breath. His long hair is a mess from the white-knuckle ride in the bed of the truck. "I think that maintenance guy got my picture, though," he says.

"No way," Nate says, turning around from the front seat. "It was too dark, and you were already over the fence when he snapped the picture, anyway."

The truck is quiet for about two seconds before we all bust out laughing, relieved that it's over and beside ourselves that we actually pulled it off without getting caught.

"Man, I wish we could have hidden out under the bleachers and watched those Taylor twits run around trying to catch a herd of greased piglets," Darien says, and that starts a fresh round of raucous laughter.

Bucky brings us back to his house to get cleaned up before we head to school. His dad is waiting for us in the driveway, a big smile on his face.

"You got 'em good?" he asks as soon as we pull up.

"We got 'em," Bucky tells him.

Mr. Redd raises his fists in the air. "Yes! Man, I love prank season." He laughs. "Wait until I tell your grandpa and the word gets back to all the alumni. They're going to love this one."

We're all still in high spirits as we drive toward Crenshaw, the last of the Crisco and pig smell hopefully washed off of us.

I'm daydreaming in Figg's class when the pink slip comes.

"You're needed in the principal's office, Julian," Figg says, handing me the slip.

"Oooooh," erupts the chorus of calculus students behind me as I throw my backpack over my shoulder.

When I get there, Bucky and Elijah are already sitting in the upholstered chairs in front of Mr. Campbell's desk. Coach Marcus comes into the office behind me.

Oh, shit.

"Thanks for coming, boys," Mr. Campbell says to all of us as Coach Marcus leans against a bookcase next to the desk.

"I got an interesting video from Ms. Eccles over at Taylor High School this morning," he says, clicking something on his keyboard and spinning his monitor toward us.

On the screen, the entire Taylor football team is chasing tiny piglets around their field in full pads. The squealing doesn't drown out the laughter or the cursing as the team fumbles around with the slippery little things, trying to get them into a makeshift pen on the other side of their fence. The moment one is caught, it wiggles out of the player's arms and flops right back down onto the field and runs away, determined not to be scooped up again.

I glance at my lap and try not to laugh. Beside me, Bucky's shoulders are bouncing up and down, and I know he's not going to be able to hold it in much longer.

"Ms. Eccles tells me that it took her team the entirety of their morning practice to get the piglets into a cage so that Mr. Redd could come pick them up," Mr. Campbell tells us, pausing the video just as one of the Taylor football players slips and takes a tumble. He's suspended in midair with his arms outstretched on the paused computer screen.

I bite my lip and try to think of every sad thing that's ever happened in order to keep from laughing, but Bucky can't contain it anymore.

He throws his head back and lets out the loudest whoop I've ever heard. "I'm sorry. I'm so sorry, Mr. Campbell, but that was just the best prank we've ever managed to pull off," he says, gasping for breath. "Throw me in detention or suspend me or whatever, but you can't deny that *that*"—he points at the paused screen—"is one of the funniest things you'll see today. This week. This *year!*"

Mr. Campbell lowers his head, and I think I see him fighting to keep his quivering lips from smiling. He clears his throat and looks up at us again. "I understand that this prank war with Taylor started long before you were born and it's a tradition that both schools have had a hand in perpetuating," he says. "But someone could have gotten hurt out there trying to catch these greased pigs. In fact, one of the maintenance staff did slip in some pig excrement while attempting to catch one of these little guys."

All of us lower our heads, not so much in shame but so no one can see us laughing.

"Brian Redd, we know *you* were involved because you so thoughtfully left a sign for your family farm, instructing the Taylor Titans on where to return the piglets," Campbell says, his voice dripping with sarcasm. "We've also got a picture of your license plate as you drove away from the scene."

"I'm sorry, sir. We didn't mean any harm," Bucky says next to me, but I know he's proud of himself. This prank will probably be talked about in his family for the next seventeen generations.

"Elijah Vance, the maintenance man managed to snap a picture of you as you were climbing the fence to get into Mr. Redd's car," Campbell says, bringing up a blurry picture of the back of someone's head on his computer screen.

My heart leaps into my throat. "That's not Elijah," I say quickly, swallowing hard and pointing to the screen. "That's me."

Elijah turns his head and looks hard at me. He narrows his eyes and shakes his head ever so slightly.

"Julian," Coach Marcus says, uncrossing his arms from his chest. "We're pretty sure—"

"No, that's me," I say. "I was the one on the other side of the fence, greasing up the pigs. It was just Bucky and me. The prank was my idea, and just Bucky and I executed the entire thing. Well, with the help of Mr. Redd's piglets," I say.

Mr. Campbell peers at me over the top of his reading glasses. "You know I can't let this go unpunished," he says.

"I understand that, Mr. Campbell. But Elijah had nothing to do with it," I say, nodding at him.

"He's telling the truth," Bucky says, nodding. "Only Julian and I were at Taylor this morning."

Coach Marcus looks me in the eye. "If that's the case, then the two of you will sit on the bench for the game against St. John's tomorrow night," he says. "If that's a suitable punishment for you, Principal Campbell."

"I think that's probably sufficient," he says. "And, boys, let's call an end to the pranks this year, okay? We've got a real chance of getting at *least* to the regional playoffs, and I really don't want two of my best players sitting on the bench for the next few weeks until the Taylor game," he says, shaking his head.

"Yes, sir," I tell him. "And I'm really sorry about all of this. If it helps at all, I told the team we were going to help Pastor Ernie and Figg clean up that empty lot on Main near Ron Redd's this weekend. I told them it was the price we were going to pay for continuing the prank war."

"I think that sounds like a great idea. Maybe in the future we can do away with the pranks altogether and *just* focus on the community service. What do you think about that, Coach Marcus?" Mr. Campbell says, folding his hands on his desk.

"I think that sounds like an excellent plan," Coach says.

"You're all dismissed. Get yourselves back to class and learn something, yes?" Mr. Campbell waves toward his door, and we all get up and go into the hallway.

Coach Marcus heads toward the gym and Bucky starts walking back to class, but Elijah grabs me by the elbow and pulls me toward the hidden space beneath the stairwell.

"Why did you do that? You were scot-free! You could have just told them it was me, and you'd be playing this weekend," he says.

I shrug. "What good would it do me to play if you weren't on the field protecting me?" I say.

"Yeah, but now you're in trouble," Elijah says.

"But you're not," I tell him.

He looks me in the eye, and I see the muscles in his jaw relax.

"We're going to make sure that Meridien sees the real Elijah. The Elijah *I* know," I tell him. "I can't do anything about what happened twenty years ago, other than make sure as many people as possible know the real story, but I *can* see to it that no one makes the mistake of judging you ever again."

Elijah reaches for me and holds my fingers in his. "Thank you."

"I won't let them underestimate you, either," I tell him. "There's way more to you than your last name. And everyone ought to see that."

Elijah leans forward and his soft lips find mine, our fingers still holding on tightly to each other. With his other hand, he grasps the hem of my T-shirt.

I reach my arm around his waist and pull him closer to me.

"You deserve at least that much," I say when we break apart.

## · twenty-eight ·

# *ELIJAH*

It's homecoming morning, three weeks since the big prank. I walk the block and a half from our apartment on Hugo Street to Rudy Street with Coley in tow, the garter I've made for Julian on a metal hanger.

"Uncajulian likes flowers?" Coley asks, her dark French braids bouncing on her head as she skips up Ms. Birdie's front stoop.

"He'll like these," I tell her.

Ms. Birdie opens the door before I ring the bell. "There's my sweet baby girl! Come on in here, you two." She stands aside and lets us in. Coley runs to the kitchen and puts her princess lunch box in the refrigerator.

"G'morning, Birdie," Coley says, wrapping her arms around Ms. Birdie's thighs and squeezing hard.

"We're going to have us some fun today, girl," Ms. Birdie says. "Go on and find Uncle Julian for me, okay?"

Ms. Birdie turns to me and gives me a hug. "Let me see those flowers, now.... Oooooh! Elijah! You've outdone yourself," she says.

"I found him!" Coley yells, pulling Julian down the hallway toward the kitchen, where I'm waiting for him.

"You sure did!" Julian says, carrying a gold-and-white garter in his arms.

I help him into his, making sure it's tight on his bicep over his football jersey. He helps me into mine, adjusting it so it doesn't cover my football number.

"I've got to get a picture of this," Ms. Birdie announces, pointing her cell phone at us. We pose at the front door, our arms around each other's shoulders, showing off our homecoming mums.

"You look like you're going to get married!" Coley singsongs, dancing around us at the front door.

We all laugh, and Ms. Birdie sends us out the door. "I'll see you both at the Taylor game tonight! Miss Coley and I are picking up your mom and Frankie at five o'clock," she says to me.

We meet Camille at the end of the driveway. She's wearing a mum the size of a small island around her neck. It is all lit up with flashing white lights and jingles with about a hundred bells when she moves.

"Wow, Bucky did a nice job," Julian remarks, pulling some of the long ribbons out and examining the baubles that are glued to them.

"He's probably been planning this mum since kindergarten." I laugh.

"He did do a good job, right?" Camille smiles down at her mum and fingers the ribbons and glittery tulle. "Wait until you see the garter I made for him! I can't wait for the dance tomorrow night."

"Hey, let's not forget about the real reason we're wearing these big flowers today." Julian chuckles. "Let's kick some Taylor ass tonight before we start worrying about the dance."

We turn the corner onto Main Street, and Julian grabs my hand and squeezes it. I squeeze back.

"Speaking of, what are our chances of beating Taylor tonight?" Camille asks. "I mean, they *did* strike first in the prank war this year, and you know what that means."

"Our prank was ten times better than theirs. That ought to count for something," Julian says, laughing. "I say we spread a new superstition that whoever does the *better* prank wins the homecoming game."

"I think we have a good chance," I say. "Their defense has no depth, and their quarterback is *way* too jumpy. He throws the ball without taking a breath because he's afraid he's going to get sacked. They're okay, but there's no way they're winning tonight."

Camille looks at Julian and raises her eyebrows. "Look at Mr. Confident over here."

"You heard the man. There's no way they're winning tonight," he says, winking at me.

I glance over at the garter on Julian's arm. I've glued a couple of tiny pigs to the bottom of one of the ribbons.

"How's Frankie doing? Is she coming tonight?" Camille asks about halfway to school. She's holding the mum away from her neck now, as if it's already become too heavy to let hang.

"She likes her classes," I say. "The school told her she'll be done with the CNA program and be able to start working at Crenshaw County General in just a few months. She's talking about moving into an apartment of her own, maybe closer to the hospital, after she gets a job. And who knows, I might go with her after graduation." I shrug, with a slight smile. "Ms. Birdie's really helping her out by watching Coley every day."

"Ugh, graduation. I know it's only October, but graduation is all I can think about! I have *got* to start working on all my applications after this weekend," Camille says.

"Tell me about it." Julian sighs. "I've got a ranked list of all the colleges I'm going to apply to, I've hit up a few teachers for recommendation letters, and I've got all of my SAT, ACT, and AP scores headed to the right schools," he says, listing everything he's managed to do in just the last week. "I'm ready. Or at least, I hope I am."

Camille laughs. "How did I know you'd basically already be done?" She turns to me. "How about you, Elijah? Any idea what you might want to do after graduation?"

I shrug and my cheeks burn. A thought started to grow in my head soon after the rest of my family got back to Meridien and I watched Frankie start taking classes, but I haven't even told Julian about it yet. I've been helping Frankie study for her anatomy quizzes, and it turns out I'm pretty good at understanding the classification of muscles and the inner workings of the nervous system, too. I started thinking maybe I could be an athletic trainer. And once I started thinking about it, it was *all* I could think about.

"I downloaded the Coastal Texas application a few days ago," I finally say. "I'll probably fill it out after homecoming. I don't know; maybe I'll even try to keep playing football. As a walk-on or something," I say to my shoes.

"As a walk-on? No way," Julian says, gripping my hand tighter. "You're good enough to get a scholarship, Elijah! You should talk to Coach Marcus about getting you some film. I can help you, if you want."

I turn to look at him and smile. "I would like that."

We get to school, and everyone is gathered on the steps, showing off their mums and garters and taking selfies with their homecoming dates. Bucky shows off a tremendous blue-and-white garter and kisses Camille about a hundred times while they take silly pictures together. I take a few minutes to really look at the garter Julian has given me. On one of the ribbons is the date of our first kiss three years ago and the date of our second kiss just a few weeks back. I try to keep my smile to myself, but it doesn't work. I give Julian a little elbow and point to the dates, and he gives me a sly smile and winks. My heart melts like hot butter.

Julian goes back to studying his garter. He pulls one of the ribbons away and points to a bit of blue fabric I have glued to the end. "What is this?" he asks.

"It's a piece of your very first football jersey," I tell him. "From when we played peewee ball together way back when. Ms. Birdie let me have it."

He looks at me, a soft smile on his face.

"It's when I knew," I say to him, shrugging.

"It's when you knew what?"

"That at the end of the day, no matter what we may have been through, I'd always have your back." I smile.

Julian reaches for my hand and holds it tight as we walk up the steps into school together.

# *ACKNOWLEDGMENTS*

Though my family and I only spent a handful of years as residents of Texas, the impact made on me by the people I encountered and grew close to will live with me forever. In a sense, this book is my love letter to Texas and the friends I left behind when we moved away. To the students and staff of Cypress Ranch High School, thank you for showing me the importance of tradition, introducing me to the spectacle that is Texas high school homecoming weekend, and helping me realize that the friends we surround ourselves with daily show us how to grow into who we were always meant to be. An extra-special thanks to JQ, KS, LP, MB, RS, KA, AR, EC, and MH. Love you, ladies.

To my brave and beautiful daughter, LB, may you and your friends always be able to find a happy ending for yourselves in the pages of a good book.

To my intuitive and empathetic son, RB, thank you for supporting your mom and for your willingness to answer endless questions about the culture of high school sports.

To my agent, Courtney Miller-Callihan, thank you for trusting me, and thank you for knowing what this book could become. It's been a long road, and you've had my back every step of the way.

To my editor, Hannah Milton, thank you for your willingness to listen and your unending commitment to making this a story that I am endlessly proud of. Your input was invaluable, and you forced me out of my comfort zone and made me push the boundaries of what I thought I was capable of.

Thank you to Ashlena Sharma for the gorgeous, pitch-perfect cover art.

To the rest of the team at Poppy/Little, Brown Books for Young Readers, thank you for shepherding me and this book through the process, and getting it into the hands of the readers that need it the most.

I don't know how anyone does this work without an intricate network of amazing friends you can call on for sprints, gifs, laughs, and support. To the Handspun sprinting crew, AP, and VAS, thank you for always showing up for me. Thank you to SW, LH, and SR for consistently keeping me upright and being my handful.

The squeeziest hug to JB for being the bestest best friend ever and my rock through this entire process. Endless tacos and leftover spaghetti for you. Always.

A big thank-you to my Stinky Petes and their kiddos for reading early drafts and offering input, kind words, and endless cheerleading.

Thank you to Mom, Dad, and Kristen for being my very first readers when I scrawled things in pink notebooks with a rainbow-colored pencil.

And last but not least, thank you, Steve. Your willingness to take me on long car rides to the beach, tell me stories about Johnny Cash, and listen to me blather about people who only exist in my head have done more for this story than anyone without a writer for a spouse will ever understand.

Steven Bietz

**Kara Bietz** was born and raised in New England but now resides in north Georgia with her family. *Sidelined* is her second novel. She invites you to visit her online at karabietzauthor.com or on Twitter and Instagram @karamb75.